When the Dark Man Calls

When the Dark Man Calls

◇ ◆

STUART M. KAMINSKY

ST. MARTIN'S PRESS
NEW YORK

Design by Lee Wade

Library of Congress Cataloging in Publication Data

Kaminsky, Stuart, M.
    When the dark man calls.

    I. Title.
PS3561.A43W48   1983   813'.54   83-2941
ISBN 0-312-86668-2

First Edition
10 9 8 7 6 5 4 3 2 1

For Peter Michael Kaminsky

When the Dark Man Calls

◇ *ONE* ◆

Crickets, millions of them, made the hot summer night cry in the woods behind the house, but Jean hardly noticed. From her bed she could see deep into the trees where the fireflies, twinkling like stars, turned the darkness into a mock sky, her private sky. She lay unwilling to remove the protection of the no-longer-cool sheet. A slight breeze puffed through the window, not sufficient to make the drapes billow, but enough to make a daddy longlegs pause and lower its body against the window ledge.

It was probably past midnight, but Jean couldn't sleep. Her legs were badly sunburned from inner-tubing on the river in her shorts. Her mother had rubbed Noxzema on them and told her that if it looked bad in the morning, she probably wouldn't be able to go to Durham to the movies. There was a Pat Boone movie downtown, and the other girls were going. Alice Parkes' father was going to drive them, and take all of them out for a sundae. Jean was determined to go even if it meant lying to her mother. She knew she couldn't lie to her father. His black eyes saw into her soul. He never said anything about going to Durham and seeing Pat Boone even though he thought modern music was a waste of the precious time God had given us.

"I won't try to force it out of you or you away from it," he said when she asked to buy a Paul Anka record. "We learn from example, from trying and doing within limits. You know what I think of such things, but if I keep you away from them, you'll long for them and make more of them than they are. I trust in time your judgment will mature."

He had said it sitting across from her at dinner, his dark eyebrows almost touching over the crinkle of his nose, his gray-flecked brown hair falling forward. Jean had the feeling that her mother saw nothing much wrong with Paul Anka. In fact, Jean was sure she had heard her mother actually listening to Elvis on the radio once. Her mother had turned off "Heartbreak Hotel" when she heard the door open, but she had been listening. Jean also knew that some of the people in town thought Lucille Kaiser was little more than an everyday-a-yes-sir housewife who did what her lord and master told her to do, minded the family and the two children and stood behind him foursquare. Jean knew her mother could get her way with the big things, the things she wanted, the dishwasher, the trip to Atlanta, sending Lloyd away to Chicago to divinity school. The around-town things and the matters of discipline she not only left to her husband, but did so gladly.

Something like a real breeze came through the window now and the curtains did billow. Far away, over the hill toward Raleigh, thunder cracked. Jean considered reaching over to turn on the radio to catch one of the late disc-jockey shows from Raleigh, probably WRAL, and find out if the rain was coming. If it was, Mr. Parkes might decide not to drive to Durham, might get Alice to call and suggest that the girls stay home and play Sorry. She could imagine Alice calling with her dad behind her, making her disappoint everyone. Jean pushed back the covers and reached toward the white Motorola her parents had given her for her tenth birthday. There was rain coming down now, and the fireflies were gone. Centipedes were curling up and the crickets hopping for cover. A crack of lightning came as Jean's hand touched the radio knob, but she never turned it on. From her parents' room across the hall she heard the closing of a window. Her father might come into her room to close her window, too, and catch her with the radio on.

And there was another sound, like a door opening downstairs. But it couldn't be a door opening.

Jean turned on her side, humming "April Love." If she were a few years younger and had a doll she really played with, not just the ones on her dresser, she'd call it "April Love." Tomorrow she'd share the idea with Alice and Susan, just drop it out as a kind of joke she thought up on the edge of the moment, as her father said. "Wouldn't that be a funny name for some little kid to call her doll, 'April Love'?"

Alice would wait to see how Susan would react, and if it was all right, all three of them would giggle a little.

There was another sound from downstairs, or she thought there was. It was hard to tell now. Barabbas the cat was out in the woods for the night, had been out there for days, would need a good flea bath when he got back. Barabbas was easy to catch since his back right leg had been broken in the woods a year earlier. But it wasn't Barabbas. And it wasn't the raccoon that sometimes came up to the house looking for night garbage. He was too smart for that since. . . Maybe her mother had gone downstairs for a drink of Coke or iced tea. Jean brushed the hair from her eyes and looked out the window. Drops of rain were hitting the window ledge and the breeze felt good, tingly on her red legs, like mint.

For about ten minutes she lay nearly drowsing, listening to the rain. Then she heard the sound of soft footsteps on the stairs. The steps were coming up slowly, carefully, quietly so as not to disturb. Jean let herself sink back into near-sleep, expecting her door to open and her mother or father to look in on her.

But it was her parents' door she heard open slowly. Jean tried to let the sleep take her, but the rain came down harder and pinged insistently at the window.

"Jeannie?" she heard her mother's voice through two doors, sounding distantly frightened or in pain.

"Jeannie?" her mother repeated. It might be a dream. She thought she heard her father mumbling and starting to come awake.

"Jean?" It had been clear and certain, a question right through the rain and the doors. It was her mother's voice and it came again, but there was that question in it, not really a calling and then that sound, like when Gus Torkias, the Greek grocer's son, had thrown the pumpkin against the school wall on Halloween. Then her mother

3

said her name again, and the sound of it sent cold terror from her neck down her back and to the secret place inside her. She thought it might go through her and make her wet the bed, and it took all her strength to keep this from happening. Then that sound again, but it was as if there had been a rock in the pumpkin.

Jean sat up, mouthed "Mommy," but didn't say it. She looked at her door, wanted to get up and lock it, knowing it was just a little chain for privacy, not knowing what was making her behave like this. Her father would think she was a baby.

But she couldn't bring herself to get out of bed. She lay back and covered herself with sheet and blanket. That was even worse. Whatever was out there, out in the hall or in her parents' room, might come in while she was lying like that, might be hovering over her right now. She was crying as she threw back the blanket and sheet and looked up at the figure. She sucked in her breath and realized that it was a chair with her new dress on it, the one she was going to wear to Durham.

"Mommy," she screamed after the breath came back, but it wasn't her ten-year-old voice. It was the voice of a child much younger. She screamed again, and the thunder and lightning mocked her.

Then she heard the footsteps in the hall. They were coming from her parents' room. They were not quite heavy, and they moved toward her door. Through her tears she watched the door, wanted to get up and run for the window, jump to the lawn fifteen feet below and run for the Pressmanns' house, but she couldn't. She could only stare at the door and try to suck in her breath. It was outside the door. She could hear it panting the way her brother Lloyd or her father or her uncle Mike did when they played baseball or carried her on their backs down the stairs when she was younger.

It stayed outside the door while she grew old. The moment never passed. It was forever. It was the story her mother had told her of the *Inferno*. She was caught there for eternity in fear, never knowing what was outside her door.

She didn't hear the footsteps go away. When forever had passed and light came through the window, the first light of morning through the trees, Jean felt something return to her. The sheet she was grasping was wet with her own perspiration. Her pajamas were wet. She pushed the sheet back, shivered once, and looked at herself. Her sunburned legs glowed red and she felt them.

"I had a dream," she whispered inside her head, knowing it was more a sob than a whisper, trying to convince herself.

She got out of bed slowly, weakly, never taking her eyes from her door. "Dream," she repeated out loud but softly, allowing herself to look at the window and see the sun. The word *dream* took on a little more strength with the light, and she repeated the word over and over as she walked to the door, repeated it till it had no meaning, *dreamdreamdreamdream*, had no beginning or middle or end.

When she touched the brass door handle, it would not turn. Her hands were too moist. She had to take the edge of her pink nightgown and use it to grip the knob and open the door. She expected nothing out there. It must be gone by now.

But the patterns on the hall carpet were there, dark and wet, and they made a trail to the stairs, and her parents' door was open and she rushed to it, wanting this over, knowing it would be over through that door, and it was.

She stopped just inside the room and saw them, and it was no dream. And then the sound came. The horrible scream from inside the room, and she wanted to run, but the sound wouldn't let her. She could only be free to run when her mind told her what the sound was, and then it did tell her and she turned and ran down the stairs screaming and out of the house screaming and toward the Pressmanns' screaming, and a devil inside her said she wouldn't see the Pat Boone movie today, and the devil told her that the sound she heard was simply the phone in her parents' room.

And the devil laughed at her.

◇ *TWO* ◆

Chicago, Illinois, January 20, 1983, 6:00 P.M.

Howard Street was crowded with backed-up buses and steaming cars. On the north side of the street was Evanston, which stretched north to Northwestern University and then beyond to the exclusive North Shore. On the south side of Howard was Chicago and Jean Kaiser, who, balancing a bag of groceries, turned down Seeley Street and began the careful walk home, avoiding a collision with a chunky Latino man whose hands were in his jacket pockets and whose head was down as he went forward like a determined tank.

With snow thick on the ground and a hazy light from the street lamps, Seeley looked like what it had probably been two decades earlier: a pleasant residential street of small apartment buildings, mostly three-story six-flats with some three-story three-flats and even a few small courtyard buildings and one or two more recently built smaller apartment complexes. But the neighborhood had been changing and changing fast. It had already begun to change when Jean and her twelve-year-old daughter Angie moved in, and Jean knew it. It was the change that allowed her to get a large old apartment for rent she could afford, but there were times when she questioned her decision.

6

The neighborhood was an uneasy mixture of families looking for bargain rents, older people on fixed incomes who couldn't afford to run, incoming Latino families hoping to find a stable neighborhood at a reasonable rent, black families caught below the dividing line between the lower and middle classes but looking at the neighborhood as a place from which they might want to climb, and, worst of all, the young men on their way from being boys to being whatever they would become. These young men got apartments in the neighborhood, tested their powers, and caused trouble.

Jean cautiously mounted a small hill of snow near an alley and managed to make it down without a fall. One small step for Jean Kaiser.

Actually, winter was the best time in the neighborhood. In the summer, the quintet of white assholes who lived across the street opened their windows three or four nights a week, blasted Rod Stewart into the night and screamed postmidnight obscenities at the moon.

When the police came, the boys of summer turned off the stereo, turned off the lights and went silent. They wouldn't even open their door. Jean had called the cops twice herself and had gotten into an argument with one young cop with a white scar on his chin. She had suggested that the police not simply ride up the middle of Seeley with their lights on when they came to check on the drug-happy gang, since there was always one jerk sitting in the window who gave those inside ample warning so that when the cop car stopped, the street was silent.

"We know how to do our job, lady," the young cop had sighed, making it clear that he had more important things to do but that he didn't mind taking a few minutes to look at Jean, who, at thirty-five, was dark, pretty, and just on the right side of being plump.

"Of all the alternatives for dealing with this problem," she had said sweetly, pushing her glasses back on her nose as she stood in her blue terry-cloth robe at the door, "you have managed to find the least effective. I wonder what you would do if this happened in your neighborhood."

"I don't live in a neighborhood like this," the cop had said.

"I see," Jean had said with a smile. "It's the price we're supposed to pay for living here and the reward you get for not having to."

7

"Mother," Angie had whispered in exasperation from the living room where she had curled up on the sofa waiting for the police.

"Lady," the cop had said. "If I don't hear it, and they don't answer the door, I've got to have a complaint. Those jerks over there are into more than a little noise. Two of them have felony convictions including attempted rape and assault. You see, we do know a little about what's going on around here. You want to come fill out a complaint? You got neighbors to back you up? You know what will happen? Even if a judge believes you, and he probably will, he'll tell those punks that they'd better stop the noise or else. He'll warn them and they won't give a shit. They'll be back the next night making more noise than ever and having it in for you. That what you want?"

Jean hadn't answered.

"Lady," he had said, looking down her robe. "Take my advice. You look like a person with some education and you got a nice kid. Find yourself another neighborhood."

So, the winter was better, though less than a week earlier she had awakened to something that sounded like gunshots and the flashing of an ambulance light.

A block and a half to go. Two children about nine or ten were going down a small snow hill built in an apartment courtyard. They were riding on what looked like a huge red pan, and their voices carried in the cold air. One kid screamed "Indiana Jones" as he tumbled over at the bottom of the hill. The other kid laughed.

Jean reached up to pull her green knit cap over her ears. She knew her nose was turning bright red. It always did in the cold. So did Angie's. So, she remembered, had her mother's.

A few people were on the street digging spaces for their cars. Carving out Toyota-sized fortresses. In the morning, they would leave chairs, wooden horses, or cardboard cartons in the spaces they had cleared, a kind of primitive claim staked out on the public street. Jean had watched from her window one night as a man jabbed a screwdriver into the tires of a car that had been parked in the street space he had cleared and staked out. She was sure that somewhere in Chicago people had fought and maybe even died over parking spaces.

More than half the cars on the street were bedded down until a chance thaw or until spring came.

Jean crossed Seeley across from her three-flat and hoped she would avoid Martha, but chance was not to have it so and Martha, bundled, a terrier grimace on her gray pudding face, looked down at her dog, who sniffed around for an appropriate place to turn a patch of white-black snow a urine yellow. The dog was a friendly enough rotund mongrel. Far from young, the unimaginatively named Pal greeted all with a small bark and friendly panting. Her master, Martha the Mad, was far from friendly.

Jean hurried to the door, pretending that she was (a) in a hurry, (b) preoccupied, (c) unable to see in the darkness and (d) busy watching the ground to prevent a fall.

None of the above stopped Martha.

"Mizz Kaiser," she said.

No help for it. Jean stopped, shifted the heavy package to ease the ache and turned to the lump of a woman who stood before her with a grim tightness to her lifeless mouth, a small tuft of gray hair on the right side of her upper lip.

The Wicked Witch of the North, thought Jean, trying to smile.

At first, for months, Jean had argued with Angie about the girl's anger with the neighbors below them in the basement apartment.

"They're old," Jean had explained, "or almost old. They live in a one-room apartment. No kids. No family. Wayne has a job cleaning up at McDonald's. They can't move out—"

"And they're both crazy," Angie finished, always getting to the heart of her own concern.

Jean acknowledged to herself that Martha and Wayne were probably more disturbed than any of the clients she was dealing with at the community center.

When they had first moved into the apartment, Jean and Angie had cleaned the old wooden floors, rented a floor polisher and sander, messed up the job, redone it, and stood back with pride. They had needed no man and had rejected an offer by her brother Lloyd to help. That very night Martha had come up with her arms folded to say that she didn't want to complain, but her new neighbors were being awfully noisy.

Jean promised to pay attention to the situation. Martha or her husband, Wayne the Broom, continued to trap Angie for the next few weeks, complaining about the noise.

"We could complain about that dog," Angie said loudly one

9

night. "When anyone comes near the place in the middle of the night, old Pal the Miracle Mutt goes nuts."

"They're scared, Angie," Jean had explained. "So they keep a loud, harmless dog."

"They're still jerks," Angie had responded with little charity.

And so Jean had bought a second-hand rug for the living room floor to cut down the noise, but the complaints from below didn't stop. For a while, Jean and Angie just stayed out of the living room, except when Lloyd and Fran brought their kids, and both Jean and Angie sat tensely as five-year-old Walter behaved like a five-year-old and rolled around on the floor. But this was different, and Jean waited with an inward sigh thinking seriously for the first time about moving. Why not? There might soon be money.

"Well?" said Martha. Her voice sounded to Jean like a poor imitation of Granny on "The Beverly Hillbillies."

"Well, Martha. My package is heavy and Angie is waiting for dinner," Jean said firmly.

From behind the window of the basement apartment over Martha's shoulder, Jean could see the thin curtain part slowly and Wayne's eye peer out at her. Ah, a trap. They had been waiting for her.

"We've had just about enough of this," Martha said, quivering with righteous indignation. "Either you turn it off or we get a lawyer."

Jean was convinced that even in a sane cause Martha and Wayne had neither the nerve, resources, or intelligence to seek legal aid.

"Martha, for what I hope is the last time," Jean said, trying to convey the patience of a television nun or judge, to touch some image in Martha's past that might relate to reason, "we have no electrical device in our apartment which is causing interference with your television set. We have no electronic game, no strange appliance. Our television reception is none too good either, and I think there may be a ham operator or a short somewhere in the building."

Martha looked down to watch Pal squat, tightened her arms around herself, and smirked, "You've got it."

I'm a pro, Jean thought, a trained psychologist, and this is a good test. I will handle this reasonably. I will sympathize with this human being.

"Why don't you ask the neighbors, the people across the street or next door, the Hellmans on the second floor, the Parks on the third floor?"

"Asked them," said Martha in triumph. "They said they have no machine."

"And I say I have no machine," said Jean, straining to keep her voice even. "Why do you believe them and not me?"

Jean thought she knew the answer to that one. Jean was, in Martha's eyes, everything she wasn't, had everything she didn't, was the focus of all her anger and dissatisfaction with the world. Jean had a big three-bedroom apartment, not a cold two-room basement flat. Jean Kaiser was not old. Jean Kaiser had a child and not a mongrel dog. Jean Kaiser had a job, an education.

From behind Martha, Wayne knocked at the window and shouted, "Tell her."

"Tell me what?" asked Jean, looking up at her own window and seeing Angie's face pressed to it. Jean wasn't sure Angie could see her, but she gave her a hopeless shrug.

"When you let Wayne into your apartment last week to show him you had no machine," Martha said triumphantly, "he saw."

"He saw," Jean repeated, shifting her package once more. Pal looked up at her and held up a paw. Jean ignored him.

"Wayne saw the extra thermostat, the one you use to hide the machine," Martha hissed.

"That's it," said Jean. "I get paid for dealing with people like you. I don't have to do it for nothing. Martha, as a last gesture of goodwill, I suggest to you that you go over to the mental health center on Touhy and talk this over with someone. Or call the police."

Jean had to admit that there was a touch of malice in her final gesture of goodwill, but even psychologists need some outlet.

"Now, just you . . ." Martha shouted, but Jean could shout with the best of them. Now the neighbors were surely hearing and straining to listen. Maybe the gang of boys across the street and the tire slasher and the alcoholic Korean landlady, Mrs. Park. All listening. Shit.

"Martha, you are sick. I want you to stop bothering me and my daughter. To stop talking to us completely. No talk. None. You avoid us and we will do our best to avoid you."

11

"Listen, you Jew bitch," shouted Martha, quivering. Pal growled uncertainly and stepped back. Wayne came out of the side door coatless.

"What are you saying to my wife?" he shouted, red of face, gray stubble on his chin. "Don't you threaten my wife."

Neither of them looked very formidable. Jew bitch? she thought. Where did she get that? It was a wacky comedy, and Jean felt like laughing through her anger. Should she deny she was Jewish? Jean was clearly fat Martha's shadow, all the things she feared and hated and resented, and there was no way to change that.

"Kike," Martha shouted, nearly foaming. Jean turned away and started into the hallway.

"Don't you turn your back on us," Wayne's broken voice came behind her.

Jean turned once more and fixed them with a stare she had seen in a Joan Crawford movie. As evenly as she could, in a hoarse whisper, she said, "If you speak to me again, either of you, or bother me or my daughter again, I will tell my brother Lloyd, who is a member of the Jewish Defense League. If I even related what you have just said, I shudder to think of what he might do."

"You can't scare us," wailed Wayne, clearly frightened.

"You damn . . ." Martha started, but Jean noticed that there was no Semitic reference this time. Pal looked from her masters to Jean as if hoping that this game would end. Jean cast a glance of sympathy at the animal before she kicked the hall door shut and went to the inner door.

Angie had already picked up the mail. No one had picked up the gathering dust, old leaflets and junk mailers on the floor. Mrs. Park, the landlady from Korea whose husband had walked out on her a year ago leaving her with three teenage kids and an ancient father, had gone quickly from dutiful Oriental wife to alcoholic with a succession of Korean boyfriends of various ages. Mrs. Park's father, who spoke no English but who had maintained the building, had moved out when the first boyfriend entered. Occasionally, Jean wondered where the old man could have gone.

Complaints to Mrs. Park had resulted in nothing, and for a while, after attempts to get the other tenants to help had failed, Jean and Angie had done some minor cleaning in the halls.

Besides Wayne and Martha in the basement, Angie and Jean on the first floor, and Mrs. Park on the third floor, the only other tenants in the building were the Hellmans on the second floor. Mrs. Hellman was a chunky, red-haired woman who worked somewhere in the Loop and was neither friendly nor unfriendly. Her son was a tall teen who was shy and unresponsive and clearly some kind of athlete since he could be seen during the summer hurrying off with a duffle bag and basketball. Art Hellman had the distinction in Jean's mind of being the most prematurely senile human she had ever encountered. He was, he said, retired, and spent his time, weather permitting, walking around the neighborhood, suggesting his hidden expertise at electronics, plumbing, carpentry and various other crafts he never seemed to practice. A slouching man with white hair and a big belly, he never recognized anyone on the street. Jean had passed him many times and said hello, only to be greeted by Art Hellman's open-mouthed blank look. He recognized her only within the apartment building.

Jean got the key out, went into the darkness of the hall, where the light on the landing had burned out weeks earlier and never been replaced, and made her way up the carpeted stairs by counting them. "There, seven," she said to herself. Angie had the door open, waiting for her.

Angie was not beautiful, Jean thought, but she might be in a few years. Her teeth were expensively braced with money from ex-hus-band Max. Her hair was long and couldn't decide if it was going to be straight or kinky. Her body was thin and verging on a decision to turn her into a woman. Angie was between a lot of things, Jean thought, and looked more like her father than her mother.

Angie was wearing an old basketball T-shirt Max had given her. It was yellow with a red number 44 in front and red lettering in back reading "Chapel Hill Recreational Basketball." It was an extra-large, like her father, and went down to her knees.

Angie took the package from her mother. The girl's eyebrows were up. Jean kicked the door shut behind her.

"Well?" said the girl.

Jean pursed her lips, took off her coat, flung it onto the chair in the hall, removed her misted glasses, and walked into the living room and jumped up in the air three times, clapping her boots on the floor and surely shaking the ceiling for Wayne and Martha and Pal, who went wild at the sound.

Jean sat on the floor, looked at her daughter and smiled. Angie giggled and then laughed. She put the package down on top of her mother's coat and laughed with her hand over her mouth, a habit she had developed since the braces had come. Jean leaned back on the carpet and let out more laughter, and Angie came into the living room on her hands and knees laughing.

They collapsed into each other's arms in uncontrollable laughter, tears coming down. Jean sat up on her elbows and bumped her head on the small table she had inherited from her mother. She laughed even louder, wondered what Wayne and Martha were making of the sound and then realized she didn't care. There was something important about the moment. It felt good and close and childish, and her daughter felt warm and changing.

"Ange," Jean said, sitting up. "How would you like to move out of Dead Man's Gulch?"

For a second Angie grew serious and looked at her mother.

"Truly?" she said. "I thought we couldn't afford to move."

Jean reached over and touched her daughter's hair.

"We're doing all right, and the CBS radio deal is a real possibility."

"Let's move," said Angie, raising her eyebrows.

"You might have to change schools," Jean warned.

"Promise," said Angie, fingering the frayed edge of the first 4 on her shirt.

"Yeah, promise," said Jean. "Cross my heart and . . . let's get dinner going. I'm starved."

They hugged once, got up and headed toward the kitchen with Angie rushing ahead to scoop up the grocery package. Why not, thought Jean, kicking her boots off and letting them drop with a thud. Max had told her that she could break her lease any time she wanted to, that Mrs. Park had repeatedly violated the lease by her failure to maintain the building. Jean had to admit that one of the primary reasons she had not moved sooner or thought of it seriously was that it had been Max's idea, and she was firmly committed to making decisions that were not influenced by him. Max had kept her from making decisions for ten years of their marriage. No, she had to be honest, to remember. Max had not done it to her. She had chosen Max because that was his personality, because she wanted someone to make decisions for her, someone to depend on, someone strong, like her father.

She had believed that when Dr. Hirsch had suggested it to her, but it took her almost three years to really feel it and another two years to develop enough sense of her own ego to rebel against it and decide to go back to graduate school, to become a psychologist.

At first Max had supported the idea, but each step toward independence had clashed with his own need to be in charge, to be a father to both Jean and Angie. It had taken Jean a long time to accept that Max and everyone else were what their histories had made them. That perhaps there were no villains preying on poor Jean Kaiser. There were just people with their own backgrounds, problems and neuroses who came together, sought each other out, and fed on each other's needs and fears.

The apartment was warm, and the old radiators were steaming noisily, especially the one in the kitchen. As they prepared a hot rice salad, mother and daughter talked of where they might move, what they might do, and for a few minutes they forgot about now and here and thought about tomorrow.

"How about coming with me to the station tonight, child?" Jean shouted from her bedroom as she changed clothes. Angie was putting the finishing touches of spice to the salad.

"Can't. Homework. I'll listen while I work," Angie said.

"I'd like you with me," Jean repeated, pulling a red cotton sweater over her head.

"I'm okay," Angie shouted back.

"I'm not worried about you," Jean lied, putting her glasses back on and coming into the kitchen, where the smell of too much oregano hit her. "I think Roger is going to make some moves on me again tonight and I'd like you there to run interference. He won't lay a hand on me if old 44 is out in front blocking."

Angie ran her tongue over her braces, and she scooped the rice into bowls on the wooden table.

"You don't need me," she said. "I've seen you with him and you can take care of yourself. I told you to stop worrying. Klinger and I will be fine."

15

Jean looked up at Klinger, a singularly stupid parakeet that Angie kept for company and talked to without hope of ever getting a reply. Klinger had been purchased with Angie's own babysitting money.

Right, thought Jean. Always put the past behind and go on with the present and the future. Assuming she could get back to the bus line and there would be no major delays, she had about ten more minutes before she left. She spent most of it going over Angie's report on her day and fantasies about where they might live.

In the middle of a mouthful of salad, the lights went out.

"Mom," said Angie in the dark.

"I'll get the flashlight and change the fuse," Jean said, feeling her way from the table.

"Not the fuse," Angie said softly.

Jean paused in front of the kitchen drawer where the flashlight was kept.

"Lights went out half an hour before you came home," explained Angie. "I went down to the basement. The fuse was okay. Someone had pulled our power switch."

"Son of a bitch," hissed Jean. "They really are crazy."

"I think they're trying to cut off the power to our secret machine," said Angie.

"You know," sighed Jean, "we might be better off if your uncle were in the Jewish Defense League instead of the Baptist Church."

Jean had no great fondness for the darkness, which was still a giant leap from the terror she had felt for years and the absolute need, for all those years, to have someone in the same room when she slept.

Flashlight in hand, she went down the front stairs into the basement, past the closed inner door of Martha and Wayne's apartment, and to the fuse box. She turned the beam to the box. She could hear the hum of the furnace behind her and smell the soapy musk of the basement. Angie was right. The switch had been thrown. She threw it back and marched to Martha and Wayne's door, where she said firmly, "One more trick like that and I'll have you both locked up in the booby hatch. It won't be hard to get a Jewish shrink to get you both certified."

Terrific, Jeannie, she said to herself. Dr. Hirsch would be proud of you. You certainly know how to keep your cool and deal with

16

those in need of help. But one thing was for sure. Angie was not staying home by herself tonight. She could pack up her homework and do it at the studio.

There are some nights when people simply should not be alone.

◇ THREE ◆

Abe Lincoln must have had an easier time getting to school, Jean decided. To get to station WSMK in Evanston, she and Angie had to backtrack to Howard Street in near arctic darkness. There was no question of using the car. The alley was under two feet of snow. If the plows came through the next day, she could give it a try, but the chances were that there would be no plow. The reason was simple: politics. The alderman was a nice young bald guy named Dennis Burke who looked vaguely like Max without the hair. Burke was a maverick, a hard-hitting independent who listened to everyone, sympathized with everyone, had the patience of a Buddhist monk and as much clout as an overripe mango. The mayor didn't like Dennis Burke, and if the mayor didn't like someone in Chicago, that person suffered. The lesson to the district was clear: If you people want your streets plowed, your garbage picked up, the alleys sprayed for rats, the police to be interested, don't elect Dennis Burke again.

Half a block from the misty glow of Howard Street, Angie took a fall and lost her books. They found everything but a pen.

"I think my braces slipped," she whispered woefully as they

crossed Howard and ran for the bus stop half a block away, trying to beat the 204 bus there.

"I'll take a look on the bus," Jean panted. They were neck and neck with the slow-moving green monster and would make it easily if Angie didn't fall again.

"You're not going to make me show my braces in public," Angie moaned angrily and stopped in the middle of the sidewalk.

"Okay, we'll look at them at the station, hurry."

They made it to the stop before the 204, but their troubles weren't over. The bus was jammed with people coming home late and irritable because of the weather. The massive rear end of a black woman carrying a Thom McAn shopping bag blocked Jean at the door. She managed a foothold on the lowest step and the driver said, "That's it. Another bus is right behind."

There was another bus. Jean had seen it. It was a 97 that would go to Skokie which would mean at least a six-block walk.

"Hold it," she pleaded. "I'm stuck." She reached back and tugged at Angie to get on. The huge-ended black woman looked back over her ample shoulder, saw the dilemma, grunted sideways and Angie made it on with no space to spare.

"Mother," she sighed, "I could have stayed home. I can still get off and—"

"No way," Jean said, pushing her glasses back and removing her mittens to grope for change. She couldn't find any so she reached forward past the fat woman and stuffed a dollar bill into the coin deposit machine.

She caught a glimpse of the driver's face and shrugged apologetically. The newspapers and television news had said that it cost the CTA millions of dollars to pay people to sort out the dollar bills stuffed into the coin machines. But since the drivers could give no change, the only other alternative was to throw people off who had the fare. Jean had seen this happen. But this driver, a middle-aged black man with a mustache and distinguished gray hair at the temples, didn't seem to mind the bill. He wouldn't be counting it. He looked downright sane, Jean thought. How could anyone be sane in Chicago on a night like this? There must be something wrong with him.

The bus door popped open at Western Avenue to reveal about ten people standing in front of the Standard station wanting to get on. One or two actually made it. Angie groaned.

"Move to the rear of the bus please," the driver said in a deep even voice as he swerved to miss a skidding Volkswagen. Jean glimpsed the face of the driver of the VW, a young woman who looked terrified as her car slid over the curb and stopped inches away from a Latin-looking man in a navy pea coat who leaped away in time, shouting something Jean could not hear.

The bus driver, however, took it all in stride. He belongs, Jean thought, in a sane asylum. Some place to muddle up his mind, make him aware of the difficulty of getting through each day. Some place to take the song out of him.

The bus moved slowly, but move it did, and by the time they got to Greenleaf in Evanston, there was plenty of room in back. People had disappeared down the fuzzy streets into the dark gray night toward their homes. Jean wondered vaguely if she and Angie should move to this area, closer to the station, farther from work, a better neighborhood where madmen and women probably didn't roam, where the streets looked plowed and the police were probably polite.

"Don't check my braces," Angie whispered, clutching her books to her thin breasts and letting her eyes wander quickly around the bus to see if anyone was looking her way.

"I'm not looking at your braces," Jean said truthfully. "I'm just looking at you."

"Looking at me," Angie sighed wearily. "You can look at me any time."

"You change a lot, kiddo," Jean said, nudging her toward the exit in the middle of the bus.

There were about a dozen people left on the bus. One was a young man with a scraggly beard who wore only a thin coat. He swayed back and forth and mumbled to himself, mad, drunk or drugged, probably the latter, thought Jean.

Passengers had given him a wide berth, but he didn't seem to notice.

"I don't know," the young man said in a sing-song voice, "what the fuck they want from me."

A tiny, well-dressed old woman with white hair and the determined face of a librarian turned to the young man and said clearly with an East Coast accent Jean couldn't place, "You keep your filthy mouth shut."

"That's me in thirty years," Jean whispered to Angie.

"Which one?" Angie replied with a smile.

The young man looked up vaguely at the old woman, trying to focus on her. "Sorry, sorry," he mumbled. "Fucking sorry, lady."

"Don't be sorry," the woman said. "Just be quiet."

"Quiet," he repeated, fingering his beard and contemplating how he might achieve this difficult end. The rest of the passengers pretended all of this was not happening.

"Mom," said Angie as they got off the bus at their stop, "do you ever get the idea we're living in Wonderland?"

"More like the Inferno," Jean said, watching the bus pull away.

"Dante," said Angie, matter-of-factly.

Jean put her arm around her daughter, and the two waited for a hole in the Dodge Avenue traffic and then hurried across.

The station was on a street with several factories behind a row of neat town houses. Trucks were always parked near the station, huge trucks to transport the electronics parts, bearings, rust removal products and seat covers that were manufactured or assembled in the squat buildings nearby. At night these buildings were dark and silent. Occasionally, Jean could look through a window and see a janitor sweeping up, but the final block was the most desolate of the journey, past the railroad tracks and a row of trucks and across a parking lot to the station that didn't look much like a station.

WSMK was housed in a small one-story building with a three-story antenna that made the station, both AM and FM, surprisingly powerful. On a snowy day, the sound carried deep into Chicago to the south, beyond Des Plaines to the west and well into Lake Forest to the North. To the east was Evanston and beyond it Lake Michigan, where the keepers of the water crib might pick up the signal; perhaps, on a night like this, it might even make it across the lake to Michigan City.

The station consisted of a small reception area painted white, with a receptionist's desk, four offices and two studios. One studio was the size of a cell Jean had once seen in Joliet prison. The other, the one she worked in, was even smaller. There was just enough room for her to sit on one side of a small maple table covered with cigarette scorches, and for her announcer, Mel Trax, to sit on the other. The clipboard in front of Mel indicated the commercials and breaks. The telephone was for him to take the incoming calls, and the two microphones were for them to share. To their right was the glass partition beyond which sat Ted Earl, the engineer. Ted was efficient, reasonably intelligent, and looked vaguely like John Mitchell. Ted was also drunk all the time, which didn't seem to affect his ability to handle the board with a few minor errors from time to time.

Mel was standing in the reception area near the desk, staring at the clipboard in his hand, mouthing a commercial, when Jean and Angie came through the door and stamped their feet on the mat to get rid of the excess snow.

Looking up through his glasses that kept slipping down his nose he reminded Jean, as always, of the stereotypical child genius. Huge glasses, small body, baby face. Angie thought he looked like Radar on "M*A*S*H," but Angie found "M*A*S*H" parallels throughout her life. Her fairy tale was "M*A*S*H." Jean had often wondered what Eric Berne would have made of that. Jean's own fairy tale, as she had told Dr. Hirsch years ago, was *The Three Bears*.

The Radar illusion was shattered by Mel's amazingly deep announcer voice.

"Hi," he said absently, with a vague smile in their direction.

"Almost didn't make it," Jean said, taking off her coat.

Mel nodded and mumbled as he looked back at his clipboard.

"Alien beings kidnapped us," Angie said, removing her own coat and covering her mouth with her hand to hide her braces and giggle.

Jean made a mental note to check the slipping braces when she had a chance. At the moment she simply gave the girl a patient conspiratorial smile.

"Right," said Mel, without looking up. "See you in the studio, Jean."

He turned and walked toward the short corridor. Then paused. "Kid," he said. "Alien beings would be sissy stuff compared to what goes on out there. Go look at the AP wire if you want something to feed your imagination."

Jean had no office at WSMK, but there was a small lounge with a Coke machine right behind the reception area. She strode over to the lounge and stepped in with Angie behind her. Jean had about fifteen minutes to go over her notes, on neat five-by-seven index cards, before the show started. Normal procedure was to start each program with about three minutes of introduction about some problem of everyday stress, and then open up for listeners' phone calls based either on her comments and observations or on whatever was on the minds of the callers.

When Jean had first started the program, the calls had not been steady. Both she and Mel had dreaded that the calls wouldn't come at all, or that there wouldn't be enough of them, so that Jean would have to stretch her responses and go off into half-remembered class lectures, passages from text books and pop literature, and glosses on conversations with Dr. Hirsch. That had proved unnecessary. True, for the first month or so, they had had to accept calls from some regulars they would have preferred to cut out, and occasionally, when things went slowly, callers were allowed to stay on longer than she or Mel thought best; but gradually, as the white lights on the phone stayed lit and glowing, the choices had been there to play with.

Roger had gloated and chortled with the deep guttural sound he always made when he was pleased. He talked about sales of local time and cost per fifteen and all kinds of things Jean cared little about except inasmuch as they indicated people listened to her. She actually didn't think a lot about the money, which wasn't very much, and she thought little about the job leading to anything else. She simply assumed that one day it would all end. The calls would stop coming, or WSMK would be sold or demolished to make way for another factory. But it didn't matter now that CBS was in the wings.

Angie parked herself on the out-of-place white sofa with pink flowers, her homework on her lap. Jean let herself plop into the matching stuffed chair in the small room. The furniture had come from Roger's apartment when he remodeled. Roger had been suggesting more and more frequently that Jean come and see the remodeling, though by now it was well over seven months old.

The walls of the small lounge in which they sat were covered with autographed photographs, almost all dedicated to Roger or his father, who was described by Arthur Godfrey in the Arthur Godfrey photo as "a true pioneer in radio." Roger's father, J.W.N., had managed to corral most of the known radio figures of the past, though Jean suspected that there were small radio stations from Gainesville, Florida to Eugene, Oregon with similar tributes to their pioneer contributions. Bob Hope, Lowell Thomas, Freeman Gosden and Charles Correll, Jim and Marion Jordan had smiling praise for J.W.N., and Roger Mudd, Bob and Ray, Steve Dahl and Larry Lujack applauded Roger. The Coke machine purred, and the small speaker in the upper-right corner of the room piped in WSMK, which was playing a Muzak-like version of "The Girl from Ipanema." Roger had thoughtfully told Mel that the music preceding Jean's show should be mood stuff rather than commercial. For WSMK the commercial stuff consisted of Vic Damone, Frank Sinatra, a little Ella Fitzgerald, some Wayne Newton, and some of the later Beatles music. Jean never listened to the radio. Angie sometimes listened, but to WLS, a soft rock station.

Jean had just removed her notes from the brown leather purse—which would need to be repaired or replaced soon before the strap broke—when Roger came in. Eyebrows raised, Angie looked up at him and over at her mother in a way that Jean found a bit too obvious.

"Ange, hi," said Roger, barely able to conceal his disappointment. "Good to see you."

"You too, Roger," Angie said politely.

"Angie didn't want to be home alone tonight," Jean explained with a smile, running her thumb over the cards to show Roger that she was busy.

"Mother," Angie said softly, shaking her head and looking down at her homework.

"Well," Jean corrected with a big smile which she knew must be so false that even the eager Roger would see through it, "I really wanted her with me tonight. I like her company on the way."

Roger took it in and accepted. He was, in truth, reasonably good looking. A little less than six feet tall, dark-haired, in good shape from hours on the racquetball court and in the weight rooms, he looked reasonably good except for his false front of confidence. The good thing about him, Jean had long ago decided, was that beyond that facade of confidence and early Tony Curtis charm was a decent guy who might be worth comforting or at least knowing. The worst thing was that he had had forty years and two marriages to build up that front, and she didn't think it would be easy to break it down. The one time he had taken her to play racquetball, she had outrun and out-thought him. She was a little younger and a lot smarter, but he had experience going for him and had beat her, though they both knew that four or five more times out and Jean would be playing him at least even. Roger had never issued another invitation for racquetball, though the club was no more than two blocks away.

"One bummer of a night out there," Roger said, looking back through the door as if the night snow might actually make its mark on the reception room. He was wearing dark slacks and a blue pull-over shirt with a little alligator on the pocket. No business meetings today.

"Bummer," Jean agreed, fingering the cards and smiling.

"Bummer," Angie agreed without looking up.

"I can see you want to go over your notes before the show," Roger said, getting Angie's sarcasm but choosing to ignore it. "Let's talk after. I'll give you two a ride home."

"I don't . . ." Jean began, but Angie had looked up and rolled her eyes back. She didn't want to wait on the corner up to her rear in snow while the wind stabbed her.

". . . want to stay out too late," Jean finished. "Angie has school tomorrow, and—"

"I understand," said Roger, putting his hands together and winking at Angie. "I'll get you right there. We should talk a bit about the CBS business. Alexian gave me a call. He wants all the tapes for this week to present to the network people."

It was Jean's turn to sigh.

"But you gave him tapes two weeks ago. How many hours of tape can they listen to? For Chrissake Roger, all he really needs is a few minutes."

"Right," agreed Roger, "but he wants to be sure himself and he wants a kind of montage of your best moments to sell them with."

Jean had vague doubts about selling her best moments. After all, her shows were not all "best moments." If she went to the network and they expected Johnny Carson for an unknown number of minutes each day, they were coming to the wrong place.

"Whatever," Jean said, looking down at her notes. "We'll talk after the show, Roger. Okay?"

"Right, I'll be in my office." Maybe he winked or waved. Jean didn't see. Since he was wearing soft-soled shoes, she wasn't quite sure he was gone till she heard his office door close.

"We weren't nice," she said without looking up.

"We did what we had to do," Angie said soberly.

"He's not a bad guy," Jean said, trying to read the words on the cards.

"He's no Charles Bronson," Angie came back. "He's not even Woody Allen."

"How about Tony Curtis?"

"Who?"

That ended the conversation. Jean managed to go over her notes and, as always, hoped for the muse or whatever to take over when the time came. Vaguely she thought of devoting one show to the problem of spontaneous thought. Where do thoughts come from? Why one thought instead of another? Why was she thinking what she was thinking this very moment instead of something else? Maybe it would be too complicated for the audience. Hell, it was too complicated for her; besides, it was time to get into the studio.

"Wish me luck, Bronco Billy," she said, pushing her way out of the chair.

"Luck," said Angie. "Can I take money for a Coke?"

"Why not," shrugged Jean, turning to head for the studio.

The red light was on over the studio door when she got there, which meant that Mel was doing a live commercial. She could see him through the glass partition, earphones on his youthful curly head, speaking intensely. She could also see Ted Earl, pipe in mouth, blissful look on his face, wave to her. Earl's face was typically pink and his eyeballs typically yellow. The light went off, and Jean went through the thick white door which always stuck on the carpet. She eased past Mel, got into the chair opposite him and reached for her earphones.

"After news headlines," Mel said without looking up from his clipboard and the yellow sheet of AP paper, "we go to a tape for muscular dystrophy, a Jerry Lewis, then a couple of others."

"Ready when you are," she said.

"I'm always ready," he said, raising his eyebrows wickedly and looking up just long enough to give her a Groucho leer.

Jean smiled at him, mumbled "Screwball," and put on the headphones to listen to the end of the final record, something by Jack Jones.

This was the time that always moved swiftly and gave her the sense of anxiety and dream. The voice of Mel, the commercial and then the introduction.

"It's nine o'clock and time for 'Psychologically Speaking,' an hour of observation and conversation with psychologist Jean Kaiser. Each night at this time Jean Kaiser turns her attention to making the mysteries of the mind a little less mysterious, and conversing with you, our listeners. This is not an attempt to solve psychological problems on the radio, but a chance to talk about the problems that are a part of our everyday lives. And here is Jean Kaiser."

In the nothingness of time between two thoughts, Jean realized how awkwardly the introduction avoided calling her a doctor while suggesting that she was one.

"Good evening," she said in the voice she reserved for clients and radio, a voice she hoped suggested that she was an interested human being concerned about their needs and giving full attention to their thoughts, fears, and dreams. "Tonight I want to talk a bit about life, dreams, and fairy tales."

She looked over at Ted to be sure her voice level was all right, but he was leaning back, puffing away at his pipe and examining a spot on the wall within his darkened booth.

Jean's professional world was filled with rules she had developed. Use as few psychological terms as possible. The real value was in the ideas, not the terminology.

At first it was hard to imagine people who could bring themselves to call a stranger for public help or conversation, but it soon required no imagination for there they were, three nights a week, anxious to talk, to be listened to, lonely people for whom she almost always felt something, even the most God-awful bores among them.

"One way of looking at any dream, fairy tale or life in general is as a never-ending conflict between the development of our own individuality and the pull we feel toward something more collective: our family, church, political party, some cause, group, or belief to invest our faith in. We are constantly pulled between being 'I' with a capital *I* and being part of some group image. Teenage rebellion is, in some ways, a healthy act of asserting that 'I,' asserting that the young boy or girl is separate from the family, parents, and society. . . .

"The pulling away from parents, family, friends, religion or social group is almost always painful and followed by a period of emotional or real wandering. In fairy tales and dreams, that wandering often takes place in the woods or a wilderness, some place where there are no people. In a sense, fairy tales, dreams, and initiations are often less painful ways to prepare us for the separation necessary for our development."

She looked over at Mel to see if he was listening but found his head buried in his clipboard.

"What often happens," she went on, "is that the person in a fairy tale, a dream, or in life will be welcomed back to the family, the 'we,' after a period of alienation. If not, the individual will often turn to a new group image. All too often the alienated individual will grasp a group image opposed to the earlier one, thinking he has shaken his dependence when in fact he is simply trading it for another one he will eventually have to cope with. The priest who becomes an atheist or radical, the teenager who runs from his or her family and joins a commune, all are attempting to balance their lives and needs, thinking that there is a simple solution, a final way to do this, rather than realizing that the change itself is part of a natural process, in either our celebration of ego or our clinging to some group image."

In the booth, Ted was nodding absently in what looked like agreement as he continued to meditate about the spot on his wall.

"In fairy tale after fairy tale, children are separated from their families to wander and face danger. Snow White, Little Red Riding Hood, Goldilocks, Hansel and Gretel. They face an animal or a monster as a result of asserting their independence or ego, are barely saved, and wind up back with their original family or a new one. A psychiatrist named Eric Berne suggested that each of us has his or her own fairy tale. Perhaps our fairy tales and dreams indicate where we are in this individuation process. Why don't we talk about your favorite fairy tales or frequent dreams with this in mind? Give us a call after these messages and we'll discuss them. Our number is four-three-nine-nine-nine-nine-oh."

"You are listening to station WSMK AM and FM in Evanston, Illinois," Mel's voice came in on cue. And then the taped commercials started and the studio white light went on.

"A bit heavy. You might get some screwy ones on this," Mel said, marking his clipboard with a pencil scratch.

"Well, it's a wild night and I hear banshees calling," said Jean.

"I hear the banshee voices calling 'Old Black Joe,'" Mel said, holding his hand up. For the first few months Jean had listened to the commercials so she wouldn't accidentally say something incongruous or funny related to them when she came back on live, but nothing had ever happened, and she had taken to removing the headphones for the brief relief of pressure during the breaks. The three lines were lighted on the phone, and Mel punched the first one and said, "Yes sir or madam, you are on the air with psychologist Jean Kaiser."

They had a five-second delay which Ted Earl monitored in the booth in case a random obscenity came through, which had happened only a few times.

"Hello Jean?" came a woman's voice, a high voice that seemed to come from someone wandering lost on a dense, foggy moor.

"Hello, yes," said Jean.

"Jean?" the woman repeated, and something about the repetition touched a deep chord in Jean, who filed it away for later examination.

"Ma'am," said Mel with mock patience, "you'll have to turn your radio down so you can hear us. You're getting an echo. Just turn down the volume on your radio. And while she's doing that, I'd like to suggest the same to other callers who get through on our lines. Remember the number is four-three-nine-nine-nine-nine-oh. Yes, ma'am, that's better now."

"Jean?"

"Yes?"

"My name is Dorothy. Not the *Wizard of Oz* Dorothy, mind you, though I've heard enough jokes about it in my time."

And I know your fairy tale, thought Jean.

"Jean," the woman went on, "I'm always falling in my dreams,

29

just like you said. Ever since I was a girl. And every time it scares me."

"And you always wake up before you hit the ground or you go into another dream?" Jean said, quite sure she had said nothing about falling.

"Right," said Dorothy brightly. "What does my falling dream mean?"

Jean didn't know what it meant, couldn't know without extensive meetings with the woman and even then might not know, but there was surely a sexual level here.

"Is anybody up on top of the . . ."

"Ladder," finished Dorothy. "Yes, a man and a broom. Come to think of it, the man is holding the broom."

Inside the glass booth, Ted Earl put his head back and laughed. Jean gritted her teeth and shook her head at him warningly, but he didn't see her. Mel just smiled at her.

"Do you recognize the man?" she tried.

"Big man," said Dorothy. "I get the feeling he could help me or knock me off but he doesn't do anything, just looks at me."

"Does he look like anyone you know?" Jean prompted. "Or knew?"

"No," said Dorothy. "My family has always had big men. My brothers and father and uncle were all big men like that, but they would help me if I were up there."

"Well, Dorothy," Jean said, now shaking her fist at Ted who saw her and tried to control himself, "that man may actually represent your brothers, uncles, or father, or maybe just strong male figures that could have helped you as a child. Were you a strong child or a dependent one, or is that even reasonable to ask?"

"Well, I loved my father," she said tentatively.

Ted was almost in pain behind the glass, and Jean thought about the Arthur Koestler joke about the woman who tells her friend that her son has an Oedipus complex. "Oedipus, Schmedipus," replied the friend. "As long as he loves his mom."

"I'm sure you did," said Jean. "I think, perhaps, that there is some connection to your girlhood in that dream since the dream goes back quite far. When you were a girl, did you get along well with your father?"

"Of course," said Dorothy, who sounded well beyond middle age. "You can ask him yourself."

"He's alive?" Jean said gently.

"Alive and well at ninety, and lives right here with me," said Dorothy proudly.

Ted's head had disappeared in the booth. Mel had his hand over his face, and Jean was torn between her feeling for Dorothy and the silliness of the classic situation.

"Well Dorothy," she said, turning her face from the two men, "you might think in terms of doing more things on your own, for yourself, letting your ego develop a little. You see the dream might be telling you that you have to get away from your father a bit more. Are you married?"

From the corner of her eye she could see Mel shaking his head no.

"No," said Dorothy. "Never was."

"Well, you might consider developing outside activities that don't involve your dad. I gather you spend a lot of time with him, taking care of him?"

"Yes," said Dorothy.

"Will you consider my advice?" she said sincerely.

"Well, yes," Dorothy said. "If you really think it might change my nightmares, though I don't see how. I don't understand science very well."

"Dorothy," Jean said honestly, "few if any people really do, including me. We just do our best. Thank you for calling."

Jean mouthed "Commercial" and Ted mouthed "Okay."

As soon as the white light went on, Jean rolled her eyes to the ceiling and said, "Come on kiddies, control yourselves. It's not funny to that poor woman. And how the hell am I supposed to keep this up with the two of you giggling like my daughter? You're both suitable cases for Freud himself. Get yourselves a copy of *Jokes and Their Relationship to the Unconscious*."

"You have to admit it was funny," Mel said.

Jean shrugged and let herself smile. "Well . . ." And the commercial ended.

"And this is 'Psychologically Speaking' with Jean Kaiser and you, sir or madam, are our next caller. Go ahead please."

31

"Jean. Jeannie. Jean," came a deep raspy male voice.

Jean froze in her chair. There was something, more than a mockery of the last caller.

"Sir," said Mel. "You must turn down your radio."

"My radio is down," he said. "Jean?"

Jean looked at the still-smiling face of Ted Earl and forced herself to answer. She knew there were still moments like this and, as Dr. Hirsch said, they would never fully go away. It would have been nice to know when they were coming, but as Dr. Hirsch had said several times, "Your mind is trickier than you are."

"Yes, this is Jean Kaiser, what can we talk about?"

"The past," came the slow voice. She looked at Mel, whose lips were pursed. Clearly nothing seemed strange in the voice to him. It was the touch of the old fear that often came without reason.

"The past is what makes the present," she said.

"Something happened to me a long time ago," he said, and she noticed that he had not given his name.

"How long ago?" she said.

"Almost twenty-five years ago. Very long ago and far away, like the old song. You remember that old song, Jean?"

There was something about the intimacy of the question that she didn't like, that she recognized from time to time in other callers, something that bordered on the obscene suggestion that came from certain kinds of people in the anonymity of their dark rooms.

"I remember the song," she said, motioning to Ted and Mel to be ready to cut this one off.

"I left something unfinished," the caller said. "Is that healthy to leave something unfinished?"

"It depends on what it is," she said, that sense of the uneasy clinging to the conversation.

"Someone I should have made contact with," he said. "There was one opportunity. One time. I acted but I didn't finish."

"I'm afraid you'll have to be a bit more specific than that," she said.

"I can't," he said apologetically. "It's too personal."

"Well," said Jean, trying to ease herself away. "Generally it's a good idea not to leave things unfinished. They prey on our minds,

32

grow, become more important than they should be."

"Like an old song you can't get out of your mind," he supplied. "Long ago and far away."

"Something like that," Jean agreed, shrugging at Mel, who made a throat-cutting gesture to indicate that the caller wasn't worth keeping on, not enough entertainment value.

"It involves a person," the caller said.

"It's often very difficult to face people from our past," she said. "And even when we can, we find it disappointing. Frequently, the person simply represents something. It's the something that we should face, and not necessarily the person. Do you follow that?"

"Yes," he said, "but it goes beyond that. And besides, I can make contact with the person."

"Well," said Jean. "I'd suggest you consider doing so, but consider the consequences to both you and the other person, Mr. . . . ."

"Yes," he said as if pondering the suggestion. "I'll do that. Thank you."

"You know sometimes we can't simply solve things by ourselves. We need help, professional help which—" but he hung up. Jean looked at the phone and at Mel, but Mel was already talking to the next caller.

"Dr. Kaiser?" came a voice from somewhere, and Jean had to struggle to free herself from the melody of "Long Ago and Far Away."

"I'm not a doctor," Jean said as amiably as she could. "I'm a trained psychologist with a master's degree and a lot to learn. A lot to learn."

The next caller was a woman who wanted to know the end of the fairy tale about the fisherman and the flounder. She was followed by a religious fanatic, who insisted on telling the entire story of Jonah, saying that people had failed to understand the underlying humor of the tale.

The rest was pretty routine. Mel signed off and signaled to Ted to go into the closing music and commercial.

"Well, said Mel, gathering his clipboard. "We've calmed them out there in cuckoo land for another night."

Jean grabbed her own notes and stood up as the voice of Lloyd

Bridges came over the studio speaker, urging her to try Contac.

"Your warm sympathy for our troubled audience is very touching," she said.

"Thousands of little time pills," urged Lloyd Bridges.

"I'm a warm person," Mel replied, raising his eyebrows in an awful Groucho imitation. "Like our creepy friend tonight."

Jean didn't have to ask which friend Mel referred to. He stepped ahead of her and opened the door as he did a shockingly good imitation of the dark voice. "Long ago and far awaay," he whispered, and Jean felt a childhood shiver run down her back.

"Great show," Roger said, taking her free right hand in both of his. In her left hand, Jean clutched her index cards. He had caught her before she made it to the lounge.

"Thanks, Roger. Sometimes it's hard for me to tell. It's just there and going, and suddenly it's over and I'm not exactly sure what I said."

"I know the feeling," he said sympathetically, and he probably did. Roger had filled in for everyone, disc jockey, talk show hosts, engineers, announcers, janitors and advertising salesmen.

She pulled her hand free and used it to straighten the cards.

"That old woman with the father might make a great clip for Alexian," he went on. "What was that, a man with a broom on a ladder? She couldn't be better if we planted her."

Jean paused and looked at him, on the verge of asking Roger what was in all this for him, but she held back. Jean was sure he had spent at least part of the past hour in the bathroom making his hair look casually natural, right down to the curl that bobbed on his forehead to camouflage a receding hairline.

Roger hoped Jean Kaiser would be the reward for his unselfish work on her behalf. But there were other things in it for him too, a chance to deal with network executives and an opportunity to claim, if she made it, that he had discovered a CBS personality.

He was half a step behind her when she made it to the lounge. Angie had her feet up with her math book propped in front of her and a can of Coke perched precariously on the arm of the couch.

"Well?" Jean asked, hoping to get a clear look at Angie's braces when the answer came, hoping they were straight and tight. A trip to Northbrook to see the orthodontist would take time from her schedule.

"That guy was a real creep," Angie said, reaching back for the Coke and bringing it to her mouth, where aluminum can clanked against steel bands.

"We get 'em like that sometimes," Jean admitted as much to herself as to her daughter, relieved that she wasn't the only one who had been disturbed by the dark caller.

"Look," said Roger, "get your coats on. I'll pick up my briefcase, get the car and pull up to the front. Say five minutes?"

"Five minutes," said Angie.

Roger skipped out and Jean watched her daughter gather her books and put on her coat.

"Three things to tell you," Jean said, putting her index cards in her purse and reaching for her own coat. The Coke machine perked up and hummed. "First, Roger is not a bad guy and he's not stupid. He's reading you loud and clear."

Angie's response was to pull her white wool knitted hat over her ears.

"Maybe he'll come with us to Dr. Sobel next time," she said. "Dr. Sobel should get a look at those teeth. They're either fake or they set Roger back half the national debt. I'm sure Dr. Sobel would admire—"

"Which brings us to point number two," Jean jumped in. "Open the mouth."

"They're all right," said Angie. "I checked."

Jean took off her glasses and smiled. "Humor me. Open up."

With a quick look, Jean sighed, "Thank God."

"And number three?"

Jean pointed to the balanced Coke can.

"The can," she said. "These hills—"

"—don't need your trash," Angie completed the Joel McCrea line from an early Sam Peckinpah movie they had recently watched on television.

As soon as they got into Roger's dark new Buick, he headed away from Chicago and toward downtown Evanston. Jean guessed

35

what was going on. There was no way he could get an invitation to the apartment for a cup of coffee and eventual, "Well, it's really getting late Roger and . . ." She would outmaneuver him and besides, there was no way he could find a parking space in her neighborhood on a night like this. So he headed into Evanston, where the streets were well plowed.

"Roger, Angie's got to get up for school and I've got to be at the center at eight-thirty. So . . ."

"Quick cup of coffee, some business, and I'll have you home in an hour. Promise." He actually crossed his heart and grinned. Since he wasn't a fool, Jean was sure he must feel like one when he behaved like this, but the poor sap couldn't stop putting it on. She wondered if, when he got home, Roger would look at himself in the mirror, drop his smile, punch himself in the head and say aloud, "Jerk, you did it again."

He pulled up right in front of The Keg on Grove Street at the fringe of the four or five square blocks that formed downtown Evanston. The temperature was dropping with a probable below-zero wind-chill and no one was wandering the streets. The wind scooped a layer of snow into the air, and the frozen shards glittered in the light from a restaurant window. The three of them plunged through the door.

"Getting colder," Roger observed, rubbing his hands together.

Behind his back when he turned to look for a table, Angie whispered, "That's who he reminds me of. One of those TV weathermen who're always smiling and telling bad jokes."

"Ange," Jean whispered back in warning, but she had to admit it was a good comparison.

Roger motioned for them to follow him into the darkness. Each table, and they were all empty, had a candle burning on it inside a dark red tear-shaped glass.

"How about this one?" he said, stopping far enough from the door to avoid the draft if anyone else came in. He warmed his hands over the candle, took off his coat, and sat down with an eager grin.

"I think I'll have a look at the menu," he sighed, reaching for the knotty-pine-colored rectangle propped between the sugar and a thin red vase with a single artificial red flower of unknown species.

Angie shot Jean a look of despair, and Jean, who caught it in spite of the fact that she had removed her glasses to wipe off the steamy lenses, said, "Roger, we really do have to get home."

He held up his right hand.

"I'll eat fast and talk while I'm eating. Promise. I said I'd have you home in an hour. Why don't you two order something?"

The waiter, a thin young man with dark hair combed straight back, came over when Roger motioned to him. He was wearing dark pants, a white shirt, and black bow tie. He looked to Jean like a solicitous apprentice undertaker. The effect was aided by the flickering candlelight that cast dancing shadows over his nose and hid his eyes.

"I'll have the whole broiled lobster," Angie said, sweetly selecting the most expensive entree on the menu, "and salad and Coke."

"Angie," hissed Jean.

"No, that's a good idea," Roger jumped in, hoping, clearly in vain, to make points with Angie, whom he must long ago have seen as the enemy. "I'll have the same."

"My father's favorite dinner," Angie said, taking a breadstick from the wicker basket on the table and cracking it in half.

"My first wife's too," Roger returned. "The two of them would probably hit it off."

"Okay, the pair of you," Jean said, fishing through her purse for her amber container of Fiorinal. A migraine might or might not be coming. She wasn't taking any chances. "Back to our corners. Sparring's over. It was one each and one even. We'll call it a draw." She turned to the cadaverlike waiter, "I'll just have a Sanka."

The waiter nodded and departed and Roger began his business, but not much of it was really new. There would be a point somewhere, and it was Jean's job to spot it when it came.

"One thing they like about you, Alexian especially," Roger said, reaching for a breadstick which he played with while he talked, "is the way you steer around the sex talk. I mean you're sympathetic, but you keep it light without letting it get dirty. That woman in L.A., what's her name, makes it too heavy. It's her voice that saves her. And the one back East, New York, Boston, Philadelphia, wherever, the one with the schmaltzy German accent, a female Doctor Freud, sells too hard."

Jean nodded through the monologue, drank her Sanka slowly,

and when the lobster came, she watched Angie ravage the carcass. It reminded her of a line Dr. Hirsch had once quoted to her as a joke, "I saw a woman flayed," he had quoted, "and you can't imagine the difference it made in her." Dr. Hirsch had been referring to the process of psychotherapy, but Jean saw only the bloody image. Angie's head came up and Jean knew the kid was capable of trying to order another lobster, even if it made her sick, just to make a dent in Roger's wallet.

"Look," Roger was saying, conducting the conversation with his baton breadstick. "We know on-the-air psychologists are not all that new anymore."

"Eat," Jean reminded him.

"Right," he said, remembering, and dug into his lobster while continuing to talk. "And almost all of them are women. Don't ask me why."

"I think one reason might be . . ." Jean started, but it was clear that Roger didn't want an answer. He was heading for something.

"The important thing is that they do want you. Alexian is sure you'll have a firm offer in a few days. The tape's not to sell you but to establish a price."

"Like a prostitute," Angie chimed in. "I'm finished."

"We'll go in a minute," Jean said, trying to put some warning in the words.

"I'm hurrying," Roger said, and he was.

The waiter appeared with a fresh pot of water and a Sanka packet before Jean had finished what she had. Business was slow.

"So," Roger finally came to the point, "it might be a good idea to think about getting a professional agent, someone to represent you."

Roger went into a bit of business about extracting a piece of meat from a reluctant pink claw, and Jean touched his arm. Angie paused in her attempt to remove a piece of lobster lodged in her braces to radiate disapproval.

"Roger, you are doing a great job. I trust you. Keep it up, okay? I'd have to give an agent what, ten percent, maybe more?"

"But a good agent can more than make up that ten percent with good deals. I think it would be worth doing."

"I'll stick with you," Jean said, giving his arm a final pat and returning to her second Sanka. Hell, she thought, I'm starting to smile and talk like him. We're an old Rock Hudson movie. "We really do have to—"

"Finished." Roger beamed, wiping the corners of his mouth with a napkin and motioning for the check as he stood up. "I'll take you home."

While Roger paid, Jean and Angie moved toward the door, putting on their coats.

"Prostitutes," Jean whispered, shaking her head. "You want to move out of Castle Frankenstein or don't you?"

Roger's nonstop chatter began again before they got back into the car. Jean wasn't paying attention to the words, simply nodding and saying "Uh huh" every time Roger paused. When he hit Howard Street and made the right turn, Roger seemed to run out of conversation. Jean had seen it with clients at the center. They'd go on, cocky, joking, angry, challenging and then suddenly they'd stop and either pull in or let the truth show through, even if only for a second with an "I'm lonely," or "Hell, I'm scared," or even, "Can you help me? I think I'm cracking up." Those were the good ones, the ones she had at least a shot at helping. She hoped Roger wasn't about to lay a confession or a need in her lap tonight.

They drove in silence the next five blocks to the front of the apartment building, where Roger stopped.

"Angie," he said softly, looking back at the girl, "am I really that bad?"

Angie gave it a few seconds and answered, "No."

"Truce?" he asked. His smile now was small and vulnerable.

"I'll try," Angie said, getting out of the car.

A pickup truck pulled up behind Roger's Buick and revved its motor impatiently.

"I'll call you tomorrow," Jean said, getting out of the car. If the pickup truck weren't there she probably would have leaned over and given him a kiss. He looked like he could use it. Come to think of it, so could she. But there was no time.

"Okay," he said. "Take care."

Angie had already dashed across the sidewalk and into the hallway. Jean followed her, remembering to close the door behind her.

The spring had been broken for months, and Mrs. Park had never bothered to fix it, or repair the furnace, or change the light bulbs, or . . . Time to move and that was for sure. As she ran to the door hoping in the darkness not to step in a pile of Pal's shit, Wayne and Martha's curtain moved slightly and the dog went into his customary barking frenzy. One of them, probably not the dog, Jean thought, had been looking out at her.

Jean fished her keys from her purse and touched her mother's wedding band, which she carried on the chain. Then the two of them went through the second door and plunged into darkness, feeling their way and counting stairs.

"I was going to have a little mother-daughter talk with you about Roger," Jean said, groping for the front door, "but I think we can skip it. What'ya think, kiddo?"

"I think we can skip it," Angie agreed.

Jean shifted her purse and got the door opened. The radiators hissed and clinked in the darkness. They usually left a small light on when they went out. Jean thought she had, but maybe she had forgotten.

"Boots off at the door," Jean said, finding the light switch and flicking it on.

Angie kicked her boots off into the cardboard Wheaties carton in the alcove and headed back to her room, clutching her books to her breast. As Jean took off her glasses and searched for something to wipe them with, she heard the heavy thud of one of the Hellmans walking above. In the back of the apartment, Angie was turning on lights.

"I'm taking a very quick, very hot bath, if there's any hot water, and then I'm going to . . ." Jean began as she kicked her own boots off and hung her coat and purse in the small closet near the door, but she didn't finish.

Angie had run back through the apartment, her face pale.

"Klinger," she shouted, looking very, very young. "He's not in his cage, but the cage is closed."

"We'll find him," Jean said confidently. "He must have found some way to squeeze out through the food dish or maybe you just let—"

"Mother," Angie said, the tears starting, "there's no way."

"Well . . ."

"I just looked all through the back. I called him."

"We'll just look more carefully, Ange. We'll start in the front and work our way back."

Jean moved into the living room and turned on one of the two standing lamps that had been given to her more than a dozen years earlier as wedding gifts from her Aunt Ellen back in North Carolina. The room was large, but there wasn't much furniture and not many places for a bird to hide.

"Klinger," Angie called, stepping on her tiptoes to examine the top of the fake fireplace and then getting on her stomach to look under the couch, chairs and desk in the far corner. Jean looked on the bookcases and behind the books. No bird.

"I'll try my room," Jean volunteered. "You check the dining room and the bathroom."

A little light from the apartment ten feet away and the hall light were enough for Jean to make out her bed and dresser. Her room was right off the living room. And hers was the noisiest radiator.

She turned on the light and saw it. Something, air escaping from her lungs, made a sound and from another room Angie shouted, "Mother, you found him?"

On the white wall about two feet over her bed was a splash of dark red, and on her pillow lay the crushed body of the parakeet, his dead eyes open, a tiny blue-white downy feather blowing crazily atop its head in a faint draft.

◇ *FOUR* ◆

It was a few minutes past midnight. Jean was tired and the young cop was marking up her floor with his wet boots. She knew that when the policeman and his partner left, she would retrace his path through the apartment, mopping up and hoping there were no scuff marks to work on. To make it worse, this was the same cop who had come when she complained about the joy boys across the street just before winter took over.

His partner was in the kitchen, a burly not-too-bright-looking man about forty with a smashed nose. The partner was talking to Angie at the kitchen table. Angie had stopped crying and was sipping hot chocolate.

"You can remove the parakeet," the young cop said, standing in Jean's bedroom. The cop's name, according to the shiny silver rectangle on his chest, was Selig.

"I thought you might want it for evidence or something?" she said, realizing that it sounded ridiculous. Jean hdn't changed her clothes. She still wore the sweater and slacks she had had on at the studio. She could see that Selig was torn between a nonprofessional interest in her and a growing suspicion that he might be dealing with the neighborhood dingaling.

"Way I see it," Selig said languidly, "the bird squeezed out, flew around in the dark, got confused and smashed into the wall. Birds are always getting splattered. My sister had a parakeet killed himself trying to go out a closed kitchen window. Downtown pigeons are doing kamikaze flights into City Hall and the Federal Building every day. I heard only a week ago a fat gray pigeon cracked right through a window at Criminal Courts. Blood and feathers all over the place."

"Officer Selig," Jean began, folding her arms in front of her and moving a step closer, not enough to make it intimate but enough to make it urgent. "First, we left a light on when we went out. It was out when we returned. Second, my daughter is sure the bird was in the cage when we left. Just go look at the cage and tell me if you see any way the parakeet could have gotten out of the cage by himself."

Selig looked tired. His lids were heavy and his eyes slightly red. He was also on the verge of needing a shave and was probably at the end of a shift.

"How'd you like a cup of coffee?" Jean asked.

"No thanks," he said, looking quickly at her bed and back again at her. "Look, my sister's kid had a hamster, fat little . . . thing. He wormed out of a space between two bars in his cage you wouldn't believe."

"Your sister's kid has problems holding onto pets," Jean said.

"This is another sister," Selig said, ignoring the touch of sarcasm.

"So the bird magically got out, turned off the light and, in near-total darkness, made a right turn into my room, ignored the window through which some light was coming from next door, and flew at about fifty miles an hour into the wall, conveniently landing on its back on my pillows."

Selig shifted his weight from one leg to the other, adjusted his cap and blew out a puff of air.

"Something like that," he said, "but I think you maybe forgot this time to turn on the light when you went out. What is it you want me to think, ma'am?"

Jean wanted to shout at Selig, throw some credentials in his face. I'm a psychologist, she thought, an intelligent human being, not a hysterical nitwit. Can't you see that? But it was clear that he couldn't see anything but a bird that got confused and committed accidental suicide.

"Someone came into this apartment when we were out," Jean said evenly. "He, she or they took the bird out of the cage, came into my bedroom, killed it by smashing it against the wall, laid it on my pillow, turned out the lights and went away."

"Ma'am, why would anyone do that?"

"I don't know. This is a batty neighborhood. Maybe the happiness boys across the street saw you coming in here after I complained about them a few months ago, and they're getting back at me."

"Waited a long time, didn't they?" asked Selig pointedly, looking at his watch.

"Okay," Jean plunged on, "the couple downstairs, Martha and Wayne Preston. They threatened me earlier this evening. The whole neighborhood must have heard. And then they pulled the power switch downstairs and turned off our lights."

Selig's eyebrows went up and he shook his head.

"What'd you argue about?"

"They're convinced I have some machine in here that interferes with their television reception. That I've got it hidden behind a fake thermostat."

"Do you?" asked Selig.

"That's not funny," Jean said, trying to keep from tapping her foot.

"Sorry, it's been a long day," Selig said wearily. "Anyone else?"

"I don't know," Jean said, unfolding her arms and looking at the ceiling. "The kid upstairs and his father are a little strange and the landlady's an alcoholic with a few grudges. . . . I'm cleaning up the mess."

She had avoided looking at the bird's body on her pillow and the spot on the wall, but she knew they were there, and she wanted the memory gone. She moved to the bed, took a deep breath, reached down and picked up the bird, did a rather adroit one-handed removal of the pillowcase and dropped the remains of Klinger inside. She would wash the wall with Ajax when the police left.

"Ma'am," Selig said, "what do you want us to do? You want me to question all these people, tell 'em it's a case of suspicion of murdering a parakeet?"

"If you think this is so amusing, why don't you tell my daughter your jokes? It was her bird. I'm sure she'll find it funny."

"Lady," sighed Selig. "We don't have anything here to report."

"How about breaking and entering, destruction of private property?" Jean held the pillow case containing Klinger's corpse away from her, wondering what she would do with it, hoping Angie wouldn't insist on a backyard burial in the middle of the night and the dead of winter.

Selig looked around the room and back at Jean before answering.

"We looked at your doors, your windows. There's no sign of forced entry. And if you're gonna ask me to get fingerprints, forget it. That costs the city a lot of money, and this place must be filled with all kinds of prints. Even if it made sense, the best you got here is possible suspicion of killing a pet bird. Lady, look at it my way and have a heart."

"Okay, that's it, you win. Pick up your partner and go protect the neighborhood or whatever you plan to do next."

"You got a phone in here I can use?" He looked around.

"I don't have a phone in my bedroom," she said, taking a step into the alcove and turning out the bedroom light.

"It's a good idea in a neighborhood like this to have a phone nearby at night."

"I'll keep that in mind, but I don't expect to be in this neighborhood much longer."

"That's a good idea," Selig said, putting his hand out. "You want me to get rid of Trigger for you?"

"His name was Klinger."

"Sorry."

She handed him the pillowcase. Selig took it, rolled it into a wad and shoved it in his jacket pocket.

"Tommy," he called to his partner.

"Okay," Tommy called back.

"Can I say something friendly or are you gonna tear my head off?" Selig said softly.

Jean shrugged and softened a little, adjusting her glasses.

45

"A neighborhood like this can get to you, you know what I mean? Something happens, a little thing and you see something bigger. I can't blame you. You and the kid move into a nice neighborhood and you'll be all right. I've seen things I wouldn't want my kid or any kid to see."

"Me too," said Jean, "but they're not confined to neighborhoods like this. Thanks. I don't know. Maybe you're right. Maybe we did forget the light and the bird . . . but I don't think so."

"So," said Selig, rubbing his eyes, "all the more reason to move."

The other cop came down the short hallway, adjusting his cap and leaving more wet footprints. "All set?"

"All set," said Selig.

"Well good night," said Selig, touching the brim of his cap. "Double-lock the door behind us and I think it'd be a good idea if you tell your landlady to get the lights working out in the hallway and up the steps."

They stepped out and both cops gave a little smile. Jean closed the door and listened to them clop down the stairs, knowing that if Wayne and Martha hadn't been the ones who came into the apartment, they were probably consumed with curiosity. Pal barked furiously, and Jean headed for the kitchen.

Angie was sitting in her pajamas, wearing a pink robe a size too small that her father had given her.

"I'm glad they're gone," said Angie, sipping the last of her hot chocolate. "That policeman was treating me like a six-year-old. I don't think he had all his smarts. Don't you have to have a minimum IQ to be a policeman?"

"I don't know." Jean went to the sink, grabbed a fresh yellow sponge, wet it and took the Ajax in her free hand. "They took Klinger with them. They'll take care of him."

Angie shrugged. "He was a dumb bird," she said softly. "But I liked him."

"I liked him too. Should we get a Klinger the Second?"

"I don't think so. Maybe when we move. Maybe we can get a cat."

"Sounds good to me," Jean said. "Your Uncle Lloyd and I had a cat when I was a girl. Picked up fleas all the time. I'm going to clean up and mop the floor once over. You finish your chocolate and brush your teeth."

"Mom . . ."

"And tonight I'll sleep in your guest bed if that's all right with you."

"I'd like that," Angie smiled. "You really think it was just an accident, that somebody didn't come in here and do that?"

The sponge was dripping. Jean looked at it, pursed her lips and shook her head.

"No, that policeman convinced me. We just had a bad day and saw shadows where there weren't any shadows."

Angie didn't look as if she had an argument welling up, but Jean took no chances. Sponge and Ajax-armed she hurried to clean out that damned spot.

This settled it. In the morning she would call Max, very businesslike, tell him that she wanted to get out of her lease, and she would spend the afternoon trying to find a new apartment. She hesitated at the door of her room, fought back a memory that wanted to surface, plunged in, turned on the light, and did what she had to do.

◇ *FIVE* ◆

Angie didn't want to get up in the morning, but she didn't want to stay home alone either, so she went to school.

"I'll be home early," Jean had said over bowls of Cap'n Crunch, which were no damn good for you but which they both liked with bananas and milk. "Maybe we'll have an apartment or two to look at."

Klinger wasn't mentioned. Jean had cleaned out the cage and put it in the front closet behind the suitcases.

"Is it okay if Elizabeth comes over after school?" Angie asked, getting her coat and white hat on. The day was gray and looked cold, but it wasn't snowing. The problem with Elizabeth Fratianno coming over was that Jean would have to walk her home when it got dark and that would cut into apartment-hunting, but Angie had gone through a bad night, and it might be good if she weren't alone, even for an hour or two.

"Sounds fine with me. Ask her if she can stay for dinner. If you like I'll call her mother."

"No thanks," said Angie, hoisting up her book bag, "We're not babies, remember? She can ask herself. Bye." And out she went.

48

Jean finished her Sanka, put on an extra sweater and her coat, and forced herself to take a look in her room to see if the spot had dried. It had, but there was still a faint, distinct outline.

The wind wasn't blowing too badly when she stepped outside, and she guessed the temperature was somewhere in the low twenties, a balmy day for a Chicago winter. She almost decided to walk, but there were too many things to do.

Art Hellman passed her, coming back from his morning walk. Jean looked at him with suspicion, but behind his thick glasses Hellman returned nothing. As usual, he didn't even seem to recognize her.

There was no thought of digging the car out of the garage, but Jean dutifully went down the snow-covered walkway next to the building, negotiating mounds of dirty ice that Mrs. Park hadn't cleared away, and went through the side door of the garage. The idea was simply to start the car each morning to be sure it would go when the alley was clear. She remembered to leave the door open. Warnings from friends and occasional news stories of people being killed by exhaust fumes in closed garages were less responsible for her caution than was the memory of Joseph Cotten locking Teresa Wright in the family garage with the family car spouting poison in *Shadow of a Doubt*. Come to think of it, Teresa Wright was in a play downtown. Maybe she could take Angie out for dinner and a show, away from the apartment. Maybe tomorrow.

When she stepped into the garage, she knew that something was wrong. She could see it, but it took a few seconds to register in the gray morning light coming through the door.

The garage was filled with garbage. The garbage covered the cement floor on both sides of her car and Mrs. Park's car. Green plastic bags had been ripped open and putrid mounds of empty Campbell's soup cans, cigarette butts, assorted letters and newspapers were all over the place. This wasn't a neighborhood. It was a road company production of *The Snake Pit*.

Don't think this time, Jean told herself. Just move. And she did. Out the door, across the small frozen lawn, up the steps past her own back door, Hellman's, and to the third floor apartment of Mrs. Park, where she knocked three times and rang the bell.

One of the two teenage Park girls came to the door. Jean couldn't keep their names straight. At first she had felt guilty about falling into the Anglo trap that all Orientals looked alike. Then one of her clients, a Taiwanese, had told her that her big problem was distinguishing between whites, who all looked alike to her.

"Is your mother home?" Jean asked evenly.

"No," replied the girl without opening the door all the way. "She left for work."

"All right. Please give her this message. Someone has dumped garbage all over the garage, on your car, my car, all over the place. It has to be cleaned up. My daughter and I will do some of it, but your family will have to pitch in."

The girl nodded and frowned. "Why would anyone do that?" she asked.

For the first time, Jean connected the mess in the garage to last night. It might be. It really might be.

"It happened before," the girl said, shivering in the open door. "Two years before you moved in. We think it was the Hellman boy and a nutty boy in the building across the alley who was his friend."

"Why would they . . . ?" Jean began. Maybe it was the Parks who were the target of this one. In this neighborhood, who could tell?

"My father, who was here then, said it was because we were Koreans," the girl said, shivering. "I'll tell my mother. I've got to get to school now."

Jean nodded, and the girl closed the door.

The trip to the community center was two buses long, but uneventful. She had a cup of tea from the machine in the hallway and made a quick call to Max before her first appointment. Usually in such bad weather about a third of her appointments didn't show up. Most of them weren't paying anyway. About half of them were Russian Jewish immigrants for whom she needed Harold, a volunteer translator who was about seventy, had a good sense of humor, spoke Yiddish and a little Russian, and even helped with the caseload since the office was short-staffed.

Max's secretary, Louise, answered on the second ring.

"Louise, it's Jean, is he in yet?"

"He's in and running," said Louise with a tolerant tinge in her voice. "How're you doing?"

Louise was about fifty, a dark, good-looking woman with six children varying in age from six to twenty-five. She was efficient, calm and unflappable. Jean liked her—and appreciated the fact that she hadn't pried or raised her eyebrows or criticized in any way during the whole divorce procedure. At one point, in fact, after it was all settled, she had said, "Let me know if I can help."

"I'll get him," Louise said. "Say hi to Angie for me."

"I will," Jean answered and waited. Then came Max's voice, steady, confident, not too deep. He sounded just the way he looked—six feet tall, well built, straight blond-brown hair and a not-too-fancy suit with a solid-colored sweater and tie. Jean would have bet money that he was dressed as she imagined him. He reminded her and probably others of William Hurt in *Body Heat*.

"Jean," he said. "Everything all right? What can I do for you?"

His first reassuring words were pure Max. Strong, reliable. He would take over and make things right. It was a good part of what she had escaped from in their marriage, his overwhelming strength. He was fine in bed, at least before things started going bad, though he had been pretty conventional. But fair is fair, so had she.

"I want to break my lease," Jean said, sipping her tea that didn't taste like tea.

"No problem," said Max. "I think—"

"Please don't tell me you think it's a good idea, and don't hint that you'd warned me about the building and the landlady and the neighborhood. I've had a rough night and morning."

"I wasn't going to," Max said gently. "You find a place to move?"

"I'm working on it."

"Okay. When you've got a place and a mover set, give me a call and I'll send a letter to . . ."

"Mrs. Park. Thanks Max."

"What's it about? You want to tell me?"

She did want to, but had no intention of doing so. Besides, Angie would be spending the weekend with him and would certainly tell him about Klinger and Wayne and Martha and whatever else there was.

"No. It'll all be fine when we move. How've you been?"

"You really want to know?" he said with a sad overworked tremor in his voice.

"I asked, didn't I?" Jean said, but she really didn't want to know.

This time he laughed, a knowing laugh.

"Jeannie, we know each other too well. I'm fine. Take care. Call me if you want me, and I'll pick Angie up about ten Saturday morning. Okay?"

"Okay, Max, I'm sorry. Like I said, it's been a rough morning."

"We have them," he said knowingly. "I've got someone on the other line. Take care."

She said good-bye and hung up.

Max was a Georgia boy who had done some graduate work at the University of North Carolina. They hadn't met there but in Chicago while both of them were going to Northwestern. The North Carolina tie had broken the ice at a party. He was perfect, strong, reliable, and almost finished with law school; and though he wasn't a Baptist, her brother Lloyd had served as minister when they married. Now it was over.

The door to her office opened and Harold put in his head of white hair.

"So, you a big network star now? Gonna get me Morgan Fairchild's home number?" he said.

"Not yet, but I'm working on it," she said. "Who've we got waiting?"

"Yuri the fury," he said shaking his head. "They're after him again."

Great, thought Jean, just the thing to start the morning: Yuri Burovsky, a fifty-year-old mechanical engineer who was convinced the KGB was following him though he could give no convincing reason why they might be interested in him among the thousands of Soviet Jews in Chicago. Burovsky wouldn't work beneath his skill level and couldn't hold a job when he got one. The damnedest thing about the man was that he loved to argue with her. So he tolerated their sessions as a forum, and because they were paid for by the Jewish Federation of Chicago, but like most Russians he didn't believe much in psychology.

"Okay, bring him in and stay close."

Harold closed his eyes in sympathy and disappeared. If things worked out, Jean would have a long lunch hour to go through the classified ads of the *Evanston Review* she had picked up and maybe time to call Lloyd. If things went well.

Harold ushered Yuri in. A small man in a dark suit, the Russian always reminded Jean of a shoemaker, though she had no idea why.

"I have a puzzling question for you," Yuri began with a sly smile, and Jean knew it would be a long morning.

After Yuri and the morning women's encounter session in which Adele Wyncoff announced for the fifth time in the last year that she was definitely going to leave Jerry Wyncoff, Jean managed to glance through the *Evanston Review* and mark five apartment leads, all of them for rents well above what she was paying. Then she called Lloyd at home.

Her sister-in-law Fran answered. Behind her was the fury of a screaming child, Walter.

"Hello, Jean? I can't hear. Walter's home for lunch and fighting with Dotty about . . . will you two please hold it down? I'm talking to Aunt Jean. Jean, sorry. Everything all right?"

"Well," said Jean. "There's good news and bad news."

"Please, no jokes before the kids go back to school," Fran answered with a small laugh as the noise behind her started to rise again. Fran was about Jean's age, a little thinner, but the two of them had often been mistaken for sisters, which pleased them both. They didn't spend a lot of time together, but when they did they got along.

"Is Lloyd home?"

"He stopped by for lunch, but he's hiding upstairs until Walter calms down. He may be on a call on the other line. I'll check. You coming out this weekend?"

"I'm apartment hunting—" she began, but Fran, with at least fifty balls in the air, interrupted to shout, "Lloyd, pick up the phone."

"Hello," came Lloyd's deep voice. "I've got it, Fran."

Fran hung up and the line got quiet. While Jean had lost almost all of her North Carolina accent, Lloyd's was still strong and re-assuring.

"It's Jean," she said.

"How're you doing? How's Angie?"

"We're fine," she said. "Well, almost. We had a little problem last night, and I was wondering if Angie could stay with you guys for a few days next week until we move out of the apartment."

Lloyd was silent for a few seconds, and then gave her the opening.

"Sure, love to have her, so will the kids. You want to tell me about it?"

She told him briefly, and he listened quietly. He was a good listener, probably better than Dr. Hirsch. Maybe it came with the job. She imagined him sitting at his desk in the house in Oak Park, probably wearing a pair of faded pants, a shirt with an ill-matching sweater and no tie. He'd be playing with his glasses and listening with his lips pursed. Lloyd resembled their father, and though he had turned out to be a minister, he never seemed to develop his dad's severity. In Lloyd's view the world was not a dark and horrible place with God standing over your shoulder ready to slap your wrist if you broke a rule. Lloyd's God seemed a reasonable human figure.

"You agree with the policeman?" he said.

"Don't know," she said.

"I don't like it much," he said. "I agree it's a good idea to get out of there. You want me to come over tonight?"

"No," she said, hearing a knock at her office door. "You've got your own life and family. We'll be fine, but if the apartment business doesn't get settled fast, I'll send Angie over for a few days."

The knock came again.

"Gotta go now," she said. "The world needs me. I'll tell you all about the CBS deal tonight or tomorrow."

"Jean." This time his tone was more earnest, with a seriousness she recognized. "I hate to ask, but this stuff isn't bringing up things from way back, is it?"

"No . . . at least not yet. I'll be fine. Gotta go now. Say bye to Fran for me."

She hung up and told her next client to come in. If it were someone she knew well, she would have finished the sandwich she had made, cucumber and butter on whole wheat, but it was someone new so she left it for later in the lower drawer next to the broken pencil sharpener.

The rest of the day went reasonably well. By ducking out early, she managed to look at two apartments, both in Evanston. One was a single bus ride to and from the community center. It was a relatively new six-flat managed by one of the big real estate agencies, which suited Jean just fine after having to deal with Mrs. Park. There were problems with big realtors who ran apartments, but she was ready to swap her present problems for them. The woman who showed her around made it clear that she was a little concerned about renting to a single parent, especially a woman, but Jean put on her best professional manner, shamefully made friends with the woman, and said she would let her know in the morning.

The woman, whose name was Ann Kruth, displayed a little more concern when Jean mentioned the problems with Mrs. Park and indicated that Jean should make up her mind quickly since there were others definitely interested, the standard line, which Jean accepted solemnly.

The second apartment was bigger, a little cheaper but on the third floor—slightly darker and older, and two buses from the community center. Both apartments were within walking distance of a junior high school, and Evanston had a reputation for good schools. On the way home, she was reasonably sure she would take the first apartment, providing she could get it. If worse came to worse, and it often did, she could bite the bullet and ask Max to pull some strings with the real estate agency. He seemed to know someone at every big agency and did legal work for most of them.

When she got home, Angie and Elizabeth Fratianno were talking seriously in Angie's room. Elizabeth was a string bean of a girl, half a head shorter than Angie. She looked like a future nun.

"I'm home," Jean announced. "How's everything? How are you, Elizabeth?"

The girls answered "Fine," in chorus.

And everything did seem to be fine. They ate frozen pizza, made popcorn and played Scrabble with Angie winning, partly because Jean refused to make crossword puzzle words like "em" and "io."

Jean insisted that Angie come with her when she walked Elizabeth home.

"Just to keep me company," she said. "And you can talk to Elizabeth a while longer."

Angie hadn't questioned it and on the way back, Jean told her about the Evanston apartment and asked if she wanted to see it.

"Take it, please take it," said Angie. "It sounds great."

Jean chose not to mention the garbage in the garage. She'd clean it up herself as soon as Max picked Angie up on Saturday.

When they got back to the apartment, the light they had left on was still on and the phone was ringing. Angie kicked off her shoes and ran into the kitchen to get it.

"Hello. . . . Hello?"

"Who is it?" Jean asked, as she removed her own boots.

"I dunno," said her daughter. "I think someone's on the other end but they aren't talking. That's okay. They just hung up. Probably one of those Mexicans who can't speak English and got embarrassed."

"Probably," Jean agreed, wondering how she would find a way to sleep in Angie's room tonight—not because the girl needed her, but because she couldn't sleep with that spot over her head and the faint memory of a ghost in the room. She also knew she'd need an appointment with Dr. Hirsch, the next day if possible.

The next day was Friday and the sun was shining—well, almost shining. It took an occasional bored glance from behind thin gray clouds, didn't like what it saw, and hid again. Contrary to popular belief, Jean knew from personal experience that things did not always look better in the morning. Angie's guest bed was too soft, and Jean felt a slight but distinct stiffness in her back. A hot shower helped, but Angie's obvious eagerness to spend the weekend with her father did not.

"Well, should I tell him or shouldn't I, I mean about Klinger and everything?" Angie asked over a second bowl of Cap'n Crunch and a glass of chocolate milk.

"Tell him what you think you should tell him or have to tell him," Jean said. "He knows about our moving. I told him yesterday. He'll take care of the lease."

Angie checked the clock, gulped some milk, hurried the dishes into the sink.

"I haven't got time to wash them," she said. "I'll do 'em when I get home."

"I'll take care of it," Jean said. "Get going. Maybe I'll have the new apartment wrapped up when I see you."

Angie clunked down the hallway and out the door. Deserving at least a massive sigh, Jean let one out and reached for the phone. It was a little early, but she didn't want to take a chance on losing the apartment because she was too polite.

Ann Kruth, the woman from the real estate company, was in early.

"I've thought it over and I really would like the apartment," Jean said.

"Fine. Fill out the application I gave you, put it in the mail or bring it to the office with a fifty-dollar deposit, and we'll start processing you right away. It shouldn't take more than two or three days, weekdays. We'll probably have an answer for you by next Thursday."

"Decorating," Jean threw in.

Phones were ringing behind Ann Kruth.

"Well," she said. "The walls were just painted six months ago. We'll see to it that they're all washed."

"The bathroom," Jean put in.

"The bathroom will be painted."

"How soon will I be able to move in? I mean I want to hire a mover and . . ."

"Why don't you just wait till I get back to you? This may take a day or so longer than I think it will or there may be some reason to consider going to another applicant. I see no reason . . . will you excuse me? I've got phones ringing all over the place, and I'm the only one here."

There was nothing more to say. Jean hung up and wondered how she could take a week or more in this apartment. Once the decision was made, she wanted to go as quickly as she could.

She called Max's office, looking at the clock. He wasn't in yet, but Louise was and took the message that Jean would appreciate his pushing a little to get her the apartment.

"It's Bellwood Realty," Jean said.

"He knows Barry Dunne there," Louise said. "I'm sure it'll be fine."

She asked Louise about her children, discovered that her son Marty was getting out of the army in a few weeks, and said good-bye.

It was too early to try Dr. Hirsch. All she'd get was his answering machine. A quick trip to the bathroom mirror to assure herself that her hair hadn't gone scarecrow over breakfast, and Jean was ready to clean the garbage out of the garage.

The job took almost half an hour, sweeping, shoveling, filling five green plastic bags she had brought, and then shoving them into the garbage cans in the yard. She could have used another shower when she was finished, but she didn't have time. Instead she washed her hands, checked her face, put back the few stray hairs that had tried to escape, and dabbed on a little of the Oh Dee Lilac Angie had given her for Christmas. It wasn't subtle but it worked.

No one went stark raving mad in her office. No one threatened suicide. There were no young girls needing abortions, and no Russians seeing KGB agents in Barnaby's Pizza Restaurant.

The first slightly bad moment came when she walked through the door of the apartment and found Angie in the living room. Usually Angie was in the back, talking to a friend or watching television. They had moved the television set out of the living room the second week they were there because Martha and Wayne complained about the noise and "viberations." Angie was looking at a school book, but the look was too intense, and it was the wrong room for studying. Jean thought she had caught a glimpse of her daughter in the window when she came down the street, but she wasn't sure.

"Fierce out there today," Jean said with a smile, her cheeks tingling.

Angie nodded.

"I think it's going to snow again, in which case we better have a lot of Ravioli-Os in the kitchen. Okay kiddo, what's going on? I can see it in your beautiful face."

"Dad's going to pick me up tonight instead of tomorrow," she said quickly and looked down at her book. "He'll be here right after work, about six."

"Okay," Jean said, slowly taking her coat off and hanging it in the closet. "Your idea or his?"

"Mine," said Angie, without looking up. "You've got a show tonight and I . . ."

"You don't want to stay here alone, and you don't want to come with me and do a Roger dodger, right?"

"Something like that."

"Sounds like a good idea to me," Jean said with a smile, hurrying to the girl and sitting beside her to give her a hug. "Let's hold off on dinner. I'm sure your father will want to take you out."

"You're not . . ." Angie tried, hugging her back.

"No, I'm not. Have a great time. I sent in an application for the new apartment, and we should be hearing some time next week."

"When we go can I put a small bomb in front of Wayne and Martha's door?" Angie asked shyly. "It doesn't have to be a real one. A nice heart attack would satisfy me."

"Not so funny, Angie." Jean got up, stretched, feeling the slight remaining tingle in her back from her night on Angie's guest bed. "That's a criminal offense. Besides, we'd need a shopping cart full of fake bombs. One for Mrs. Park . . ."

"And don't forget the jerks across the street," Angie added.

"There aren't enough bombs, Angie," Jean said. "You'll just make yourself unhappy wishing there were. These people are taking up too much of your time, and they're not worth it."

"You get that from Dr. Hirsch?" Angie asked, closing her book and following her mother into the back of the apartment.

"Probably," sighed Jean, "but I hope I thought it up on my own. I do have a few original thoughts, not many but a few. By the way, I wore the Oh Dee Lilac you gave me for Christmas and got some compliments."

It was not quite a lie. Harold, with his slight Yiddish accent, had said, "I think you spilled your yogurt or something." And Diane Noleggi thought she smelled something burning "or somethin'."

Jean checked to see that Angie hadn't packed too much for the weekend and forgotten her tooth brush or math book.

Max pulled up in front of the building at six on the button in his white Mazda and hit the squeaky horn. There was no place to park. He shrugged to them through the window. Jean nodded and held up a finger to show that Angie would be down in a minute. Their eyes held each other's for a while. He gave a slight smile and then Jean shrugged. Whether she was shrugging over their whole past together or just the moment neither could tell for sure.

"Bye Mom," shouted Angie, struggling into her boots and clinging to her overnight bag.

Jean left the window to hug and kiss her daughter.

"Dad'll take me to school on Monday," she said. "Have a good weekend. I'll try to listen to your show tonight."

"Forget it," Jean beamed, holding the door open to give the girl a bit of light down the darkened stairs. "Get your father to take you to a movie instead."

She closed the door and remembered her idea of taking Angie to a play. Well, they could do that next week. Now Jean was alone in the apartment with the radiators, the Hellman footsteps and a few things to do. She changed quickly, put on a recently purchased pink wool sweater and maroon slacks, and left, being sure to leave both the living room and kitchen lights on. The walk to Burger King was about four blocks, but a cheese Whopper with extra tomato was exactly what she needed for energy and morale.

An overweight kid in his twenties with dark curly hair looked her over carefully as he lingered over a burger in the next booth. Jean caught his eye, lifted her eyebrows wearily, shook her head and went on eating, which discouraged him.

She caught a 204 bus with time to spare and got to the studio ten minutes early.

"Where's my fan club?" Mel greeted her at the coffee machine. His cheeks were pink, probably from the cold, and with the large round glasses he looked more than ever like a boy genius, probably a math whiz.

"Angie's spending the weekend with her father," Jean said, accepting the reinforced paper cup from Mel.

"What is this, tea or coffee?"

"I don't know, but it's hot," Mel said, heading toward the studio. "Five or six minutes."

"Be right there," she said.

She didn't hear Roger come in behind her and almost spilled the hot drink when he stepped in front of her.

"Sorry," he said. He, too, was casually dressed tonight in dark slacks and white turtleneck sweater—something soft, probably cashmere. "I've got news." His smile was that of a child waiting to be coaxed to tell his mom he won the spelling bee.

"Are you going to share it with me, or do you want me to

guess?" she said, taking another sip of the liquid.

"Alexian came up with an offer. You start on a one-year contract with WBBM in Chicago, a three-nights-a-week, one-hour local slot. If it goes well, they renegotiate your contract and add a five-minute taped network slot and syndicate your series. You get fifty thousand dollars for the first year, before renegotiation."

"Fifty thousand dollars?" she repeated. This time she did spill the liquid, but it missed her and splattered on the thin brown carpet.

"Only the start," Roger chuckled. "I talked to a local speakers' agency. With that kind of exposure, he can get you four or five speaking engagements a month in the Midwest alone for a thousand plus expenses."

Jean shook her head.

"I can't believe this. I'm getting seventeen thousand dollars a year for treating people privately and I'll get all that for bullshitting three hours a week."

"Right," agreed Roger, "and you don't have to give up your regular job either. In fact, Alexian thinks it's a good idea for the time being if you continue to be a practicing psychologist."

"Roger, I . . ."

"Neither can I," Roger said, smoothing his dark hair. "Let's celebrate after your show."

She only hesitated a moment. With Angie away, there was no way she wanted to turn him down.

"Why not?" she said. "It's on me."

"Hold it. Let's wait till the first check actually comes. Then you can take me to the Petit Bergnon," Roger said, giving her a hug.

It felt good, and Jean didn't push him away or force him to shake hands.

"Roger, thanks. Really. A year ago when you asked me to do the show I never would have thought . . . Hell, we'll talk about it later."

"Later," Roger agreed, holding her hand.

Jean adjusted her glasses and her sweater and moved down the hall with her notes. She had jotted them down while eating her lunch that afternoon but now she couldn't bring herself to come back to earth. Then she remembered her subject: the biochemical roots of meditation, though that wasn't what she would call it on the air.

Ted Earl gave her a yellow-eyed smile and waved his pipe in her direction. He was nodding his head to the end of the Barbra Streisand record.

"Roger told me about CBS," Mel said, giving his notes a last look. "Congratulations. Maybe you can bring your faithful announcer along with you. I'm not proud. I'd work for double my present salary."

He was joking but he was also serious.

"I'll see what the situation's like, Mel," she said. "If I can, I will, but it doesn't seem real yet."

"Fair enough," smiled Mel. "Here we go again."

Mel did the news headlines—OPEC raises oil prices, governor vows to fight property-tax increase, higher temperatures—then a live commercial for Minute Maid Orange Juice and the show's introduction.

Keep your mind on it, Jean told herself. Stay with it.

"It's nine o'clock and . . ."

A deep breath, look at the notes, get ready.

". . . here is Jean Kaiser."

"Good evening," she said and grinned at Mel who grinned back. "I read an article the other day that's causing a small stir among psychologists. A team of researchers at a major Boston hospital has suggested that the human body has a chemical defense mechanism that keeps us alert to danger, a mechanism that goes back to our primitive beginnings. When danger arises, the chemical comes to our aid and gives us extra energy to run or fight. The problem in our hectic modern society is that the mechanism all too often is called into play when our situation is such that socially we can neither run nor fight. That builds up an excess of the run-or-fight chemicals in our body and keeps us tense and neurotic.

"What these researchers have discovered is that there are techniques that can restore the chemical balance so that we can cope with the tension. Their tentative conclusion is that techniques such as meditation, the Oriental technique of relaxation, actually affect the body chemicals and restore calm and a degree of both mental and physical health and well-being.

"So," Jean said, looking up from her notes. "The question

tonight is: What, if anything, do you do to relax? Have you tried some form of meditation? What do you think of the whole idea and, as always, what is on your mind either related to or not related to this question?"

It had sounded a little too formal to Jean. She had stuck too closely to the cards but she had feared moving away from them and losing her concentration. Fifty thousand dollars was a hell of a lot of money.

"Our number is four-three-nine-nine-nine-nine-oh," came Mel's deep voice. "And our lines are open. So dial us and tell psychologist Jean Kaiser what you think about meditation and how you cope or fail to cope with the tensions of modern life."

A transcribed commercial for TWA came on, and Ted Earl's voice crackled into the small studio.

"I meditate with a warm bottle of J and B Scotch. Keeps me very tranquil."

It sure does, agreed Jean, watching the studio light, which went to red, indicating they were back on live. The four buttons on the phone were all lit and flashing.

Mel pointed to the dancing lights and winked. Then he picked up the phone and pressed one of the buttons.

"Hello, you're on the air with Jean Kaiser."

"Jean," came the enthusiastic voice of a woman, "I listen to you every night."

"Thank you," said Jean, who was on only three nights a week. "What's on your mind tonight?"

"I don't know about that meditation business," came the woman's voice, "but television helps me. I lose myself in television. Especially a good comedy like 'Three's Company.'"

"Well," Jean began, "I'm sure that helps, but I think the idea of meditation might also help you to get rid of social pressure, to relax, and if you can, simply not to think about anything. Just listening to yourself breathe for ten minutes without thinking of anything else can help."

"Well," the woman laughed, "if I want to hear breathing, I can listen to my husband snore any night. I'm afraid it doesn't relax me a bit."

"Do you have a lot of tension? Do you want to give your name?"

"Connie," she said. "I've got a malignancy in my hip. Lost my right leg two years ago. Now they may have to take the other one. And my husband isn't exactly a big banker."

"I'm sorry," said Jean, pulled out of her own joy. "Maybe your doctor could suggest some ways you could relax."

"Drugs," Connie said. "They give me drugs, tranquilizers."

"Well, that's not what I had in mind, but your situation is a bit beyond the ordinary and I suggest you take your doctor's advice."

Mel was making a sour face. Connie was the kind of "down" caller who caused people to turn off their radios or change the station.

"Thank you very much, Connie," said Mel. "We have to move along now. The board is lighting up with calls." He punched Connie off and someone else on. "Sir, you're on."

"You are so right," came a slightly high-pitched male voice. "You really are."

"About what?" Jean asked.

"Meditation," the man answered. "I've been doing it for three years. Of course I'm still nowhere near Nirvana, but I'm able to deal at a distance with . . . things."

"What kind of 'things,' Mr. . . . ."

"Block, Arthur Block," he said enthusiastically. "I'm a poet. I spend my days running my father's safety glove company, but I'm not really there. You know what I mean?"

Mel nodded vigorously to show he knew what Arthur Block meant.

"You mean you are sort of outside looking at yourself while another part of you is writing poetry," Jean tried.

"Exactly," Arthur agreed.

"Do you get along with your father, Arthur?"

"Sure, he retired to Florida three years ago. We talk on the phone every day."

"But you don't enjoy running the glove company?"

"I'm not there," he explained again. "I meditate. I'm somewhere else."

Jean looked at the flashing lights on the phone and realized she should hurry this one up, but she also thought she might be able to help him. She had classified him among the more than fifty percent of callers who wanted help and didn't know how to ask for it. Some called in asking for help but not for what was really troubling them.

"Well, Arthur, it's commendable that you can control the difficulties and pressures of your job, but you have to spend, what, seven, eight hours a day working?"

"Sometimes more," he said.

"That's a lot of physical time you may be wasting, isn't it?"

This was sticky territory and she wanted to go slowly, carefully. She didn't know this man, his background, what made him behave like this, but the symptoms were common. As much as Roger and she told others that she never diagnosed and treated, only discussed, she knew she did far more than that, and she thought by and large that she did a lot more good than harm.

"One thing meditation, concentration can teach you is to live each moment, enjoy each moment, not escape from it," she said. "Do you follow me, Arthur?"

"Sure, but you can't just walk away from your responsibilities," Arthur came back.

Mel put out his palm and let it drop noiselessly to the small table, indicating that this one, too, was getting too heavy.

"Well," Jean said, nodding to Mel. "I think this point is worth your discussing with someone, a priest, clergyman, a good friend. Have you got someone like that?"

"I don't know," mused Arthur.

"Are you married?" Jean tried.

"My wife's downstairs watching 'The Price Is Right' or something," he said, summing up what they shared and didn't share.

Mel was signaling for a cut with his finger across his throat and his hand indicating the board.

"We'll have to interrupt here for a brief commercial message," said Mel. "And then back to our calls. Remember the number is four-three-nine-nine-nine-nine-oh." A commercial for Hamm's Beer came over the studio speaker and Mel whispered, "Nowhere near Nirvana. Sounds like the title of a best seller." Then, into the phone: "Hello, 'Psychologically Speaking.' We'll put you on as soon as the commercial ends."

Jean took a deep breath, hoping to get a little more wit into the next response, a little more drama without that melancholy touch. She tried to ignore the feeling that again she had failed someone because air time did not permit discussing matters in depth. The commercial ended and Mel said, "And now back to the show. Sir, you're on."

"Jean," came the soft male voice.

Jean's fingers pushed down on the table, bending her knuckles white. One word wasn't quite enough, but it sounded like the man who had called on Wednesday, the one Angie had called "creepy."

"Yes," said Jean, trying to keep her voice even.

"I talked to you on Wednesday," he whispered. "You remember?"

Jean looked over at Mel, who now recognized the voice, shook his head, rolled his eyes and mouthed, "That one."

"I remember," she said.

"Long ago and far away," he said.

"I remember," she repeated. "And what did you want to talk about today? Have you tried some form of meditation?"

Something, maybe a laugh came from the caller.

"Maybe," he said. "I took your advice. I made contact with that person from a long time ago. Would you like to know more about it?"

"If you want to talk about it, certainly, but we do have to move along. We have a lot of callers tonight," she said.

"I won't take long," he said. "I just had to talk to you. A little bird told me to call."

Jean closed her eyes. Coincidence, coincidence. Don't go back to it.

"I paid a visit to my friend from long ago, but she wasn't home," he said sadly. "So I left her a message. I wanted to be sure. You understand? You know, a bird in the hand? Was that the right thing to do?"

"What was the message?" Jean's throat stuck, scratched.

"Only that I remembered her and that I'd be seeing her again soon."

"I'm sorry sir, but I didn't get your name."

"I think I'll just call myself Paul," he said. "My friend might be listening, and I still want to give her some surprises. It's been so long. Twenty-five years. And I do want to see her again, soon."

"Well, Paul, I'd like to discuss this with you further," she said, controlling her voice. "Why don't you leave your telephone number and—"

But the line went dead. She looked at Mel, who had a puzzled-little-boy expression. He signaled to Ted Earl for a commercial three minutes early. When the green light went on, he leaned over and touched her hand.

"You okay, Jean? You look as if . . ."

"I've talked to a ghost? Tell Ted to hold the tape of that last caller. I want to hear it again. I'll be all right. Just keep punching the calls and talking to me during commercials."

The puzzled look continued on Mel's face, but he nodded yes and got ready to go into the next call.

But he's locked up, Jean thought. He's locked up forever, forever. It can't be him.

And then the next call came through.

◇ *SIX* ◆

It took less than five minutes to get through to the North Carolina State Police.

Roger had wanted to question her when she asked to use his office and phone immediately after the show, but there was something in her face that made him step back. Now he sat in his leather swivel desk chair looking at her with curiosity and concern. She stood holding her side with one hand and the telephone with the other. The man who answered the phone had the soft, familiar North Carolina accent of her childhood. He turned her over to someone who sounded more like the Bronx, but the man she got after him returned her to the accent.

"Ma'am," he said. "Lieutenant Wayland retired one year ago last August. He's back in Winston-Salem. Yes, ma'am, we've got records on our cases going back to the thirties, but I'm not at liberty to give out information. Thank you ma'am."

Roger considered asking a question when she hung up. His mouth opened, but Jean was back on the phone before the words came out. This time it took about four minutes to find James W. Wayland in Winston-Salem.

"Hello, Wayland here," came the voice, much higher than she had remembered it.

"Lieutenant Wayland?" she asked.

"Retired by law," he said. "Just Jimmy Wayland now. Who'm I talking to?"

"My name is Jean Kaiser," she said. "You probably don't re—"

"The Carrboro killings," he said. "You were the little girl. I'm not likely to forget you for the rest of whatever days I got left. How are you?"

Jean bit her lower lip, played with her glasses, and answered, "I'm fine, or was till today. Lieu—Mr. Wayland . . ."

"Jimmy," he said. "Call me Jimmy."

"Jimmy," Jean said. "Is he still in there? Is he still locked up?"

"Parmenter? I don't know," said Jimmy Wayland. "I guess so. Tell the truth, I don't even know if he's alive."

"Jimmy, can you find out for me? Can you find out if he's in there, and if he's not where he might be? I know it's a lot to ask but . . ."

"It's nothing to ask," Jimmy said. "I've got a garden that takes care of itself, a house that really doesn't need any more fixin' and a wife who thinks she has to come up with projects to keep me amused. Glad to find out for you. I'll call you with it in the morning."

"How about calling me with it tonight? I'll give you a number." She gave him the number of Roger's phone and waited. There was a brief silence.

"You think he's out?" he said.

"It could be."

"You sit there, and I'll get back soon's I can. But Parmenter is a name from antiquity. May take some doin'. Then again it may not."

They hung up and Jean looked at Roger.

"He's going to call me back," she said.

Roger nodded.

"Might be a while," she added.

"Want me to order a pizza?"

"Sounds all right." Jean gave him a small smile. "But use another phone and another line. He may call back soon."

Roger nodded. "Extra sauce, extra onions, right?"

"Right," she said.

The pizza came in a little under an hour. It was reasonably hot, large, and just the way Angie liked it, but Angie wasn't there. Jean nibbled and Roger consumed. Roger was respectfully silent and Jean talked. She owed him some explanation.

"I'll make it brief, Roger," she said, still unable to sit. Her hands were again hugging her breasts as if it were cold in the slightly over-heated little office. "When I was a kid my parents were murdered. I was in the house when it happened."

Roger almost dropped the slice of pizza from his hand.

"They found the man who did it. He was in the woods about thirty yards from our house. This was back in North Carolina. His name was Parmenter, Ben Parmenter. He was drunk, covered with blood. Axe was right next to him. He had just come back from Korea and had been treated for what they called battle fatigue. He had been drifting around the country. He didn't remember killing them, but he did remember my father's face looking at him. Gave a good description. Lieutenant Wayland handled the case. I remember him as a bear of a man with a rough voice who was very gentle with me. I had neighbors and relatives, but he sort of put an arm around me for a day until Lloyd flew down from Chicago."

"What happened to Parmenter?"

"They put him in a mental hospital. Back then they called them hospitals for the criminally insane. They may still call them that. They showed me a picture of Parmenter once to see if I knew him. I remember a scrawny man with wide eyes and a tuft of dark hair sticking up on his head like Stan Laurel."

"Then?" Roger asked gently.

"I did the only reasonable thing a little girl could do," she smiled. "I withdrew, almost catatonic. I had near fits when the phone rang. There had been a phone ringing in my parents' room when I found the bodies."

Roger pushed the pizza away.

"I found out later that it was my brother calling from Chicago. It was Saturday morning, and he always called the family then. But that didn't help. It was a long time before I could handle a phone ringing. Lloyd brought me to Chicago. My parents had left us a little money and Lloyd sold the house. Our Aunt Dottie came and took care of me while I went through the world's duration record for psychotherapy with Dr. Leon Hirsch."

"I've heard of him," Roger said.

"I got better," she said. "Remember the Laurel and Hardy joke from one of their movies? They haven't seen each other for years and Ollie asks Stan how he is and Stan answers, 'Remember how dumb I used to be? Well I'm better now.' I got better and with those years in therapy I began to study psychology. I got married to Super Max, who could protect me from imagined Parmenters, had Angie, got even better and decided to stand up by myself. And here I am waiting for a phone call from out of a nightmare."

Roger stood up and took a step toward her. He was going to take her in his arms, but Jean stopped him.

"Not just now, Roger. I'd fall apart, and I might wind up letting you take care of the whole thing. Maybe a little later, okay?"

"Okay," he said, sitting down again. He reached for a pizza slice and so did she. Then they listened to Mel Trax's disc jockey show from ten to eleven. This, thought Jean, is the time to meditate. But she couldn't. She kept seeing that photograph of Parmenter looking like Stan Laurel.

The phone rang just after eleven, and Jean grabbed it.

"Yes?"

"Mizz Kaiser? Jimmy Wayland here. I got your answers. Parmenter was released about three weeks back. I talked to his doctor. Doctor said he was harmless, talked about having a mission to make things right. Doctor's convinced ol' Parmenter couldn't hurt a weevil if it was chewing on his last cotton boll. Parmenter's got born-again religion."

"Where is he?" Jean said softly.

"No need to worry. He's living with a sister and he reports in to an analyst every week. Doc back here is keeping tabs on him, says not to worry."

"Jimmy, where is Parmenter? Where's his sister?"

71

"Chicago," he said. "Her name's Bratcovick, Ellen Bratcovick."

"Jimmy," she said evenly. "I live in Chicago."

"Shit," sighed Jimmy. "I think you'd better call the police there."

"I will," she said. She looked at the black phone, for an instant forgot what it was there for, and came back.

"Give me a call if you need me," he said. "And take care. You give the police up there a call. He's been bothering you, hasn't he?"

"I'm afraid so," she said.

They said good-bye and she hung up.

"So," she said, looking at Roger. "First I call Lloyd and tell him the good news. Then I tell Max. Then I call the Chicago police. Then maybe I have a nervous breakdown."

"Think you could manage a cup of coffee first?" Roger tried.

She took his hand. "Sounds like a good idea to me."

They met Mel in the lobby after she had made her calls. Both Lloyd and Max had wanted her to stay with them. More protection. The only one who didn't want to rush over and protect her was the policeman she had talked to. He asked her if she knew where the police station was on Clark Street north of Devon. She knew. He told her to stop by there next morning. She agreed and hung up.

In the lobby Mel gave them a look of concern.

"Roger, we've got to do something about our music policy. For Chrissake, I'm falling asleep during my own show."

"I like the music, Mel, and so do our listeners," Roger said.

Mel shrugged and walked away, doing an imitation of Liza Minnelli singing "New York, New York."

"I don't want to go home, Roger," she said as he reached for the door. "Not till tomorrow morning."

He could have said something cute or clever or suggestive or made a little face, but, thank God, he didn't. He nodded with understanding. Jean squeezed his arm, and they walked into the cold night air.

In the morning she wrapped one of Roger's terry-cloth robes around her, found some eggs, bacon and juice in the well-stocked kitchen, and made breakfast. Roger came in in blue nylon pajamas, hair tousled, looking a little sheepish.

"Good morning," he said, not sure of whether to come to her. She grinned, straightened her glasses and took a step away from the sizzling bacon to kiss him quickly. He smiled and sat down.

The apartment didn't really look as if anyone lived in it. It reminded Jean of the model apartments that management keeps in large buildings to lure in tenants. Roger's was done in masculine brown with muted oranges and a little black here and there.

At first she had taken the tour of the place, said it was "very warm," and then they had talked, first about the new radio show, then about Roger. Strangely, they didn't talk about Jean's problem at all. He was willing, she knew, but he welcomed a chance to talk about himself.

"The only time I've talked to another human being about my last marriage, I mean really talked, I paid for it. I mean I paid a shrink to listen, and I watched the damn clock, worrying about how much it was costing me and if it would eat into the alimony." He smiled and went on, Jean occasionally confusing wife number one with wife number two. One of them had gotten remarried. The other hadn't. The whole tale took about forty minutes, with Roger drinking a beer and Jean a Sprite. They sat on the suede sofa in his living room, looking out at the stream of traffic on the Outer Drive. The cars were scattered streaks of light. When Roger had moved to the stereo, Jean had half-risen and said, "No music, please. We don't need music behind us for everything we do in life. We don't need our senses divided. We don't . . . we don't need me preaching. That's what we don't need."

They probably would have talked, hemmed and played games all night if she had waited for Roger, twice-wed rollicking Roger, to make any move.

"Roger," she finally said, putting down her second Sprite. "I don't have it in me to play around. I'm tired. I'm still a little shaken. I'm having trouble absorbing what the CBS deal means, and I'd very much like to get into bed with you."

She thought she had handled the moment pretty well. Roger had certainly responded well though she had led the way.

"You sure you've been married twice?" she said at one point when they climbed under the cool blankets.

"Why would I lie about something like that?" he asked reasonably.

Her own experience wasn't all that extensive either. She could, counting Roger, add up all the men she had been in bed with on a little more than one hand. Manuel, whom she had met in college before marrying Max. She had thought him a rough ghetto Mexican fighting his way to respectability. She found out later that his family owned a dozen fish canneries, and he had never worked a day in his life. After Max there was The Runner. That had only been one time and she couldn't remember his name. She had met him at a party Dr. Hirsch had given. The Runner was about forty at the time, well built, dark and almost bald, with a nice tan. Then there was Al Hershkowitz. That had gone on for almost four months until Al got a job in Seattle and left her the lone psychologist at the center. She had been happy to see him go, though she had played it sadly and suggested that he should shave his beard even if it did make him look young. She always thought of him by his full name, Al Hershkowitz. Finally, before Roger, there had been two nights with Dr. Noel Venazoni in San Francisco during an American Psychological Association Convention. Venazoni had lived up to his reputation as an expert on early childhood and Erikson therapy, but as a lover he could have used Freudian analysis.

For a thirty-five-year-old woman unmarried for the past two years plus, she didn't think she could be ranked among the sexually overactives, but neither did she worry about it much.

Roger had been warm, gentle, tender, and both anxious and willing to do what she wanted. That was apparently what she had needed.

The breakfast was fine, the orange juice a little lumpy because they had forgotten to thaw it out till morning, and the conversation cautious. Roger was wisely assuming nothing from the night before.

"You want me to come with you to see the police?" he asked.

"If you're not busy, you can drive me there, wait till I talk to them, and then drop me at home. But I'd rather you didn't come into the station with me. All right?"

She took a bite out of the sandwich—scrambled egg, bacon and cream cheese on an English muffin—and he asked her if she made sandwiches out of everything. She gave him a quick smile, assuming a double meaning, but Roger was asking a straight question.

"When I can," she said. "Picked up the habit from my big brother when I was a kid. Roger, thanks. I needed you last night and this morning."

"You've got cream cheese on your chin," he said, finishing a bite of egg. "You want me? I'm here." He held out his arms, offering more than Jean was interested in at the moment. It was time to establish a little distance again.

"We'll see how things go. The next real test is how you're going to take it when I beat you at racquetball."

"I'll learn," he smiled. "I'm more worried about Angie."

"Me too," agreed Jean, but they meant two different things.

Later Roger dropped her in front of the stone-on-stone-on-stone new police station a few miles from her apartment. "I'll be across the street at the International House of Pancakes," he said.

It was warmer today. Might even get up to the low thirties. Might even turn the snow into dirty slush puddles that would have to be navigated around. She hurried into the police station and to a woman in blue uniform behind a counter. She told her story, in brief, to the thin blonde with a nose like Bob Hope, and the woman directed her down a corridor to a door marked "Investigation."

She went in. The room was neat, clean and fluorescent-lit, with thick, narrow ceiling-to-floor windows that couldn't be opened. Detectives, victims and criminals alike were at the mercy of the air-conditioning and heating system.

"I help you?" a roly-poly man in a rumpled blue suit asked her. His crew-cut hair was gray and long out-of-style. He had a folder under his arm, and his collar was chafing one of his three folds of neck fat.

Jean told her tale again as quickly as she could. He half-listened while looking through his files and cut her off midsentence to shout across the room.

"Abe, you wanna take this one?"

Then the man with the fat neck excused himself, picked up the phone and started dialing.

There were six evenly spaced desks in the room. Four were occupied, one by a woman in a dark suit and three by men. She eliminated the woman, whose name was probably not Abe. The woman was typing something. Two of the men were talking to people sitting at the chairs near their desks. Jean tried to tell by looking at them if they were criminals or victims. She couldn't. It was like standing in the Piazza di Spagna in Rome on her honeymoon with Max and playing the game of trying to guess which passersby were Americans, which were Italians and which were something else. Then they would try to catch a snatch of conversation. They were wrong almost all the time. The differences between cultures were fading. Maybe the same thing was true for criminals and victims.

At the last desk, far back in the corner, a thin man who looked like he was about sixty sat talking on the phone. His hair was short, gray and curly, and he wore suspenders. He waved at Jean and she came over to him. He pointed to the chair and she sat.

"Then book him," Abe said to whomever he was talking to. He sounded Jewish, his voice a resigned sigh. Whoever was on the other end spoke, and Abe said in a mild sing-song, "Then don't book him."

The person on the other end obviously went on, and Abe looked at Jean, giving a shrug that said, "What are you going to do with some people?"

"The way I see it," said Abe, "you either book him or you don't book him. It's not like you've got a whole lot of options, Bart, and I'm not going to make the decision for you so you can say, 'Hell, Abe Lieberman told me to do it this way.' You're a big boy, Bart. You got a big gun, a big belly, a big wife. Book him or don't book him. You're welcome."

He hung up the phone and looked at Jean with sad eyes.

"Some people don't wanna grow up. So they spend their lives playing cops and robbers. What can I do for you?"

She told him. About her parents, the dead bird, the phone calls,

76

Parmenter in Chicago. And he listened, nodding his head every once in a while to show he was paying attention. When she finished, he said, "Excuse me a second."

Lieberman dialed a number. He looked more like the pop of a mom-and-pop neighborhood grocery than a cop. Maybe he was a cop because there were almost no more mom-and-pop groceries. Jean tuned into his conversation, assuming it was about her, and heard Detective Lieberman saying: "A bland tomato sauce will be fine. Because I don't like spicy stuff and you know it. When I eat veal, I want to taste veal, not my hot tongue. Thank you. Me too. I won't be late. I promise in blood. You can have the small toe of my right foot if I'm not on time. Good-bye."

Then to Jean: "Who needs the small toe of a right foot, right?"

Jean was obviously not amused. Lieberman sat back and looked at her.

"You think I'm building something that isn't there, don't you?" she said, ready to argue, to plead her case.

"No, if I were in your place, I'd do the same. Who needs dead birds in their bed and maybe crazy people calling them?" he said sympathetically. "I've seen almost everything in the past twenty years, and I've made almost every mistake. It's easier and better for my conscience to follow it up than be sorry later if you're right. Besides, it's Saturday morning, and things are a little slow. Want some coffee? It's not half bad. New machine."

"No thanks," she said. "Someone's waiting for me at the restaurant on the corner."

"You're not Jewish," Lieberman observed. "That's all right. You act a little Jewish." He reached for a form of some kind and added, "In case you didn't recognize it, I meant it as a compliment."

She went through the whole thing again slowly, and he typed with two fingers, asking questions, getting information.

"If it's Parmenter," she said, "how did he find me, get my address? My phone is unlisted. I'm not in the book."

Abe smiled.

"Part of that is easy," he said, rubbing his nose. "This Parmenter goes back to your little town, looks in an old newspaper, finds out

77

maybe you came up here with your brother. So he comes to Chicago, picks up the phone, asks for Jean Kaiser and bingo, the nice lady tells him the number is unlisted, letting him know that you do live in Chicago. Then through your brother . . . There's a hundred ways."

"So what will you do?" she asked.

"Find this Parmenter's sister, nose around, try to make up my mind if it's him and what he wants. Not much I can do outside of that. Usually I find or try to find murderers after they've murdered. We haven't got much here, but I'll look and give you a call at that unlisted number or at your office. Meanwhile, don't spend a lot of time at home alone. Just in case."

"I won't. Thanks."

He nodded and started to dial another number.

"Pleasure meeting you," he said. "You're a nice looking lady, and you've had enough troubles in your life. I'll call as soon as I've got something."

That was it. Jean made her way out of the room, which was now filling up with people, though not so tightly that they had to play "excuse me" past each other. She felt better. Maybe it was Abe Lieberman's willingness to take her seriously while still treating the whole thing as if it were routine and could easily be handled.

Roger was nursing a cup of coffee when she came in and joined him at a booth.

"Okay?" he said.

"I think so," she said, reaching out to pat his hand.

"What would you like to do? I mean today?" he asked.

"I'd like to get in a time machine and go back and change history. If you can't swing that, how about a late-afternoon movie?"

"You got it," he said, finishing his coffee and motioning to the waitress for the check.

Yes, Jean decided, she definitely felt better. She looked out the window and saw that something resembling rain was falling.

Before Roger made too many assumptions, Jean mapped out the day. They would stop at her apartment, where she'd pack a few things. They might even make a try at getting her car out of the garage later if the rain kept eroding the snow. They would then take in a movie, after the Saturday matinee when the kids were gone, and she would drive herself to her brother's in Oak Park, that is, if they got her car out. Roger nodded in understanding. He wasn't going to push.

There was a parking space about half a block from her apartment. She spotted it and grabbed his arm. Roger revved up, went over a mound of melting ice and bounced gently to a stop.

"Now all we have to do is worry about getting out of here," he said.

Martha and Pal were outside in the rain as Jean and Roger dashed past. The rain beat on Martha's blue plastic umbrella, and Pal barked, wagging his tail.

Martha tried to pretend they weren't there and looked, Jean thought, a little frightened. When they were in the hall, Jean wondered at the look and then figured it out. Martha thought Roger was her brother, that the Jewish Defense League was coming to break windows and heads.

Her phone was ringing as they made their way slowly up the stairs. During the day there was a little light from a small window on the landing. Jean opened the door quickly, kicked her boots off and turned off the light, which she had left on. The phone kept ringing. She took a deep breath and picked it up.

"Jean?"

"Max?"

"Angie and I were getting worried about you," he said. "We called last night."

"I stayed with a friend," she said. "I didn't want to be alone here last night. I'm sure Angie's told you the whole tale."

Max handled the implication of staying with a "friend" without missing a beat and said, "I called Barry Dunne at Bellwood Realty this morning. He'll push the deal. You should get a call about the apartment on Monday."

"Thanks Max," she said. That was probably the millionth time she had thanked him for something. She had meant it all the other times, and she meant it this time, though she felt a touch of "damn it, I should have done it myself."

"Angie's downstairs at the deli," Max said. "I'll tell her you're all right. Can she reach you there?"

"I think I'll stay stay with Lloyd and Fran tonight and tomorrow night," Jean said, looking around at Roger who, still wearing his coat, was seated at the kitchen table.

"She'll probably call you there later. Jean, if I can . . ."

"I will," she said. "Bye Max and thanks again."

She packed quickly. The spot over her bed was still there, more faint than the day before, but it would never go away. It needed a new paint job, which it was unlikely to get as long as Mrs. Park owned the building.

Outside, by the garage, Roger did a little slush-shoveling in the rain while Jean got the car started.

"Smells like a team of turtles died in there," Roger said when she opened the garage door.

"The rain will help," she said. "Listen, I'll drive my car. You drive yours. I'll meet you in the parking lot at Lincoln Village before the show, about four, okay?"

Rain had flattened his well-groomed hair and run down his neck. He would surely go home and take it easy for a while. Then they would see Burt Reynolds in *Paternity* and go their separate ways.

He touched her hand and ran down the alley, splashing into black puddles and probably ruining an expensive pair of shoes. Jean got her '74 Aspen out without worrying too much about hitting the sides of the garage. Both sides of the car were covered with scrapes and scratches. Jean's forte was not getting out of narrow garages.

With nothing much to do, she went to the library, dropped by her office and called Dr. Hirsch for an appointment. She didn't get the machine. She got Dr. Hirsch and felt a childish weakening of the knees. It had been more than a year since she last talked to him and she had forgotten, at least in part, the power that his voice held for her. Hirsch said that, coincidentally, he had a cancellation his next hour and she could come in if she could make it. She could make it.

The rain had eased a bit by the time she made the turn at Hollywood off Sheridan Road and drove onto the Outer Drive. Traffic wasn't too bad so she stayed on the Drive all the way to Jackson instead of going down Michigan Avenue. She took a chance that the underground lot on Michigan would have some spaces. It did. The barrier wasn't up. She looked for a parking space as close to the

Monroe pedestrian exit as possible. In the past she hadn't been particularly worried about parking here, even with the two or three murders in the past year, but today she didn't want a long walk through that cool, damp and not too brightly lit tomb of cars.

The rain had relaxed to practically nothing when she caught the light in front of the Art Institute, leaped over a nearly oceanic puddle at the curb, almost said "Olé!" to a bull of an Oldsmobile that she barely danced away from, and made it across the street. She hurried to the building on Wabash and through its entrance, which was always a little dark because it fell under the shadow of the elevated train tracks, and which was doubly dark today because of the rain.

Jean made it to Dr. Hirsch's office on the ninth floor with ten minutes to spare and let herself into the typically small waiting room. There were only two chairs, a single table with a lamp and an assortment of magazines including *US*, *The New Yorker* and *Psychology Today*. Patients were not supposed to meet each other. Their appointments were spaced an hour apart and they left from a door that led directly into the corridor so they wouldn't have to meet the next patient. The system wasn't foolproof. Over the years Jean had arrived occasionally at the exact moment when a patient was leaving Dr. Hirsch's office and stepping into the corridor. When Jean was just finishing her therapy, about a dozen years ago, one woman in her forties had been before her for about a year. They got to the point in their meetings where they felt able to nod at each other. Then, one day, another woman had come through the door from the appointment before her, and Jean asked Dr. Hirsch what had happened to the woman Jean knew.

"She committed suicide. Pills."

That session and the next two had been devoted to the woman, suicide, and the ultimate value of psychotherapy.

"I'm a guide," Dr. Hirsch had explained, "with a small flashlight. We're in a massive maze. I say, 'Keep going to the right, and we'll eventually get out of this,' but you and my other patients have to make the decisions and I never know for sure what will be in the beam when we turn each corner. I sometimes have a good idea, but it might be something so frightening or upsetting that the patient runs away and gets lost again. Now, in the hope that I have not mangled that metaphor beyond common sense, let's go on."

And they had continued, and on the whole, though Max and Lloyd had both had doubts, eventually, gradually, Jean felt better. She went through all the expected stages she would later read about. For almost a year she was hopelessly in love with Dr. Hirsch and wanted to call him Leon. He had told her that if such intimacy was essential, she should call him Michael, his middle name. He also pointed out that in case she hadn't noticed, he was about five feet four inches tall, considerably and comically shorter than she, that he was at best homely, with a clichéd hook nose and ears that stuck out, that he was happily married and much, much older than she. "It will pass," he said. And it did.

A movement of chairs inside the office behind the pebble-glass door made Jean put down the copy of *US* with John Travolta grinning at her. The outer door opened and the patient left. About two minutes later Dr. Hirsch opened the door and told her to come in.

The office was much the same as it had always been, with but a few changes. Now there were photographs of Dr. Hirsch's grandchildren, two girls, in addition to his wife and his own two daughters. But the biggest change in the office was Dr. Hirsch himself. It had been several years since she last had seen him, and now he looked old and even shorter than the five-four he had claimed. His suit was dark and neat, and he pulled on his trouser legs as he sat across from her and raised his eyebrows.

"You've got a question?" he said.

"Just . . . I'm sorry . . . but you look older."

"There's a very good reason for that," he said, leaning back. "I am older. I'm sixty-eight years old. And ten years from now I'll be seventy-eight if I'm still here. My hearing is good since I haven't listened to rock music all my life. My eyes are only slightly worse than they used to be, and my brain makes up in the accumulation of knowledge what it loses in the aging process. At least that's what I keep telling myself. Now it's your turn. Why are you here and what shall we talk about?"

Dr. Hirsch was not a Freudian, Jungian, Adlerian, Gestaltist, Behaviorist or anything else. He took from each what suited him. He had told Jean once, "We've been doing this psychiatrist business for less than a hundred years. They've been building cities for thousands of years and they still don't have that right. We're still putting the whole thing together."

Dr. Hirsch's patients sat across from him or lay on his black leather couch. They paced the small room or stood in a corner. They talked to themselves or they conversed with him. He seldom told them what they should do and frequently led them to make decisions. He also clearly enjoyed his work.

Now Jean told her story once again, only this time she included the dark feelings of the past. She sat across from him, looking in his face, which was attentive but didn't respond to details of the tale.

"You used to have dreams about this Ben Parmenter," he said when she finished. "You having them again? Recently? Last night?"

"No, but that memory of the room, my room the night my parents were killed. It still flashes in sometimes like a series of snapshots put together and flipped so they seem to move. All jerky."

"And . . ." Dr. Hirsch went on reaching for his jar of hard candy and offering one to Jean. She turned it down. "If the police find out he did these things and send him away, you'll feel better?"

"Of course."

"And when you move in a few days you'll feel better?"

"Oh . . . you mean he could find us there too if they don't get him or if they do and he comes back. I still want to move. That neighborhood, our neighbors. I want out. Angie wants out."

"Good reasons," agreed Dr. Hirsch, sucking away. "So why do you feel guilty about moving?"

"Do I?"

"Do we keep asking each other questions or does one of us stop and answer? We finished with the doctor and patient relationship a long time ago. We're talking as friends, colleague to colleague, or whatever. I think you should answer," he said.

"I do," she said, blowing out. "I'm running. I'm not handling the situation and I'm letting men help me again, asking them for help, even you."

"So," said Dr. Hirsch reasonably, "ask a woman. You have women friends?"

"I didn't have many a dozen years ago, and I have fewer now,"

83

she admitted. "The last time I had close female friends was when I was a little girl."

"I remember," he said.

"So, what do you think, Doctor? All this time, all these years. All the reading and training I've had, and I'm still a dependent little girl, right?"

"You asked me another question. Try answering it."

"Okay," she said, removing her glasses. "No. I'm not but when something comes to shake me up, something like this, I run for cover, for protection."

"You want my advice?" he asked.

Jean's somber look turned to a smile and then a laugh.

"I assume you're not thinking of resuming therapy," he said, returning her smile, "and even if you were I'd have one hell of a time working you in on a regular basis. Our time is almost up, and, Freud forgive me, we are friends. You can't kill ghosts. You have to learn to live with them. Exorcism is for Hollywood. You should know that. I'm sure you do know that, but sometimes you can't feel it, and that's more important than knowing it. You don't have to prove anything to me, to your brother, your ex-husband, the ghosts of your parents or yourself. You've got to get used to living with yourself and your past. That's the psychological situation. The immediate pragmatic situation requires that you get out of that apartment and hope the police are efficient. There, that's the longest speech I've given since last year at the APA."

"I'll try," she said.

"Don't try," he said, looking at his watch. "Let it happen and then think about it. Meanwhile, now that you're going to be the new Johnny Carson and inflation is here, you can give me a check for seventy-five dollars."

"I knew I shouldn't have told you about that CBS deal," she said, fishing her checkbook out of her purse.

"That's the dilemma," he said. "You can't even hold back your financial status when you talk to your therapist, not if you want the whole thing to have a chance at working."

She made out the check and handed it to him.

"Thank you," she said, getting up and putting her glasses back on. Dr. Hirsch, still sucking his candy, got up too, and took both her hands in his.

"I'm here. You've got my home number. You want to get together, I'll always find an opening or make one. If you promise not to have a breakdown, Dorothy and I will even invite you and Angie over for dinner. No charge."

"Sounds good," she said, feeling like crying.

"No, it sounds specific," he said, reaching for his calendar. "Sunday night. Make it six-thirty so Angie won't be up too late. You remember how to get to my house?"

She nodded.

"If there's a problem with that date, I'll get back to you." He opened the door to the corridor, and out she went.

◇ *SEVEN* ◆

She had hoped the movie would carry her into never-never land, away, for an hour or two, from too many things to think about. She was great at giving advice to people over the radio on how or why to meditate, but she was lousy at doing it herself. Besides, the movie wasn't very funny. Burt Reynolds looked tired and whined a lot, and New York looked too clean.

Dinner with Roger was all right. He wanted to talk about CBS and Alexian, but he had long since run out of anything to say about them. She had already told him about Detective Lieberman and Parmenter. Beyond this, which didn't surprise her, they seemed to have very little in common. Roger was enthusiastic about Burger King, but when they got there he ordered a straight burger with ketchup and a small Coke.

"If we're going to keep seeing each other socially," Jean had said between mouthfuls of Whopper with onion and double cheese, "we're going to have to find something to share besides business talk and a bed."

"Right," he said. "I liked the movie."

He took a small bite of the burger.

"And if you don't like the burger, don't fake it, please," she went on. "Get yourself a nice steak or whatever it is you're really thinking about eating."

"Tuna salad," he said with a smile. He had gone home and changed into a new pair of dark slacks, a new pink shirt, a new blue sweater and a brown Italian windbreaker.

"You look like you just stepped out of an ad in *Playboy*," she said. He shrugged.

"You like basketball?" she continued. "I know we don't like the same music."

"Sure I like . . . hell. I can take it or leave it. But baseball . . ."

She shook her head and with the last mouthful of Whopper still in her mouth shook her head negatively.

"Bores me. Too slow. We'll work on it. I'm being too aggressive for you, aren't I?" she said, reaching out to touch his hand with one hand and wiping her mouth with a napkin in the other.

"No," he said sincerely. "That's one of the things I like about you."

"Me too," she said. She considered another Whopper, remembered her unflattering mirror and said, "Let's go."

In the parking lot, with an Oriental kid on a motorcycle watching, she gave him a kiss and told him she would see him on Monday before the show or if something came up he could call at her brother's or at her office on Monday morning. She wasn't planning on going home.

The rain started again when she hit the Eisenhower Expressway and she drove carefully to the beat of the windshield wiper through the blur of darkness and automobile headlights. When she pulled up in front of her brother's home the rain had ended and the temperature had started to drop again. By morning, if not sooner, the rain would freeze and driving conditions would be somewhere between a Three Stooges short and Dante's *Inferno*.

Five-year-old Walter, wearing glasses that were duplicates of his father's, waved at her from the window and then looked disappointed.

"Where's Angie?" he asked when she stepped into the house. The place was an old three-bedroom Victorian house, warm with a lot of varnished wood.

Lloyd took her coat and gave her a small hug.

"Angie's with her father for the weekend," Jean explained.

"How are you doing, Jean?" Lloyd said. She gave a look intended to show that she was holding her own.

"Why didn't they both come with you?" Walter insisted. His brown-yellow hair was straight and tumbling over his eyes. He pushed the hair away.

"I told you, Walt," Lloyd said. "Aunt Jean and Uncle Max are friends, but they don't live in the same house any more."

"That's bad," said Walter. "I wanted to show Angie my 'Dukes of Hazzard' colorforms."

"I think Angie will be spending a few days with you this week," said Jean, turning to greet Fran, who came in looking a little tired and very thin. She was about forty and had the air of someone who expects to be given another chore and will take it willingly while letting you know it is a chore. That judgment, Jean thought quickly, accepting Fran's hug, is unfair. Fran was a decent person who, if Jean gauged it right, did not spend a lot of time in speculation or criticism of Jean's private life.

"Where are the girls?" Jean asked, moving into the living room.

"Staying with a friend overnight," Fran explained. "Would you like something to eat?"

"No thanks, I had dinner." She stepped over an unidentifiable Lego construction on the living room rug. "I'll have coffee when you do. Sanka."

"Uncle Max," declared Walter, "is not a nice person."

"Uncle Max is an okay guy," Lloyd said, lifting Walter up and tickling him.

"Your back," warned Fran. "Tomorrow's Sunday. You want to limp to the pulpit and have everyone think I wrecked you with depravity?"

Lloyd put Walter down.

"Uncle Max," the boy declared, "is a pimp."

The three adults looked down at him, and Walter, pushing his hair away again, returned the look.

"What do you think a pimp is?" asked Lloyd.

"I'm not sure I want to hear this answer," sighed Fran.

"A pimp's a bad guy," said Walter. "They said it on 'Rockford.' And a bad lady is a ho-kur."

"That's hooker," corrected Lloyd. "And there's more to it than that. Besides, Uncle Max, I repeat, is not a bad guy."

"He's not," agreed Jean.

"Build something out of Legos and start thinking about getting ready for bed," Lloyd suggested.

Walter decided he would rather spend the time watching television, and turned to head for the stairway that led to his room. He took two steps and stopped.

"But sometimes a bad guy can look like a bad guy and not be on television," he said.

"Got anybody in mind?" Lloyd asked.

"The man in the car behind Aunt Jean when she parked. He got out and went to her car and looked at it and looked at me. He looked bad."

Jean and Lloyd exchanged glances as Walter turned and started up the stairs.

As casually as he could, Lloyd called out, "Walt, what'd the man look like?"

"A skinny, skinny," he said. "An old skinny without a hat and white hair and big eyes."

Lloyd moved to the window and looked out.

"No one there," he said. "And there's no car parked behind you. Probably just a neighbor and my son's overdeveloped imagination."

They talked in the kitchen, Jean going over the details of the last few days: CBS, the trip to the police, and, without being too specific, her time with Roger.

"Do you really, I mean, like him a lot, or . . ." Fran began.

Jean shrugged and sipped her generic decaffeinated coffee, which tasted just fine.

"Let's just say, I like him. And let's, for a while, talk about you guys."

They did. Fran talked about how their oldest daughter, Lucille, named for Jean and Lloyd's mother, would be going to college the following fall. She wanted to be a forest ranger. The girl was hefty, healthy-looking and fresh-faced, as well as a good student. Neither

Lloyd nor Fran understood the desire, but they both supported it. The other daughter, Dorothy, was named for the aunt who had taken care of Jean when she came to Chicago from North Carolina. Aunt Dotty, who died while on a tour of Spain with her women's club, had been strong and chunky. Fifteen-year-old Dotty was well built, dark and pretty. She looked more like Jean's daughter than Angie did. Lloyd had started to tell about the possibility of moving to another church when the phone rang. Lloyd paused and took it.

"For you," he said, handing it to Jean.

She took the phone. "Hello?"

"Abe Lieberman. The detective you talked to this morning."

"I remember," she said.

"I'm pleased," he responded.

"How did you find me?"

"Brilliant detective work," he said. "You told me you were spending the weekend with your brother. You gave me your brother's name in the report. You even told me where he lived."

"Did you find him?"

She looked at Fran and Lloyd, who grasped what the call was about and waited silently.

"He wasn't that hard to find," said Lieberman. "His sister is in the phone book, or rather, her husband is in the book. They live over in Logan Square just on the line, you know, where the parkway is, Latinos on one side, Poles and whoever on the other."

"I know," she said, wanting him to get to the point.

"I went down there, talked to the lady who is not, let me tell you, partial to the police. And I talked to Benjamin Joshua Parmenter. You're right about one thing. He's a ding-dong. Jesus this, Jesus that. Hockin' me a tchynik about how he has a mission in Chicago. God gave him a mission."

"That sounds—"

"You should see him," Lieberman continued. "First, his voice isn't low. I know someone can disguise a voice, but frankly, I don't know if Parmenter has the brain for it, know what I mean? Still, it's possible. But possible isn't probable. He denied calling you, denied the bird business, denied any great interest in you though I must admit he knew who you were. He's a skinny little thing. I'm not a

Mike Rossman and I could take the schlemiel with one hand."

"Does he have white hair and a car?" she asked.

"White hair, shaved at the side, sticks straight up," he confirmed. "And he has a car though for my money a 1959 Chevrolet is more in the category of antique."

"I think he followed me out to Oak Park," Jean said. "I think my nephew saw him."

There was a long pause on the other end, and someone said something behind Lieberman about his dinner getting cold.

"I suppose it's possible . . ."

"I know," said Jean, "anything is possible, but do you think it's likely?"

Lloyd was listening and nervously nibbling on the final crumbs of a peach pie in the aluminum tin. Fran motioned to Jean, asking if she wanted more coffee and Jean nodded that she did.

"I don't know," Lieberman admitted. "I'm going to talk on Monday to the psychological social worker he checks in with and see what I can find out. But I can't do anything beyond that. I've got no provable crime, nothing. That sister of his may not be ready to appear on 'Meeting of the Minds.' . . . You know that Steve Allen show?"

"I know it," Jean said.

"Good show," Lieberman went on. "She may not be ready for that, but she knows how to yell police harassment. I'll talk to the social worker, but at this point, that's all I can do. You let me know if anything more happens or you get a good look and find he is following you. Then maybe I can do something. I gotta go now. I'll call if I have anything, and you know the number at the station."

He hung up and so did she, dropping her shoulders and holding up her hands.

"I got most of it," said Lloyd. "Fill us in on the rest."

She did.

"So," asked Fran, rinsing the last cup and taking the empty pie tin from under Lloyd's hands, "what next?"

"You could try talking to him," Lloyd said. "It might work, unless he's a Lutheran, in which case all hope is lost. Unless he's a Calvinist, in which case it's even worse."

"We can do without the church humor," Fran said, hitting him playfully on the head with a dish towel. He caught his glasses as they came off.

"Maybe he's Jewish," Lloyd persisted, trying to coax a smile from his sister. "Then you've got a chance. He'll talk, might even be reasonable.

> "The only man that e'er I knew
> Who did not make me almost spew
> Was Fuseli he was both Turk and Jew
> And so dear Christian Friends how do you do.

"William Blake had a way of getting right to the point, which is what I better do. I've got a sermon to finish. Should I ask?"

Jean smiled. "I'll come to church but you know—"

"You're not really a Christian any more," he finished. "I know. I know. As the hunter said when he shot the tiger, 'Tyger, Tyger my mistake, I thought you were old William Blake.'"

"Enough Blake already," Fran said. "Go write your sermon."

He excused himself. Jean and Fran talked in a little more detail about Roger and her feelings, interrupted once by Walter, who decided he wanted to go to bed so he could get up early enough to see the "Tarzan" rerun.

Then the two women watched a rerun of "Saturday Night Live" for a few minutes till John Belushi came on as the Samurai.

"It'll be all right," Fran said as Jean walked up the stairs with her overnight case. "At least that's what I'm supposed to say in a situation like this. It's minister-wife talk. I guess what I really mean is that whatever is going on or whatever isn't going on, we're with you. Am I making sense?

"You're making more than sense," Jean said. "Good night."

Jean took a long bath, a very hot long bath with her eyes closed, toyed with the idea of playing with Walter's yellow plastic water pistol at the edge of the bathtub, then washed and got out.

She was spending the night in her nieces' room at the front of the house. She closed the door, pulled the covers back from the bed near the window, and turned out the lights. Then she went to the window, where she pulled back the curtain and looked out. Her car was there in the light of the corner streetlamp. There were other cars on the street but nothing that looked as if it might be a 1959 Chevrolet and no one who looked like a scrawny, thin man with white hair.

On Sunday morning, they were up early, with Walter pleading to stay home and watch "Tarzan."

"We'll be back for 'Tarzan' or most of it," Fran told him. "Lloyd?"

"Unless I get carried away, which is not very likely," he agreed.

Lloyd wore his regular black Sunday morning suit and played with the thin sermon, its three sheets clipped together. It reminded her of her own notes for her radio show, and that reminded her she had a show the next day that she felt obliged to do, and this, in turn, reminded her of who might call.

The morning was cold, the streets icy and the conversation minimal. Lloyd took the congregation of no more than 150 through the service and a brief sermon drawn from the book of Daniel. There were no references to William Blake, on whom Lloyd had written his doctoral dissertation two decades earlier. He was an expert on Blake's unique religious thought and had even had an offer at one point to teach at Southern Methodist University because of his scholarship, but he had turned it down to stay in Chicago.

Walter missed about five minutes of "Tarzan," according to him the best part, where "Tarzan screams and you see all the animals going nuts."

Lucille and Dotty showed up around lunchtime, and Lloyd had to spend some time talking church business with an old man introduced as George Mosthrin.

The day went quietly and calmly. There were no calls to Jean, no hassles, only conversation: mainly about forestry—Lucille growing very intense on the subject—and the way women's bodies change—about which Dotty was intense. Jean didn't look out the window for strange men that night, but she had looked around during the day, both at church and at the house, the one time she had stepped out to get some air on the porch.

She slept well, which surprised her, on the extra bed in Walter's room, had an early breakfast with the family, said good-bye, promising to bring Angie back soon, and went for the door, her overnight bag in hand. Fran hurried to her at the door.

"You don't have to be Wonder Woman, you know," Fran said softly. "We want to help."

"Thanks," said Jean, taking her sister-in-law's hand.

Lloyd and the kids shouted good-bye to her again from across the house, and she went carefully down the icy stairs and out into the gray, cold morning. There was a chance that the car wouldn't start. It had sat outside for two nights. And the windows needed scraping. She reached over to the glove compartment after she threw the bag into the back seat, extracted the scraper, put it into her pocket and started the car. The engine resisted for a second and then went on. Jean sat back with some relief and fed gas to keep it going. That was when she first really looked through the front window.

On her windshield right over the steering wheel was a large black cross. It was painted with magic marker and not particularly straight lines, but it was definitely a cross. She reached up to wipe it off but it was on the outside, under the ice. With the engine turning over, idling comfortably, she got out and scraped the ice off, jabbing at reluctant patches, anxious to get down to the cross. The cross wouldn't rub completely away, but enough of it came off so that she could see through it. She looked around the street, up and down for the old Chevy, a glimpse of the man, but there was none. She considered running into her brother's house and asking for help and comfort, but something was overlaying her fear. It was anger. A what-the-hell painful anger, a trembling anger that sometimes got her into trouble.

"Okay, Buster," she said softly but aloud as she got back into the car. "That's enough."

She wasn't sure how, but she was going to talk to Parmenter. She had been running from him for almost a quarter of a century, asking people, men, to stand in her path, blocking him out, but now it was time to put this demon away.

Something murmured in her stomach, told her fear was coming, but she ignored it, turned the radio up and drove to her office through the heavy morning traffic, refusing to listen to that reasonable rumble, which had now risen to her chest.

◇ *EIGHT* ◆

Since Max was dropping Angie at school and Jean had brought enough clothes for work to Lloyd and Fran's, there was no need to stop at the apartment, which was just as well. Not that she really expected anything to be wrong there, but the prospect of running into Wayne or Martha and Pal, or Art Hellman or Mrs. Park, or, heaven help her, the Bowery Boys from across the street, was more than she thought reasonable to bear. So she went straight to the office.

Nobody was sitting on the bench outside her office. Harold was having a cup of coffee and talking to Ida Schwimmer in the nook where the machines with coffee, Coke, ice cream and candy sometimes yielded up their promised treasures for appropriate coins.

"I was just telling Ida you've been looking like you need a vacation," Harold said, spotting her. "You want a cup of this?"

"Yes, thanks," Jean said. "I've got a couple of phone calls to make. Could you bring it in and let me know when someone comes in for an appointment? I think we've got one of the Gimmelman twins first."

"Robert, right," agreed Harold, looking for some coins.

Ida Schwimmer, well below five feet tall and well over one hundred and fifty pounds, looked at Jean with concern. Ida had been through four husbands. Two had given in to heart attacks, one had moved to California, and the last, Mr. Schwimmer, was still holding his own.

"I think the problem," Harold had once confided to Jean, "is that Ida likes skinny men, and she likes to get on top. You know what I mean? You'll excuse me talking dirty, but I'm being clinical."

Jean had trouble fantasizing the benign Ida, well into her sixty-fourth year, pulverizing husbands with sexual fury. If she took phone messages and handled office business the way she handled husbands, it was truly an impossible image. Ida would rather talk than do, look than act.

Jean's first call was to Detective Lieberman who apparently had just walked in the door.

"Lieberman," he said and then grunted as if trying to ease a weak back into a comfortable position.

"It's Jean Kaiser. When I left my brother's house this morning, I found a cross painted on my car window with magic marker."

There was no answer, just silence. There existed the possibility that the news had overwhelmed Detective Lieberman, but she doubted it. She had her own script worked out for this conversation.

"Are you there?" she asked again.

"I'm here," he said. "Did you think for a minute that it might just be kids fooling around? Or a nut in Oak Park? You know Chicago hasn't got the market on nuts cornered. Did you look at any of the other car windows near you to see if they had crosses?"

"No, I didn't," she admitted as Harold came in bearing hot liquid and lingered uninvited to listen. "But it is one hell of a coincidence. You and an ex–North Carolina state trooper tell me that Parmenter has gone religious. My nephew sees a man who looks at my car and sounds like Parmenter, and someone puts a cross on my window."

"And," Lieberman went on, "the bird, the calls . . ."

"Somehow I expected the conversation to go this way," she said, sipping the hot drink, "but I wanted the information on the record. I'll try taking care of my own responsibilities for a while."

Harold nodded approval, though she was sure he didn't know quite what the conversation was about.

"If that means you plan on playing a little 'Hart to Hart' and going for a little chat with Parmenter," Lieberman said, sipping something, "forget it. You can't go around harassing. I still think you're a nice girl—"

"Woman."

"All right, a nice woman, but I'm a couple years from retirement. My wife is a woman. To me everyone under fifty is a girl. So, you're a nice woman. I don't want you to get in trouble, and besides from what's on my desk, I got a busy week shaping up."

"What are you drinking?" Jean asked.

"I don't know," said Lieberman. "I think it's coffee."

"Me too," she said. "Good-bye."

"Don't do anything," Lieberman said. "Just call me if anything happens. I started a file. I'm a good listener. Good-bye."

When she hung up the phone, Jean pushed her glasses back on her nose and looked around the small office. The walls were white brick blocks. The black desk was small and metal with a single photo of her and Angie at Great America amusement park. Her psychology degree was framed on the wall in a three-dollar Woolworth frame. One of the fluorescent lights overhead was threatening to pop and was making a sputtering sound that might merit consideration as long-term torture in a Turkish prison.

"I think it was anti-Semites," said Harold. "Maybe even the Klan or the Nazis. There's Nazis out there in places like Oak Park."

Harold was leaning over, whispering confidentially in case some spy might be hiding outside the window.

"You work for Jews," he explained. "They gave you a warning."

"I don't think so, Harold. But I'll bear it in mind."

Harold shrugged a suit-yourself shrug.

"I'll see if the Gimmelman armageddon is waiting," he said and out he went.

A call to Ann Kruth at the real estate office confirmed that Jean and Angie could move into the new apartment the following Monday, one week, no sooner. Jean thanked her and promised to bring over a month's security deposit and the first month's rent in advance. Then she spent ten minutes trying to find a reasonably inexpensive mover who could do the job. She hadn't yet found one when Harold ushered Robert Gimmelman in and left.

"Well, Robert," she said, trying to ignore the pinging fluorescent light. "How are you today?"

Robert was homely with wild hair like Larry in the Three Stooges. At the age of sixteen he had the round hard stomach of a truck driver, the result of an addiction to Coca Cola and junk food. Robert even carried his own two-quart plastic bottle of Coke with him in his book bag.

"This time, Miss Kaiser," he said, pacing the floor in front of her desk, "I'm really going to have to kill him."

By the time Robert left, fifty minutes later, on his way to Mather High School, Jean was fairly confident that she had persuaded him not to kill his twin brother. Actually, neither she nor Robert thought that homicide was a viable option, but that was the game plan they went through, which kept them from making any great progress on the boy's many problems.

Before the next case was brought in, Jean, with trembling fingers, found the name Bratcovick in the Chicago phone book. Detective Lieberman had told her it was there. What he hadn't told her was which Bratcovick. There was a full column of them, and no Ellen. Lieberman had said she was married. Step two, how many Bratcovicks lived in Logan Square? She checked three possibilities before the next clients were brought in.

It was a couple for marriage counseling. She had never seen them before, and the husband, a dark little man in his forties wearing a dark European sweater and smoking when he entered, proved to be as much trouble as he looked. The woman with him, carrying a baby, was hefty, or as Harold would say, *zaftig*, reasonably good looking but frightened. They were Russian immigrants.

She accomplished nothing with them. The man was clearly there because he was not yet wise to what was required and what wasn't in this country. As soon as he understood that he didn't have to be there, his minimal grasp of English began to disappear except for one devastating thrust when she asked him why he thought he couldn't live with his wife any longer.

"You married?" he asked, jutting his chin out.

"No, but I was and I've got a daughter," she said.

"What happened your husban'?" he asked, leaning forward.

"We got a divorce," she admitted. "There are circumstances in which—"

"Aha," said the man in triumph, revealing a poor mouthful of large teeth.

The wife said almost nothing. The child began to cry. The couple said they would return on Wednesday. Jean knew there wasn't a chance in Siberia that she'd see both of them again, though she might be dealing with the wife.

When they were gone, she started dialing Bratcovicks. There was no answer at the first and none at the second. A woman answered at the third.

"Yes?" she said.

"Ellen Bratcovick?" asked Jean.

"Yes," the woman said with suspicion.

"My name is Jean Kaiser," she said, watching her hands. "And I—"

"I know who you are," the woman interrupted. "Leave him alone. You'll only make him worse. Do me a favor? Leave him alone." And she hung up.

Leave him alone? Someone's perspective was a bit screwed up. Okay, she told herself. Sit back, take it easy and describe how you feel. Be honest. Right, honest, she thought. I'm trembling and on one level I'm sorry I made the call, sorry because it made a further contact with Parmenter. His sister might tell him I called. He might come after me. Wait. She wanted this contact, this confrontation. She had lived all this time with the dry fear of this man, and she would probably live with it for the rest of her life if she didn't face it. It wouldn't simply go away. Dr. Hirsch had never promised it would, as she, in turn, had never promised any clients in the last six years that she could take away their pain and fear. All she could do was make them aware of it, help them to deal with it in terms they found realistic, and give them some basis for getting on with their lives and not being stifled by the guilt, hate, fear, need or whatever drained them.

But she was forced to put the matter of Parmenter aside for more of her clients. Philip Sean Berke, a gnome of a man born in Ireland, one of the wandering and almost lost Jews, who had been involved in petty crime and was without a community to turn to; Michael Portman, an eight-year-old who had started seeing her almost a year ago, unwilling to speak and angry over his father's abandonment of himself and his mother, an abandonment that, Jean had confirmed early, Michael blamed on himself; Ruth Levitt, nicknamed by Harold "The Gypsy Princess" because of the gaudy old-world dress she affected in spite of the fact that she had been born in Skokie. Ruth was thirty-seven and trying to go back to the hippie image she had missed by being an obedient Jewish daughter.

Later Harold wanted to talk to her about one of the families he was trying to help, but Jean had to hurry to catch Angie at school. They were, damn it, going home to the apartment. Scared or not. She wanted the whole thing cleared up before they moved.

"I've got to catch Angie at school," she said, taking Harold's hand. "I'll come in a little early tomorrow and we'll talk about it."

"I'll bring some sweet rolls," Harold called to her. "You like prune Danish?"

"No," she called back, dancing past Ida Schwimmer and almost clobbering the little woman with her flying purse.

"Cheese, it'll be," he called.

"What's all the yelling?" yelled Ida.

The last thing Jean heard was Harold saying, "So, what is this a synagogue we can't talk?"

The streets were still icy and the traffic slow even though it was a good hour before the start of evening traffic. When people started leaving their jobs for the night, they'd head north and west and south to the suburbs or the far neighborhoods. But Jean worked on the Northwestern edge of the city and headed east for her daughter's school and home. She arrived about five minutes late and Angie, with overnight bag and books, was walking toward the bus stop, slumped down with the weight. Elizabeth Fratianno strolled alongside her daughter.

"Hey, kids," Jean shouted, pulling up next to them and opening her window, "you want a lift or are you doing penance?"

100

Angie gave an enormous sigh of relief, opened the back door, and threw her things in, motioning for Elizabeth to join them. The two girls bundled into the back seat, and Angie leaned forward with a cold-cheeked hug that almost made Jean weep sappily.

"How would we be doing penance?" Elizabeth asked, puzzled.

Elizabeth was a good Catholic girl. She didn't yet have the disposition or experience to be anything but a good girl.

"It was just a joke," Angie explained, still sitting forward.

In the rearview mirror Jean could see Elizabeth's thin face slowly accepting but not understanding.

"What's that on the windshield?" Angie said, pointing over her mother's shoulder as she started the car forward.

Jean shrugged. "Kids, I guess. How was your weekend?"

"Great," Angie said. "We ate at Arby's, bowled. I got a ninety-nine, went to a show yesterday, saw a double feature, *Halloween* and *Halloween Two*."

"You've seen them both before," Jean said.

"I like them and Dad hadn't seen them."

The two girls leaned back and let Jean chauffeur while they talked about school, friends, and about a boy—briefly, before Angie said, "Shut up," giggled, slapped Elizabeth's hand and looked up to see if her mother had heard.

Jean tuned them out as she turned a corner, felt her rear wheels slide on a patch of ice, and waited in that thin slice of time for her rear fender to bounce off a blue Buick parked to her right. The jolt didn't come. The girls hadn't noticed and were babbling on. Just as Jean began a sigh, a slur of Elizabeth's words cut into her awareness.

"What funny man with white hair?" she said over her shoulder.

"Oh Mom," Angie said with an air of great exasperation. "Just some nutty guy outside the school. Just before you came. I think he wandered over from that halfway house in Evanston. You know they come—"

"What," Jean cut in, trying to keep her voice even and conversational, "did he do?"

"Mom," Angie answered. "He wasn't a sex pervert or anything like that. Just a harmless nut."

101

WHEN THE DARK MAN CALLS

"He said, 'Tell her to read my message,'" said Elizabeth.

"No," Angie corrected, "he said, 'heed my message.' A religious nut."

"Did he say anything else, do anything else?"

"Mom, we told you. That's all he said. He looked around like some kind of bird and ran away with his hands in his pockets."

Jean had planned to invite Elizabeth for dinner, but the conversation changed her mind. Instead, she dropped the girl off at her home, a small frame house about four blocks from their own.

"I'm afraid you'll have to come with me to the studio again," Jean said as soon as Elizabeth closed the door.

"Oh Mom," she said. "I'll be all right. I talked to Dad about it. Besides, I've got a little work and I want to watch some television."

"We'll talk about it later," Jean said, thinking the girl would be a little less willing to stay alone when darkness fell and the memory of the weekend with her father had faded.

They found a parking space not too far from the apartment, since it was still early. Angie didn't question why they weren't going into the garage.

No sign of Pal, Martha or Wayne around as they walked down the sidewalk, trying not to slip on the ice or the piles of dog droppings that looked like the remnants of bombing raids.

They kept chattering, about Lloyd and his family, about when they were moving, about anything, as they went into the apartment. It wasn't bad, and nothing seemed out of place, though Jean tried not to look. Angie skipped into the back of the apartment with her bundles, and Jean made a quick survey of the place before being satisfied that they had no visitors.

Stepping into the living room, she had heard below her the voices of Wayne and Martha in argument. Nothing unusual about that. The Hellman apartment was silent. She walked to the front window and looked across at the first floor apartment where the boys of summer lived. The window was dark, but it was early.

Then she looked down the street in both directions, but there was no white-haired man in a parked car.

Jean opened a couple of cans of tuna packed in water, mixed it with too much mayonnaise the way Angie liked it, sliced a huge white onion, and made sandwiches for dinner which they washed down with generic cola. Angie had put on her number 44 Chapel Hill shirt, and Jean suggested that she might take it off so they could get it cleaned. Angie resisted the suggestion until she dropped a blob of gooey tuna on the shirt.

Pulling out some notes from an old psych class, Jean went over them quickly and jotted down a few things for the show. The man who had talked to Angie and Elizabeth might not have been Parmenter, but when it came time to go, Jean insisted that Angie come with her. Sensing something quite serious, Angie agreed.

"But only on one condition—no going out with Roger for coffee or anything. No business talks."

"Agreed," said Jean. "But I thought you were going to make an effort to get along with Roger. He is going to be around, you know."

Angie looked up abruptly and said, "Don't rush me. He isn't all that easy to take sometimes."

Jean agreed with that. When they left, Martha and Wayne were still going at it in their little apartment.

"Love," Angie said, pointing to the windows, behind which the noise level rose.

"Need," said Jean.

When they got to the station and parked, it looked like it might be a normal night. Inside Mel Trax walked past them and nodded with a Coke in his hand. The big change was in Roger, who joined them in the lounge, a soft smile on his face and a well-pressed tan suit on his shoulders. He took Jean's hand and gently said, "Hi, everything all right? Hi Angie."

Angie caught something new, a touch of intimacy, and let her eyes drift from one to the other of them. Jean gave him a smile back and removed her hand so she could take off her coat.

"I'm fine," she said.

"You look great," Roger returned, and Jean caught Angie's attentiveness.

"I better go over the notes, Roger, and I'm afraid that after the show Angie and I have to get home rather quickly to start packing."

The disappointment came into his eyes, then passed and returned through his grin.

"I understand. Remember, Alexian tomorrow. You know how to get to CBS?"

Jean reminded him that she had been there a few times and promised to meet him at two in the afternoon.

He looked undecided, then leaned over and kissed her cheek.

"I'll see you, Angie. Your mom's going to be a big star." He turned and left, and Jean stood for a few seconds with her back to her daughter before turning around. Then she looked over her shoulder and saw Angie sitting cross-legged on the lounge, her tongue in her cheek, her arms folded.

"I told you everything I did on the weekend," Angie said. "Did you tell me everything you did?"

Not by a long shot, kiddo, Jean thought, but said, "Everything that was important. Have a Coke. Ruin your teeth and read your book. I'll see you in an hour."

Jean hurried past Roger's partly open door and into the studio, where Mel was waving for her to sit down and Ted Earl roused himself dimly from his reverie to wave his pipe in her direction.

"You cut it close today," Mel said, raising his eyebrows and looking more like Radar than ever.

The opening went well, better than last Friday's poorly chosen meditation topic. This time she talked about good and evil as relative terms. How something that was clearly right on one day in one context would be wrong on another day in another context or, to make it even more complex, two perfectly reasonable people might be at odds over whether something was good or bad. She gave some examples ranging from the international, nuclear energy, to the personal, divorce. Mel nodded approval, which was a good sign since she hoped, but never told him, that he represented the imagined male audience she was trying to reach. Her sister-in-law Fran represented the female audience.

The calls went well. One divinity student who happened to be listening while doing his homework called to argue, with some passion, that good and evil were absolute. Another caller, a woman, wondered whether it was good for her old mother, who was in pain with cancer, to live and whether it might be evil if her life were eased away. This was the stuff of radio drama and Jean talked the woman through the suggestion of euthanasia, careful not to say that she

104

thought the woman was actually contemplating it and getting the woman to agree to talk to her clergyman the next day.

"You're on the air with Jean Kaiser," Mel said as the next call came in. But he quickly put his hand over her microphone and mouthed, "It's him."

Jean took a deep breath and nodded to Mel that it was all right. She had been expecting it, waiting for it, and, though she had to admit that she was shaken again, she was ready.

"Jean?" he asked softly, deeply.

"Yes," she said evenly, "Paul?"

"That's right," he said. "I had to call you. I made contact with my old friend. I mean I left my friend a message, actually saw my friend."

"Well that's good Paul," she said, looking at Mel, who tapped his forehead and made a face to indicate that the nut wasn't worth the time. Jean shook her head. "You said your friend is a woman."

"Oh, yes, a woman," he said. "A very lovely woman, a voluptuous woman. She was only a girl long ago and far away."

"So, you spoke to her, talked to her face to face," Jean went on.

"No, not yet. I'm still a little—"

"Afraid?" Jean cut in.

"No," Paul laughed, a whispery laugh. "I'm just not ready."

"I'm sorry Paul, I think you are afraid. Fear can lead to evil or one's own sense of it. Are you a religious man, Paul?"

There was a pause on the other end of the line. Jean had him backing up for the first time since his initial call a week ago.

"Yes," he said finally. "I've had a long time in a far away place and I was visited by Jesus, who gave me a mission."

"And is your friend a part of this mission?" she asked, ignoring Mel's eye-rolling suggestion to cut it off.

"Yes, I'm afraid so," he said almost sadly.

"I've got to get on to other calls Paul. To be candid, I think hiding is a little less than heroic at this point."

She nodded to Mel to cut off the call before Paul could reply, and she launched into the next interchange.

When the show ended, Mel immediately said, "Hey let's not let that guy through the next time he calls."

"He might not be calling again," she said, standing and turning to Ted in the booth. "How much trouble would it be for you to put together on one tape all three of that guy's calls?"

Ted turned his yellow eyes to her and nodded to indicate that it would be no great problem.

"I don't think you should talk to that creep," Angie greeted her.

"I hope you mean the guy on the phone, old Paul."

"Yeah, I wasn't digging at Roger. Roger, apparently, is now something special and beyond criticism."

Jean, coat half-on, looked at Angie, who made a sour face.

Jean responded by crossing her eyes and saying, "Look, Barbra Streisand."

Angie tried to hold back a giggle, but she couldn't and her braces gleamed.

"Cut it out," Angie laughed. "I'm serious."

"That, my friend, makes two of us."

Roger didn't rush out or accidentally come into the hall to greet them, and they made their escape. Before going home they stopped at the all-night Jewel at Howard and Western, picked up some groceries and a stack of flattened cardboard boxes for packing. When they got to Seeley there were no spaces on the street. Reluctantly, Jean went to the garage and was relieved to find that it was not piled with garbage.

The lights were on in the apartment, as they had left them, and everything looked fine when they dumped their cartons in the kitchen. When Angie went to raid the refrigerator, Jean checked the door locks and followed her.

"Scrabble and hot chocolate?" Jean said. "Tomorrow we pack."

"If we can watch the news too," Angie agreed. She had changed into a red T-shirt with white script saying, "Some People are Just Too Cute."

Jean agreed, lost the game, ignored the news and kissed Angie good night before deciding to read. She read a hundred pages of a spy novel by someone named Granger and then went to bed, in her own room. It wasn't easy, but she did it. And she had a dream that almost eluded her when she got up.

It was a dream she had had when she was a little girl. She had been listening to a scary story on the radio in her room back in Carrboro, and when she turned the radio off and went to sleep, she dreamed that a giant bird, a vulture or eagle, perched on her headboard, looking down at her upside down. And now the dream was back.

She woke heavily and with difficulty at Angie's voice saying: "Mom, get moving, we're gonna be late."

Jean forced herself up and looked at the wall over her head. The dark irregular circle was still there, but fainter.

◇ *NINE* ◆

While hurrying through a cup of decaffeinated coffee and a bowl of Cap'n Crunch with a few canned peaches mixed in, Jean made a list of things to do:

> Talk to Harold
> Pick up more cartons for packing
> Pick up tape for packing
> Meeting with Alexian/Roger, CBS
> Pick up Angie at Elizabeth's
> Make rent deposit

Angie's request to have dinner at Elizabeth's, where she had a standing invitation, was a further incentive for Jean to do the thing she had left off her list. She decided it would be better not to think about it, just go ahead and do it.

"I told Elizabeth we were moving soon," Angie said, gulping her too-chocolatey chocolate milk. "From what you said, I think it's only about ten minutes by bike or one bus ride. You think we won't be friends when I transfer? I mean Elizabeth and me?"

"Don't know," admitted Jean. "Probably, but you'll meet new kids too. Which reminds me, I've got something to add to the list. I've got to call your principal, Mrs. . . . ."

"Miller," Angie supplied. "I'm late. I gotta run. You'll pick me up at Elizabeth's?"

"Between seven and eight," said Jean, accepting a quick kiss from her daughter, who clomped down the hallway and flew out the door.

Jean did the dishes, looked at herself one last time in the mirror, decided she looked a little tired but pretty good. She had settled on her white long-sleeved lacy blouse and a blue skirt for the Alexian meeting, but after putting it on, she had switched to her light green suit and an even lighter green blouse with the amber necklace.

"You'll do," she told her mirror image, but the image gave back only a faint smile.

As she headed toward the community center, she turned on the radio to WBBM, the local CBS news station. It had started with a straight news format about five years ago, but had gradually begun easing into a news and talk format—fine with Jean, since she would soon be part of it.

El Salvador, a drop in the Consumer Price Index (one of the mystical terms she never understood, like Dow Jones), a Latino gang murder of a twelve-year-old boy, a baseball trade between the Cubs and the Pirates.

She was five minutes late for her first appointment, and she had promised Harold to be early. Harold had not forgotten. He was sitting in her office at the client's seat, drinking.

"Harold, I'm so sorry, the traffic was hell," she said, hanging up her coat.

"It happens," he said. Take it easy for a few minutes. Here, I brought you Danish."

Jean had forgotten about the promise of a Danish, but there was no getting around it.

"Great," she said, pausing to wipe her glasses on a Kleenex. "I didn't get a chance to eat. I'm starved."

Harold nodded his gray curly head and gave an understanding little smile as he handed her the huge sweet roll.

"Great," she repeated, taking a bite. "We'll take a few minutes. Who's waiting?"

"Yuri," he said, taking the final bite of his own roll. "He can wait. I want your advice about the Kleins."

They talked about the Kleins for five or six minutes while Jean finished her roll and hot liquid. What Harold really wanted was confirmation that he was doing the right thing by pushing Howard Klein to take a part-time job. Jean reassured him, and he left—more satisfied, Jean noted wryly, than most of her patients.

She had cancelled appointments for the afternoon, but the morning ones made up for it. Yuri, she decided, was getting no better. In fact, he was getting worse. He hinted that the office might be bugged, talked of finding a new route to the center, of possibly wearing a disguise; Yuri was beyond Jean's help.

"I think I have someone who can help you, Mr. Burovsky," she said, writing down the name and number of Dr. Martin McCann. "He's a psychiatrist and—"

"Hmmm," hummed Yuri suspiciously. "First, I got no money for a psychiatrist."

"Harold and I will find some way—" she began.

"Second," he jumped in. "I'm not in need of a psychiatrist. I'm in need of FBI but they won't listen on me."

"But Mr.—"

"Third," he went on, holding up three fingers, "I don't believe so much in this psycho, psycho business."

Jean was about to speak, but Yuri was standing up now with another finger raised.

"Fourth," he said triumphantly, "how I know he's not KGB, huh?"

"Can it really hurt to talk to Dr. McCann?" she said.

"Perhaps," said Yuri, straightening the lapels on his worn suit jacket. "Perhaps I could engage him in converse and discover."

"Discover?" Jean asked, regretting the question even before the word emerged.

Yuri sat silently, crossing his arms and smiling smugly. Jean stood up and Yuri, still smiling, rose too.

She ushered him out and asked Harold to set up the appointment with Dr. McCann. Before her next client came in, something struck Jean. I wonder, she thought, if I come across to Lieberman or that cop Selig the way Yuri comes across to me? Do they look at me with sympathy and want to get away? But no, Lieberman had believed the calls. She picked up the phone and dialed the radio station WSMK. The secretary, Marion, who worked only during the day, said Ted hadn't come in yet, but she would remind him about the tape Jean requested.

"I heard about CBS," Marion added. "Good luck."

"Thanks," Jean said, and they hung up.

When noon came Jean wasn't hungry, but she had made up her mind. It was on her way downtown, and she had almost two hours. She drove through the old Jewish neighborhood of Albany Park and then into Logan Square, where Latin faces started to mix with heavier, Slavic ones. The weather was still cold, but it was lunchtime and a few people were out.

She found the street without too much searching, and drove slowly, looking for the address and, at the same time, for an old blue Chevrolet. She didn't spot the Chevy, but she did find the house. It was one of a line of dark two-story apartment buildings with slanted roofs, all close together with thin passages leading to back yards and alleys. The street was narrow, and the somber buildings of old red brick and gray wood blocked out much of what daylight there was. She parked, sat for a minute or two taking deep breaths, and then got out of the car, looking up at the building. No curtains quivered, and she could see no one through the windows.

Marveling at herself, Jean walked up the six worn cement steps and looked at the names next to the two doorbells. One, printed in blue ink, read "Bratcovick." The other, typed, read "Provska." Half hoping there would be no answer, she rang the Bratcovick bell. The ringing inside came from the first floor. She waited a few seconds and rang again. Again no answer.

Well, I tried, she told herself with some relief, and was turning to go when the door opened.

"Yes?" a woman's voice said.

Jean turned to look at her. She was a burly woman, a little taller than Jean, wearing a very faded blue dress and a green sweater. The sleeves of the sweater were rolled up as if she had been in the middle of cleaning walls or floors or making bread. The woman's face was a ruddy red and her hair, pinned back, was a mixture of brown and gray.

"Mrs. Bratcovick?" Jean asked.

"Yes," the woman said, and then something flitted across her gray eyes.

"You."

"I'm—" Jean began.

"I know who you are," the woman said angrily, standing straight up, but then she repeated her words and the anger was gone, replaced by a sad knowledge. "I know who you are."

"I've got to talk to your brother," Jean said. "I've got to know what he's doing and why. I've got to get him to stop. He has to understand that this will just get him into trouble."

"He hasn't done anything," the woman said, rubbing her hands together. She looked down when she spoke.

"You mean you don't know if he's done anything," Jean said softly. "Is he home?"

"No," the woman said. "He goes out. I don't know where he goes."

"Can I come in? Just to talk?"

The woman hesitated and looked over her shoulder back into the apartment.

"Come in," she said wearily, and Jean entered.

The apartment was dark. Very little light penetrated the few windows and the heavy curtains didn't help. The woman led the way, and as they walked Jean could see dozens and dozens, maybe hundreds, of little plaster statues no more than a foot high, on tables, mantelpieces, chairs and on newspapers on the floor. She couldn't make out the shapes clearly, but they seemed to be human.

The kitchen was a bit brighter than the rest of the house. A heavy wooden table, solid wooden chairs, worn linoleum, a dripping sink. On the wall was a religious calendar, and on the table were two more of the plaster statues. One was a grotesque crucified Jesus, slumped in agony, his eyes enormous, bulging. The other was a man, a thin man, lying on his back, a heavy stone on his stomach and a man sitting on the stone, apparently reading a newspaper.

"Did you . . ." Jean began, nodding at the statues.

"No," the woman said. "Ben did them. Does them all the time. Spends all the money he gets on plaster. Started doing them in that place he was in. He's good at it. Even sold a few. Tea, coffee?"

"A little tea," Jean said, still wearing her coat.

Mrs. Bratcovick paused for a second, looking at Jean, probably comparing herself to her visitor and coming up the clear loser. She filled a battered metal kettle with water and put it on the stove before turning and sitting across from Jean.

"My husband's at work," the woman explained, sitting heavily. "He's got a tavern over on Division. Ben cleans up there mornings, nights."

Jean nodded, not knowing what to say next, but the woman looked away. She wanted to talk. Jean knew the look. Maybe her husband, living in this dark world, had long ago given up listening, if he ever had at all, and her brother was more in need of help than a possible confidante.

"You got a daughter. We got no kids," the woman said, looking over at the kettle. "He thinks it's me, but I think it's him. Doesn't matter though. I don't think he wants any kids any more, and now we're too old."

Jean nodded, assuming this was the woman's roundabout way of getting to her brother.

"My family, Ben's and mine, are from England way back," she said. "My husband's people are from Czechoslovakia. Never been very good at fitting in, but Ben's been a disaster at it. Ben's a poor soul. Just to look at him . . ."

"I've never met him," Jean said. "I was just a little girl."

The kettle started to boil. Mrs. Bratcovick got up heavily, with a grunt.

"I know all about it," she said, serving tea. "You want a cookie, I got some cookies, those little vanilla wafers."

"No thank you," Jean smiled. "Do you think your brother will be back soon? I've got an appointment downtown."

The heavy woman took some tea and looked at her guest again, a guest who dressed like that and had appointments downtown.

"He's been through the devil's own time," the woman said.

Jean felt like saying, so have I, but she held back.

"Ben was never quite right as a kid, always jumpy. Then when he went to Korea . . . He shouldn't have been in the army, missus. Then none of it would have happened. He's not a bad man."

There were tears in the big woman's eyes, but she pulled them back.

"I'm not saying he's easy to live with, and I'm not saying my husband is all that happy about it, but if people will leave the man alone, he'll make his way."

"Mrs. Bratcovick, I'm not here to bother him. I think he's been bothering me, calling me on the phone, following me and my daughter. I've gone to the police."

"I know," said the woman, helping herself to a vanilla wafer, looking at it and nibbling. "A little Jew policeman came and talked to me and Ben and Pete, my husband. Pete didn't like it much. Ben's not all right, but he wouldn't hurt anyone."

Jean withheld the impulse to remind her that her brother had murdered Jean's mother and father.

"I really want to talk to him," Jean said. She finished the weak tea and pushed the cup away. "I can come back on my way from downtown or stop by in the evening."

Mrs. Bratcovick looked up in fear.

"You can't come when my husband's home. You've got to leave Ben alone."

"And he's got to leave me alone, me and my daughter," Jean said firmly but quietly.

The woman rose again and turned toward a door at the back of the kitchen.

"Come with me," she said.

Jean hesitated and then followed the woman to the door.

"This is Ben's room," she said. "Maybe you'll understand."

She turned the black painted knob and pushed the door open. A window with a thick gray curtain let in a beam of dusty light. Jean stood in the doorway, looking over the heavy woman's shoulder. A bed, neatly made, a small table with tools and an amorphous plaster statue with its ice-cream-stick skeleton showing through, and walls covered with religious pictures, paintings of Jesus, all of them of the crucifixion. The paintings, all cheap reproductions and cutouts from magazines, filled every inch of wall.

"Here," said the woman, "look at this." She stepped into the room, motioning Jean to follow her, which she did, and then closed the door. For an instant Jean was afraid she had walked into a trap, but the woman pointed at the closed door and said, "Look."

It was a thumb-tacked newspaper page, yellowed by time and lined by folds. There was the headline. There were the pictures of her father and mother. There was Lloyd as a young man, little more than a boy, looking lost as the photographer took his picture, and there was the ten-year-old Jean clinging to her Aunt Dottie in the yard.

"Ben says he's got a mission," the woman sighed. "Says God gave him the word and he came up here with a mission. I'm not much for going to church. My husband's a Catholic, but he doesn't go to church either. Ben, he knows the good book from cover to cover and back again."

Jean stared at the newspaper and then looked around the room.

"Mrs. Bratcovick, can't you see? I'm the mission. What does your brother want from me?"

The other woman looked around the room, too, and shook her head.

"He's not out to hurt anyone," she said. "He's become, I don't know, almost holy. You know, spiritual, like a holy man. I let you in to talk to you, ask you not to bother him, scare him. You can't talk to him, bring all that back up."

The woman had taken a step toward Jean in the small room. Her strong arms were out pleading, but there might have been a threat too.

"I can't let you bother him, don't you see? Now that you've seen how he lives, can you understand?"

"I think so," agreed Jean. The woman grabbed her wrist, and Jean pulled back, freeing herself. "I've got to go now."

Jean turned and opened the door, stepping into the kitchen and out of the closeness of the small room. Mrs. Bratcovick was right behind her.

"My life hasn't been all that much," the woman said. "I'm not good-lookin', and I don't have downtown meetings or a little girl, but I've got a brother who needs me and I'm going to take care of him. You understand?"

The woman's voice had risen as she talked and Jean turned to face her. There was a moment of silence, and then Mrs. Bratcovick reached down and grabbed a cookie, which she shoved into her mouth. Her eyes went wide and angry now, and with a mouth full she repeated, "You understand?"

"I understand," Jean said gently. "I'm going."

She expected the woman to follow her to the front door, but she didn't. Then she imagined her standing in the kitchen, finishing the box of cookies, a wild, angry, protective look in her eyes.

Jean stepped carefully, trying not to bump into the tables of statues or trip over the ones on the floor. She hurried out of the darkness into the gray afternoon and closed the door behind her. A sparrow on the black metal porch railing looked at her, chirped, and flew away.

Jean went quickly to her car and got in, locking the doors. Visiting Parmenter had not turned out to be such a good idea, but she was still committed to it, especially after seeing his room and meeting his not totally stable, and very protective sister. Ben had become the child Ellen Bratcovick would never have. Jean looked at the dashboard clock. She would have to hurry to make her appointment at CBS.

As it turned out, parking wasn't as big a problem as she had anticipated, not if she was willing to pay two and a half dollars for the first hour. In the lobby she identified herself to the black man in uniform. He made a call, gave her a pass, and said, "That's room three-oh-three."

The building was relatively new, very modern and uncurved inside with soft wall lights and thick carpets. She almost bumped into Johnny Morris, the former Chicago Bear who was now a CBS sportscaster. He smiled, showing perfect teeth that she hoped were real, excused himself and walked past. She ducked into the small elevator with a young red-haired woman who was looking at a sheet in front of her and closing her eyes to memorize it.

Roger was waiting in the hall, leaning against the wall, super straight and super clean in a light gray three-piece suit she had never seen before. Roger didn't seem to wear anything more than once. He had been looking at the elevator and let his eyes close in thanksgiving when he saw her.

"That's what I call cutting it close," he said, giving her a quick hug and a kiss on the cheek before consulting his watch.

"It's what I call being right on time," she said, as he turned to open the door to 303 for her.

"Here she is," he announced to a secretary in her late forties with her dark blond hair tied in back and pulled away from her scalp. She had the tight skin of someone who has had a facelift.

"I'll tell Mr. Alexian you're here," she said, halting her typing and lifting the telephone on her desk.

There were two men in the office: a frail white-haired man wearing a yellow turtle-neck sweater and, behind the desk, a burly, not-quite-fat bearded man, about fifty, in a black shirt with a white tie. He was holding a crustless sandwich and chewing.

"Jean," said the bearded man in the hoarse whisper of a man who talks too fast and too loud. He spoke through a mouthful of sandwich. "Bob Alexian." He held out his hand, and she took it. His grip was firm. "This is Andy Browder, publicity and promotion." The white-haired man nodded and smiled. Roger stepped over to shake Browder's hand and Alexian said, "Andy, this is Roger Nash. I told you about him."

"Pleasure," said Browder with a smile. His face was deeply tanned. He must have arrived from some place else, Jean thought, unless he was Indian, or spent a lot of time under one of those sun-lamps that would soon turn him into a mummy.

"I hope it's all right if I eat while we talk," Alexian said, pointing to his sandwich, a can of Coke, and something in a white carton that Jean discovered was potato salad. "I couldn't get out for lunch. You want something to eat? Either of you? Some coffee?"

Roger and Jean declined and sat down in the two chrome-and-black-leather chairs opposite Alexian, who continued chewing away. Andy Browder sat on a matching settee off to the side.

"Roger told you what the deal is," Alexian said, still holding the red and white can in his hand, "and you agree?"

Jean looked serious and nodded.

"Good," said Alexian, raising his eyebrows and then examining his potato salad before dipping into it with his white plastic fork. "We've got publicity, a few things to iron out. Our plan is to get on

117

the air some time late next month. How does that sound?"

"Fine," said Jean.

"Good," said Alexian, wiping some mayonnaise from his beard. "Now we can get down to some basic business. You're a good-looking woman, Jean. You know that had something to do with our going with you instead of some of the others around the country."

"I thought I was also doing a good job on my show," she said, trying not to sound testy. In fact, she chuckled a little when she said it and looked at Roger, who seemed to be telling her something with his eyes.

"Of course," said Alexian, "that was the number one concern, but we're looking down the line a year or so, and we're looking at television appearances, local and national. Joyce Brothers is getting a little long in the tooth, and Carson and the others are going to be happy to talk to you about . . ."

"What's wrong with kids today, nuclear fear, drugs, cults," Andy Browder supplied.

Alexian shook his head and fished something out of his teeth.

"No," he said, "lighter, lighter. What's new in morality, the growing-up problems of test tube babies, why people don't stop smoking in spite of the fact that it's killing them. Do you find this kind of talk distasteful, Jean?"

Jean looked up at him and into his brown eyes. She knew it was an important question.

"No," she said simply. "I'm just a little overwhelmed. A few weeks ago I was an underpaid and underemployed psychologist—and now this. My only conditions at this point are that no one puts words in my mouth and I have the right to turn down any promotion, publicity, whatever ideas that I find objectionable."

Alexian looked around for something else to eat and settled for the remnants of potato salad, which he got by spearing them gently.

"Fair enough," Alexian said, looking at Browder, who nodded in agreement. "You can back out of the contract with two months notice, and we can do the same. But we're not planning that. We're planning for things to get bigger and better. Can you take a little criticism, constructive?"

"A little," she said, smiling.

"Good," said Alexian, now dropping the empty cans and cartons into an unseen wastebasket under the desk. "First, you photograph too plump. Right Andy?"

"That's right, Jean," Browder admitted sadly.

"But I'm—" Jean began.

"I can see you are," said Alexian with a pleasant smile. "But it's a question of how you look in a photograph, on television. Are you willing to shed five or six pounds for this?"

The image of Ellen Bratcovick, lumbering through her dark apartment, munching on cookies, hit her. This wasn't the conversation she had expected. Then she remembered the money.

"I guess," she said.

"The hair," Browder said and Alexian nodded.

"You don't like my hair?" Jean said, looking at Browder.

"Your hair is beautiful," Alexian said. "We just want one of our people to make some suggestions on cutting it and give you a little advice on clothes. If need be, we'll make a reasonable contribution toward wardrobe."

For radio? she thought, but they had already answered that. They were thinking beyond radio.

"Let me think about all this," she said.

"Of course," Alexian said. "We've got an agreement. These are only suggestions that we think would affirmatively affect your future. Don't get me wrong. We're not doing all this because we want to turn you into a Cinderella. We think with a little time you can do some good things for this station and even the network. You think about it. Another thing we'd like you to think about is the content of your shows."

She couldn't contain the suspicion in her look.

Alexian smiled and pointed at her while he turned to Browder.

"I told you," he said. "She's got that whatever it is, pride, spunk."

"Mr. Alexian," she said with a smile, "I'm sitting right here in the first person. What about the content of my shows?"

Roger reached over to touch her arm and keep her cool, but she ignored him.

"You have a tendency to get a little too intellectual," Alexian

119

said. "I've listened to your tapes. Meditation, things like that. You know how to talk to the callers, but your lead-ins get a little well, I said it, intellectual. What would you feel about having a professional writer do your intros? You give him or her the subject matter, even tell them what you want to say and they write it, subject to your approval. Is that fair?"

There were several ways to read this offer. One way, the way Jean chose, was that she wouldn't have to do that work. She had never enjoyed rushing through the cards, trying to put an opening in order.

"Worth a try," she said.

Roger sat back relieved.

"We're moving right along," Alexian said, stifling a belch. "Now I'm going to say something that might offend you."

She thought that he had already done that, but she nodded cautiously.

"Never be afraid to talk down to the audience," he said. "That surprise you? The rhetoric of this business for years has been, 'Don't talk down to the audience, respect them.' That is a sanitary truck full of garbage. Listen to your own tapes, any call-in show. Ninety-nine point nine percent of the people who listen are lonely people with nothing better to do. They want to be talked down to. They are not the people you'd have over for dinner and conversation. And the ones who are listening who you might invite over never call in. They just listen to hear the others act out a drama with you as the focus, the . . ."

"Juggler," Roger supplied.

Alexian didn't much care for the word, but not having a better one he lifted his hands to indicate "whatever."

"Am I lying?" Alexian said, leaning back and fixing his eyes on her. "Am I being clean?"

"A bit rough maybe, but there's a lot in what you say," she admitted.

"Then," said Alexian rising and smiling to show large straight teeth, "we are in business." He held out his hand to shake hers and Roger's, and Browder moved forward to do the same.

"We'll be in touch through Roger to work out the details," Alexian said.

Roger led her into the outer office and closed the door. The blond secretary was talking to a nervous man in his fifties with a briefcase clutched to his chest and a bushy gray mustache. The secretary nodded and answered the buzzing phone, probably Alexian asking her to send in the next victim.

In the hall Roger said, "Well?"

"I want to think about all this," she said. "Oh, I'm sure I'll do it, or at least start. It's too damn tempting not to, but Robert Alexian is a bit overwhelming. I'd hate to be locked in a bedroom with him."

"He doesn't like women," Roger said. "I mean sexually."

"That," said Jean, "is a relief."

They moved to the elevator with Roger gleefully going on. "I'll work things out with them, wangle a good producer and see what's going on with this writer idea. I suppose Browder will get in touch with you directly about the rest. As Alexian said, 'We're in business.'"

Jean pushed the button for the elevator. There was no one else waiting on three.

"Do we bother to ask if Mel can come in on this?" she said softly.

"I'll see what we can do," said Roger. "I'm going to lose him soon anyway. He's too good to stay with WSMK—he's going to get an offer sooner or later from someone who can pay him more. I'll try. Now what about us?"

She looked at him. He was scanning her face intensely.

"We go slowly?" she said.

"Weekend? Friday, Saturday, Sunday?" he said with a smile.

"If Angie spends the weekend with Max, we'll see," she said. "Why not?"

He kissed her even though the elevator door had opened. From the corner of her eye in midkiss she saw two or three people step around them. She pulled away, took his hand, and stepped into the elevator.

This time he pulled away.

"I'm going to stick around here a while and see if I can get things moving," he said, stepping out of the elevator. "I'll call you."

The doors closed on his smile, and down she went. The door of the elevator was mirror smooth. Jean looked at her reflection. Plump? Hell, she'd think about cutting back on the food and, as soon as the weather cleared, she would go back to jogging. Before that, she'd get more serious about playing racquetball with Roger, but she was beginning to think that she might not ever get really serious about Roger.

Back in her own neighborhood, she went to the Jewel, picked up another armful of cardboard cartons, tape, and a dozen eggs, and headed home.

She pulled into a space on the street, knowing that she still had to get Angie after dinner, and began to lug the cartons, eggs, and tape toward her door, going slowly to avoid a disaster on the ice. An eye was definitely looking at her from the basement apartment. She looked back and the eye disappeared. The game plan was to fix a final to-hell-with-cholesterol-omelet, put some boxes together, and go on with the packing. She had arranged for a mover for the next Monday, and everything had to be ready to go. What Jean needed now was a dull evening that would not require her to think; but as soon as she pushed through the door of the downstairs hallway, she saw that the hope of a quiet evening was gone.

The two men were in their twenties, one tall and lean, the other stocky. The stocky one had the start of a beard, or maybe he had just forgotten to shave. The tall one had vacant eyes and long, straight, dirty blond hair. Both wore jackets too light for the weather.

"We'll give you a hand," the lanky one said, stepping forward.

Jean recognized them. They were two of the gang that lived or hung around across the street. The noisemakers and supposed drug takers and dealers. They weren't just in the hall waiting to give help to women in need.

"No thanks," Jean said, trying to decide whether to pretend she had forgotten something and go back out the door, leaving her cartons for ransom, or to brave it out and try to get past. It didn't matter. The tall one stepped in front of the outer door and closed it. The stocky one stood in her way.

"Okay," she said wearily. "You two can't imagine the kind of day I've had or, for that matter, what kind of week. What's going on?"

"We've got a question," the stocky one said. "Couple months back the cops were hassling us. We just heard you were the one complaining. And now there's cops around again asking questions."

122

Jean could imagine who they heard it from. Just a word dropped by Martha when she and Pal were out fouling up the neighborhood. In fact, Martha had complained loudly and long about these people, but had never called the police.

"You heard right," she said. "You might even remember that I complained to you one day when you were sitting in the window, and you thought it was pretty funny."

The stocky one was rubbing his hands together and bouncing slightly on his heels.

"Now if you'll just step out of the way and let me go by . . ."

"We noticed you before," said the lanky one behind her. "You're a good-lookin' lady."

"With a temper and a big mouth," added the one in front of her.

"All right," she said, removing her glasses. "You did your *Blackboard Jungle* routine. I'm properly frightened, and now you can go away while I have no real complaint against you. I'll be moving in a few days, and then you can have the whole territory for yourselves until the cavalry rides in, if it ever does."

She stared in the stocky one's face, which was slightly pink. The conversation wasn't going the way he wanted it to.

"I think maybe we're gonna all three go in that dark hallway over there and get acquainted real friendly like," he said. "Maybe when we're good friends you won't feel so fuckin' smart."

"Hey Carl," the lanky one said, his voice uncertain. "Maybe we—"

"I'm gonna take the lady in the stairs over there," Carl said evenly without taking his eyes from her, "and get friendly. You can come too, if you want, or you can watch the door. And the lady isn't going to scream, or I'm gonna have to hurt her."

"This is stupid," she said, trying to remember what one should say in a situation like this. "It's not even night. People are coming in and out of here. This—"

Carl, the stocky one, grabbed her and she decided to scream, but his hand was over her mouth. It tasted gritty with the faint hint of tobacco. She lifted her knee toward his groin but he turned away, taking it on his thigh.

"You want it that way," he said. "Fine with me."

His right fist pulled back and she closed her eyes waiting for the blow, but it didn't come. Instead she heard a knocking and a familiar voice.

"Excuse me," said the voice. "Can I come in?"

The stocky one pushed her against the wall. She hit hard, and the air poofed out of her lungs, but she didn't fall. Detective Lieberman, a good foot shorter and forty years older than the two, was trying to push his way into the hallway.

"Old man," Carl said, "turn your ass around. Get out of here, and forget you saw anything."

Lieberman's sleepy eyes looked at Carl and then at the young man at the door, whose left hand went into his pocket. Lieberman shook his head, looked as if he were going to take the advice and leave. He put a hand on the door before he turned around, as if to ask a question, and threw his knee forcefully between the legs of the tall boy, who let out an awful shriek and went down.

Carl took one step toward the little man and came face to face with a gun. Lieberman touched something and the gun clicked. Carl stepped back, pulling in his breath.

"Don't get crazy," he told Lieberman, putting his hands up.

"No one's going to get crazy," said Lieberman, still sleepy-eyed. The tall boy rolled on the tile floor in a fetal wail. Lieberman looked at Jean. She nodded to indicate she was all right and put her glasses on. Lieberman advanced on Carl, who dwarfed him. The pistol went up to the young man's neck.

"You're a very lucky young man," Lieberman said quietly. "You almost made a bad mistake. You know who this young lady is? You heard of Sam Giancanna?"

Carl nodded. He had heard.

"You heard of Cosa Nostra? You go to the movies? You read newspapers? You do something besides play cops and robbers? This young lady's the late Mr. Giancanna's niece. You fool with her and you and your friends wind up in a car trunk with your hands tied behind your backs with coathangers and a hole through the back of your head and the roof of your mouth. You hear what I'm telling you?"

"I hear," said Carl.

"Good, now apologize to the lady, pick up that heap of shit you came in with and pray she never sees you or any of your friends again, ever. Something happens to this lady, even if you don't do it, my friends and I are gonna come looking for you, and most of my friends are bigger and meaner and younger than I am."

Lieberman tapped Carl gently on the side of the head with his gun to get him started. Carl grabbed his buddy's arm, lifted him up, and left. The tall boy groaned into the street.

Lieberman put the gun away.

"Let me help you with those things," he said, reaching for the cartons. "Then maybe you can give me a cup of coffee."

Jean was drained. She wondered why she didn't cry.

"Thanks, I . . ."

"You want to thank me?" he said. "Pack these cartons and move some place safer. That's what you're going to do, right?"

"Right," she said, finding her voice. "Why didn't you arrest them?"

He opened the second door for her and said, without looking back, "If they think you're protected by the police, they'll be back at you and twice as mad. They know what the police can and can't do. If they think some crazy organized mob of hot-blooded Italians is protecting you, they'll stay away. They saw *The Godfather*."

"I'll take your word for it," she said, following him through the door and into the dark.

"Good. Lead the way through this catacomb and we'll talk."

She waited till they got into the apartment and the kitchen before she began to shake. She was determined, however, not to cry, at least not in front of him.

"You all right?" he said soothingly, turned his eyes away and looking for or pretending to look for a spoon or something.

"I think they had rape on their mind," she said, sitting at the table and putting her head in her hands.

"I think so too," he said, finding a spoon. "Their minds won't hold very much. They keep it simple. Here, have some coffee, the real thing, at least the real thing with little flavor buds or whatever. And some sugar too." He heaped in three spoons of sugar.

She lifted her head up.

"I'm going on a diet," she said, trying to stop him from spooning sugar. "I look too fat in pictures."

Lieberman was shaking his head.

"I told my wife you were a skinny thing. You're right. It's a crazy world. You said that, didn't you?"

"No," she said, taking a sip of coffee, "but I thought it."

She calmed down, and he suggested that she call someone to stay with her even though he was sure the "dreck" wouldn't be coming back. She decided that she didn't want anyone there but her daughter, and Lieberman looked at her with respect.

"You've got guts," he said, toasting her with coffee. "You've also got education and good looks, but I'm a little concerned about your common sense. You know why I just saved your virtue?"

"No, I . . ."

"Mrs. Bratcovick called to complain that you were harassing her and her brother, that you forced your way into her house and threatened her. Having seen Mrs. Bratcovick, I am naturally skeptical about you forcing her to do anything, but I am convinced you went over there in spite of my advice."

"I went over there," she admitted, drinking more coffee. "Parmenter talked to Angie after school yesterday. He was waiting for her."

"What did he say?" Lieberman asked, his hand tightening on the cup though his voice remained calm.

"That 'she,' meaning me, should heed his warning." A shiver ran through Jean and she was sure he saw it.

"You want me to make you an egg or two?" Lieberman asked.

She said she would eat when he left, and Lieberman nodded sleepily before telling her the good news. He had spoken to the psychologist in charge of Parmenter's release. "The man, his name was Fred Acound, said he was seriously considering recommendation that Parmenter be returned for treatment. It seems he is not only not improving in the bosom of society but deteriorating, which, having witnessed our little encounter downstairs, should be no surprise to anyone. He doesn't think Parmenter is dangerous, but who knows? So, my advice is stay away from Mrs. Bratcovick, stay away from Parmenter, be sure someone is with your daughter all the time, and he should be on his way back to North Carolina in a few days."

"Sounds good," she said. "Thanks."

"A servant of the public meets an enemy of the people," he said. "You sure you'll be all right? I was on the way home. My daughter's coming for dinner with her family. You want to come along, pick up your daughter?"

Jean put on her glasses and looked at him.

"No thanks, but are you for real?" she said with a weary smile.

"All right, look a gift cop in the mouth," he sighed, matching her weariness. "I thought I might get a little free psychological advice about my retirement. I heard you on the radio the other night."

"Then you heard him call," she said.

"I heard," he admitted. "But I couldn't swear it was Parmenter. Sounded more like his sister."

"I've got tapes of the conversation," she said.

"Let's hope we don't need them. You're gonna pick up your girl? I'll walk you to your car and look tough."

He did. She arrived to pick up Angie early enough to watch her come out of the school door, and she mentioned nothing about what had happened. The two of them stayed up too late packing, talking and planning, Jean relating the meeting with Alexian, and Angie making jokes about her mother winding up on a revival of "Charlie's Angels."

That night she checked the doors and windows and pushed a few packed boxes in front of both the front and back doors. Lieberman had convinced her about Carl and his friends, but there was more out there, much more. In spite of it all, she slept, a dreamless sleep.

◇ *TEN* ◆

The center was closed on Wednesday, a Jewish holiday—Jean couldn't remember which one. She got up early anyway, made herself and Angie breakfast, which consisted of French toast with powdered sugar and syrup and a large glass each of grape juice.

"You've got something on your mind, Angelina," Jean said as the girl silently finished her juice and remembered to wipe away the purple stain on her upper lip. "It's too quiet around here this morning."

"Can I stay home today?" Angie said. "There's not much happening at school, and I could help you pack."

Jean considered it seriously for a few seconds, and then shook her head.

"No, with moving and going to a new school and my new job I think you're going to miss enough school in the coming months. Besides, that isn't what was on your mind."

"How do you know?" Angie pouted.

"I'm a psychologist. I studied for years. I watch people all the time. I'm supposed to draw them out, help them, remember?"

"I think," Angie said after a deep breath, "that Daddy is going to get married again."

It shouldn't have come as a surprise. It had been two years, more than two years, and she had expected it in a way. In another way, she had held onto that germ of the idea that they might try it again, though she knew it wouldn't work.

"Anyone I know?" Jean asked casually.

"No, her name's Phyllis Yomo or Yogurt or something like that. I heard him talking to her Sunday," Angie said softly. "You want to know more?"

"Not today," Jean said.

Angie went on anyway. "She was nervous about meeting me, Dad said. That's what gave me the idea it was serious you know."

"And what do you think about it?" Jean said, knowing she was sounding as if she were in her office guiding a client.

Angie shrugged.

"I don't like it. It doesn't seem right. You know?"

"Just try to be nice to her when you meet," Jean said gently.

"You mean not the way I am to Roger. How do you feel about it?"

Jean's mind was full of feelings about many things. This was the week of chaos. Maybe Freud would have seen it coming, but she hadn't. How did she feel?

"Jealous," she admitted. "Not of Phyllis Yogurt and your father, but of you and me. If they get married, you'll spend a lot of time with them, hopefully get to like her. It's what I'd want, but I can't help feeling jealous. Honest enough answer?"

Angie nodded and showed her braces in a pained smile.

"Are you thinking of marrying Roger?" she asked, getting to the other thing on her mind.

"No way," she laughed. "But that doesn't mean I won't be seeing him a great deal, or that I'll never get married. It's not unheard of, marriage. You might even want to consider it at some distant point in the future. Now get going so I don't have to write your teacher a note."

At ten on the dot Roger called, told her about further details he was working on in the contract with Alexian, and volunteered to come over and help her pack. She turned him down politely, saying she would see him at the station later, that she had errands to run. A decision would have to be made about Roger. It wasn't fair to jump into bed at night and then turn cold in the morning. Considering the events of the past few days, she was fairly sure that she would get together with him again but that it would be nothing lasting, and a time would come when Roger could get hurt. Shit. She had packing to do.

Once or twice, actually four times, she went to the window and looked across the street. No one moved in the apartment of the boys who had visited her the night before. She was convinced that Lieberman's act had worked partly because the violence had been real.

Who would have thought the old man had so much blood in him? she thought. That wasn't quite right. Wasn't that what Macbeth said about the king? She turned on the radio, letting a talk station with a raspy-voiced host who riled his callers keep her company till the knock came on the door. She was in the middle of packing a drawer full of clothes, and had decided to leave Klinger's empty cage in the apartment when the knock came, and she went rigid.

"Who is it?" she called, looking around for a potential weapon.

"Mrs. Park," came the reply, a high-pitched squeal.

Jean opened the front door, but didn't invite the landlady in.

Mrs. Park was slightly shorter than Jean, slightly older, slightly thinner and possessed of a handsome Oriental face with eyes that were beginning to sink from worry, responsibility and alcohol. She wore a housecoat, a faded wraparound with a lost pattern, and she clung to herself in the cold of the dark hall.

"You moving?" she asked, peering over Jean's shoulder at the boxes.

"I'm moving," Jean admitted. "My lawyer must have gotten in touch with you by now."

"You have lease," Mrs. Park said. "You cannot break lease."

Mrs. Park's English was deserting her as she grew more excited. Jean stepped back to let the woman in out of the cold.

"I'm sure my lawyer told you," Jean said patiently, "and you and I have discussed it many times. This building isn't maintained. You don't clean the halls. You don't change the lights. I was assaulted in that dark hallway yesterday."

"Assaulted," Mrs. Park repeated. "I do not believe."

"You don't fix the boiler, the basement tubs have been backed up for weeks and the place smells like a toilet. You don't shovel the walks. Half the radiators don't work. There's no point in going on. If you feel you have a case, have your lawyer talk to my lawyer."

Mrs. Park was still shivering even though they were now inside the apartment, where it was reasonably warm.

"You have been bad since you and loud daughter moved in," said Mrs. Park.

"We have been unhappy," Jean said, "but you don't know what bad is. Either you are closing your eyes to a situation you don't wish to comprehend or you are unaware of the caliber of disaster in this community, to quote *The Music Man*."

Mrs. Park looked completely puzzled for a few seconds and returned to anger.

"You not get back your deposit," she said.

"Mrs. Park, knowing you, I don't think you've got it to give back. I'll consider it a donation, a low enough price to pay to escape. My sympathy for you long ago disintegrated into exasperation. Simply put, that means I am purposely and rather meanly speaking in a way you will have difficulty following. The result is I don't like myself very much at the moment. I really can't say that it has been nice knowing you," Jean said softly as she opened the front door.

Mrs. Park said something in Korean, which came out as a kind of hissing spit. Jean was sure it did not suggest a friendly farewell and good wishes for the future.

Maybe I deserve that, she thought, closing the door and returning to her packing. When the next knock came, even harder about ten minutes later, Jean feared it was Mrs. Park returning with a new supply of threats in English and hysteria in Korean.

"Yes," Jean shouted, pushing a Chase and Sanborn box full of clothes into a corner.

"It's Lloyd," he said through the door. "Can I come in, or do I have to spend a reasonable time out here getting used to total darkness?"

She hurried to the door and opened it. Her brother, tall, broad, his hair falling over his eyes and his glasses misted on his nearly Greek nose, stepped in. He was wearing jeans, a gray sweat shirt and a blue down jacket Fran had bought for him when his own decade-old brown wool jacket had refused to be repaired again.

"How did you know I was home?" she said, closing the door behind him.

"Jewish holiday," he said. "I know a little about religion, remember. Can I make myself a cup or two of coffee, or have you packed everything?"

She followed him into the kitchen, where he put on a pot of water and turned to look at her. It was the face of her father, but a softer face, and it occurred to Jean that Lloyd right now was just about the age her father had been when . . . a shudder ran through her. Lloyd saw it.

"What's wrong, Jeannie?"

"Bad night," she said. "What brings you here?"

He went to the refrigerator, found nothing to his liking and turned to her, rolling up the sleeves of his sweat shirt.

"I could tell you I was in the neighborhood and just stopped by to say hello," he said, raising his eyebrows. "Truth is Fran and I were worried about you. Anything new on Parmenter?"

She told him everything, the visit to the Bratcovick apartment, Lieberman's news about Parmenter possibly going back to North Carolina, the meeting with Alexian, Max's possible coming marriage and even the encounter in the hallway with Carl and the lanky young man.

"And you're angry?" he asked, looking over his glasses. He poured hot water in her cup and his. He had chosen a cup Angie had made in day camp with a drawing of Wonder Woman on it. She took a spoonful of dark crystals, and he did the same while she thought about his question.

"Confused, scared, I don't know about angry," she said. "Aren't I supposed to forgive everyone and leave it to God's judgment?"

"Don't mock me, little sister," he said with a grin. "I think God gave people a choice, and then he sat back to see how they would exercise that choice. That's the road of life we walk down. We make choices, we exercise our will, and God determines whether our choices are good or evil, and we know whether our choices are good or evil and we are responsible. That, Jeannie, is a rough condensation of a sermon I often fall back on when all else fails. Nope, it's you and the other descendants of Freud who gave man the out. Nobody's responsible for anything. We're just victims of forces beyond our control.

> "Whate'er is done to her she cannot know
> And if you'll ask her she will swear it so
> Whether 'tis good or evil none's to blame
> No one can take the pride no one the shame."

"Let me guess," she said, looking up with a smile. "Blake?"

"On the button," he admitted. "How about I help you pack for a while? Then if we feel like talking, we talk, if not we don't sit around trying to fill the silence. I'll tell you Walter stories and you can tell me about Angie's braces and if she's discovered boys yet."

"If she has," said Jean getting up, "and I think she has, she's not ready to admit it to anyone but Elizabeth Fratianno."

They worked for about an hour, talked a little, and made Jean feel much better about the day, the week and the future. Lloyd piled a box on top of a stack and stood back.

"Walter would love to climb on that," he said, pointing at the stack.

"Bring him over before Monday and he can, but I've been thinking seriously again about sending Angie to you till then. The problem is she'd miss school."

Lloyd put on his jacket and zipped it and then found his boots, pulled them on and began lacing them.

"With all that money you're getting, you can stay at a motel or a hotel," he said. "There must be a few not too far away so you can get to work and get Angie to school."

"Yeah," she agreed, "but I'm a little worried about disruptions for her. She might find it fun, but . . ."

"Ask her," he suggested, putting on his hood. He looked like a mountain climber about to tackle Everest.

"I will," she said and gave him a hug before he went through the door with her thanks for having stopped by.

She wandered slowly to the living room window to watch him drive away, and to wave at him again and smile to show she was all right. He didn't look up but went right to his station wagon across the street. That was when she looked back down the street and saw the old blue Chevy and caught a glimpse of white hair beyond the spot of sunlight that masked the front window of the car.

There wasn't any doubt. It must be, had to be Parmenter, and he was here watching her, waiting for her. She thought of opening the window and calling for Lloyd to stop. Her hands went out and began to do just that, but her mind caught and stopped her. Lloyd was starting his car. Parmenter's face was still not visible. She turned, grabbed her coat and purse and went out the front door, into the dark hallway, down the steps and outside. The day was sunny and deceptively cold. Lloyd pulled away without seeing her, and she made no effort to stop him. Instead she stepped into the street and started to walk toward the blue Chevy, which couldn't escape the one-way street without passing her.

The sun still hit the front window, but she was sure now that Parmenter saw her. He started his engine and she trotted forward. A public street, sunny day, late in the morning was the perfect place to confront him. It might not be totally safe, but it was in her favor, and she was angry. He really was right there in front of her apartment, in front of her and Angie's home.

She was no more than twenty feet from the Chevy when he stepped on the accelerator and banged into the car behind him, jerked forward and came out of the space and into the street in front of her. She moved between two parked cars, prepared to stare him down. Parmenter didn't drive past her. He began to back up quickly, recklessly scratching a white van on one side and making it to the corner.

"Not that easy," she said to herself and ran for her car, thankful that it was parked nearby on the street. He'd have a start on her but she was going after him, not quite sure what she would do but feeling a new sense of control.

It felt frightening, terrifying maybe, but good. She started the engine without warming it up, cut across to Damen and headed south hoping to cut him off. At Rogers, in front of the exterminator store with the picture of an ugly bug, she looked around, saw nothing and was about to quit and turn around. Instead, not wanting to give up the feeling of pursuit, she drove down a block to Touhy and spotted him. He was a full block away, headed east toward Clark Street. She decided to follow him.

Now I'm watching you, she thought with satisfaction, wondering if she were a bit hysterical and not much caring. He turned south on Clark and so did she. She stayed a good block behind him, knowing that he knew her car, had painted a black cross on its window. From time to time she could see his wild white hair.

He drove through the white Appalachian decay of northern Uptown and then the black decay of south Uptown. At the fringe of the chic shops of New Town he hesitated at a corner, decided, she thought, whether to turn right and head for the Bratcovick apartment or to go somewhere else. The decision took a while, and a car behind him hit its horn to hurry him up. He turned slowly to see who was honking at him, and Jean slumped down in case he looked back and spotted her. Then he turned and drove. He had some place to go.

Five minutes later he parked not far from the Newberry Library near a Cadillac dealer and got out. He didn't bother to put change in the street meter. Jean pulled into an empty space across the street, jumped out and stuck a quarter in the meter before following him.

Parmenter wore a jacket far too light for the weather, and no hat. His hands were plunged into his pocket, and his white-haired head bobbed. Others hurried to get out of the cold. He walked slowly and she followed.

He stopped at the bright lights of a porno movie theater, which, Jean could tell from the titles, specialized in all-male pictures. Parmenter moved to a door next to the theater that, in contrast, had a red flashing light saying GIRLS, GIRLS, GI . . . The RLS of the last call were burned out.

Four young men came down the street from the other direction, coming north, and pushed past Parmenter through the door that promised girls. Parmenter followed them. The choice was now Jean's, go back to the car and wait, or follow. She crossed the street when the traffic cleared a bit, hesitated for just a beat, and opened the door.

There was a dark, narrow wooden stairway, wide enough for only one person to go up at a time. Faded posters of women, some of them looking as if they dated back to the Second World War. There were voices upstairs ahead of her and the smell of rotting wood and dry urine.

She went up and came to a level space where a flat table was covered with red linoleum held on with thumb tacks. A man sat behind the table, a thin, dark Latin man with a thin mustache, dark hair and one massive pock crater on his left cheek. He looked as if he were trying out for a road company of *El Grande de Coca Cola*. The man looked up at her with mild surprise, but he had probably seen all kinds.

"You wanna ticket?" he asked.

She nodded and he shrugged.

"Three bucks," he said. "Movie and live show."

She got her wallet out, handed him three singles and found herself in a small theater, about fifty seats. The smell was even worse inside. The movie screen was old and torn. Adhesive tape had been used to bind a tear right in the middle where perhaps a patron had lost control and flung himself in madness or ecstasy at the image. Jean found a seat at the back and looked for Parmenter. His white head caught the reflection from the screen four rows ahead of her, and she sat back to watch him and look at the screen.

The pornographic film wasn't quite as old as some of the posters on the stairway but it certainly predated her own birth. It was explicit but corny with grunts of passion and fake ecstasy. The quartet of young men in the first row laughed and made nervous jokes. Parmenter sat silently. She thought, when there was a lull in the film conversation and the boys' joking, that she heard him talking to himself or the screen.

The movie lasted about ten more minutes, and the lights went on, not brightly enough to reveal the patrons clearly to each other, but on. A thin girl came out on the stage wearing a flimsy see-through gown. One of the boys in the front row whistled softly and was promptly hit in the ribs by a companion trying to cut the uncool behaviour. Jean could now see that there were several more men in the theater, who had been slouching so low when she came in that she didn't notice them. The thin girl gave them time to pull themselves together from the wild excitement of the film and told them that the

136

live show was through a door on the right through which they could pass for another two dollars.

"You part of the show?" asked one of the boys, the one who had whistled. He seemed to be high on something.

"I'm part of the show," she said with a tired smile.

Parmenter didn't turn around, but one of the slouching men did. He was about fifty, bald and well dressed. He looked like a businessman, maybe a librarian or car salesman, who had taken a chance and now was afraid he'd be caught. He looked at Jean, made a funny sound, and then hurried down the aisle and back out of the theater, looking away.

The rest of the audience, including Parmenter, followed the girl and coughed up two more dollars. Jean waited till they had gone through the door and hurried up, two dollars in hand. The thin girl, who wore too much make-up and had the dry look of the teenage addict, gave her only a slight curious look and took her money. Then the girl disappeared. The boys pressed forward into the new room with dark drapes and no light except for a dull spot hitting a stage barely big enough for a person to stand on. Parmenter and another man stood off to the side. The room was small, but Jean stayed back behind Parmenter, watching him, as the Latin-looking ticket taker languidly walked to the platform and announced that they were now going to see Lolita, the teenage wonder of the Orient, who had just come to Chicago to escape the horrors of war in her native country, where she had learned the arts of pleasing a man.

He ducked behind a curtain, and the sound of Oriental music came from a low-fidelity tape recorder. The thin girl came out, made a few moves while the boys nudged each other and Parmenter watched, transfixed. The girl didn't really bother to keep time with the music or move against it. First she dropped her nightgown and, seconds later, both her bra and panties came off, revealing an almost anemic body.

Then the light went out and the music stopped abruptly.

When the lights came back on the girl was gone, and the Latin man was standing in her place, saying they could pay another dollar and go back into the theater for a new and different movie.

By this time, one of the boys was beginning to catch on.

137

"Hey, what kind of shit is this?" he said.

"No shit at all," said the Latin man with a smile. "We deliver what we promise, and there's more in store."

The boys had a conference, seemed split but decided they had had enough and looked around for an exit. They bumped past Jean at the door and one of the boys said, "Why ain't she in the show?"

That made the remaining undecideds, including Parmenter, turn toward her. For the first time, she was face to face with the man who had killed her parents, smashed their faces with an axe, torn their bodies. This was a moment, she knew, that she had wanted and dreaded, and the most horrible thing about it was that Parmenter looked at her blankly. He was a thin, pale old man, his mouth open, his eyes puffy and slightly sad. Then recognition came, and his mouth dropped open.

The other two men in the room looked at her and scooted past as Parmenter stood transfixed.

"Lady," came the voice of the Latino man who stepped into the room. "You're slummin' or a narc or vice, right? Whatever you are, you're bad for business so how about I give you your money back and you go away, okay?"

Parmenter looked at the man as if he were speaking in a foreign language and then back at Jean.

"You too, nut case," he said to Parmenter, "only you don't get your change back. You probably came in your pants twice, right? Now out, both of you, I gotta go collect. That door."

Parmenter followed the man's pointing finger, looked back at Jean and shuffled quickly through the door. Jean ran after him, and found herself in total darkness.

Her first reaction was no reaction at all. The door had sprung shut behind her giving her the sensation of being gobbled by the great void. It took her breath like an unsuspected punch, but she managed to catch it and the sob of fear welling behind it.

Her second reaction was close to total panic, a desire to reach for the door behind her, tear through it if it was locked. She actually turned and reached for the place where a knob should have been but wasn't. The impulse to scream came up like bile in her throat and someone said, "No."

The "no" stopped her and the scream. The voice was familiar, her own.

"No," she repeated aloud, pushed away from the warm wooden door, and turned into the blackness.

There were no footsteps. If she couldn't see, neither could Parmenter.

"You can't get away from me," she said, hoping to hear something to indicate where he was, pushing away the panic telling her he was only inches beyond. She pressed her back to the door.

Breathing. Low breathing. In the darkness it was difficult to tell how far away it was or in what direction, but she was sure it was a distance in feet and not inches.

"Talk to me," she said softly. When no answer came except for the breathing, she let her voice rise and insist, "Talk to me. You wanted to face me. Here I am."

Feet moved, a shuffling, scraping. Jean pushed back against the door and automatically lifted her hands to where Parmenter's face might be if he ran at her. But if he was searching for her, he was blundering in the wrong direction. She could hear him hit something. Some boxes fell. His voice squealed, "Ow."

In the instant she realized he might be looking for a light switch, she also sensed that she could now see, not much, but something, vague gray dots, rather like an enlarged, faded black and white photograph in which you can see only the dots.

"No," came another voice in the dark and this time it was Parmenter's. Parmenter was panting now, moving along the wall, crashing into objects, making his way toward her. Like a maze, she thought.

Then came the click and the light, a small yellow naked bulb dangling from the ceiling of the narrow room. As dim as it was, the light froze Parmenter who looked around frantically, at first unable to find Jean, then finding her. But his eyes didn't rest on her long. They continued to circle the walls and take in the posters hung there.

At first Jean couldn't take her eyes from the man. His eyes were wide open as he stepped back and tripped over a box that sent him into an absurd dance step to keep from falling. Then Jean looked around. Her first thought was to find a weapon, but her eyes couldn't help following his gaze.

She could only see the posters nearest her. The others, those close to Parmenter, were in shadows beyond the power of the dirty bulb. It was a hallway of pornography. Enlarged dusty photographs of women and men coupled with animals, exploring bodies with fingers and mouths. Some of the people, she realized, were not normals but deformed and what made the display even more horrible was its age. The enlarged pictures were all old, judging from the costumes, hair styles, even the grayness of the prints, they were at least fifty years old, possibly much more. She wasn't looking at some recent perversion but something that might be timeless, something that generations had paid to see.

"No!" Parmenter screamed and stood in the center of the hallway forcing himself to look at Jean. Half in and half out of the shadow beyond he looked at her with the same look he had given to the posters and she could sense that he was deciding, not with his brain but with some whimpering instinct, whether to rush at her or away from her.

His right hand came up, possibly to gesture, and it came in contact with one of the posters. He pulled it back instantly as if it had been burned, looked down at it, thrust it under his left armpit and whimpered as he turned, took four or five steps down the hallway, and threw open the far door. Jean ran after him not looking to right or left, not touching the walls, pushed open the door and found herself on a fire escape with Parmenter who was looking down, unable to decide what to do or which way to go. They were about two stories up, and for a second Jean thought he might actually jump rather than turn and face her.

The wind came through the alley, blowing his hair. To Jean it looked as if he were on white fire. A strand of her own long hair fell across her lips. She brushed it away.

"What do you want from me?" she said. "What do you want from me and my daughter? Why have you been calling me? Haven't you done enough to my life?"

Parmenter's Adam's apple jumped as he gulped. Bristles of white hair covered it. He turned to her, and something came into his eyes, a resolution. Jean felt fear and reached back for the door, but it had no handle on the outside.

"I'm doing what must be done," he said finally. Jean tried to discover the voice on the phone in his words but couldn't be sure. The voice had whispered. This man was shouting. "They came to me in that place for years, bringing the face, telling me, telling me about you, how I had to come and do what must be done, to make it right and final. Jesus he came, John and Peter, they came too."

"And Paul?" she said, reminding him of the name he had used when he called her.

"And Paul," he repeated sadly, "the wisest of them all. They all told me I must come here and find the face before I could be cleansed of the blood that was on my hands. And General William Booth came to me with a big bass drum and said, 'Are you washed in the blood of the lamb?'"

Jean edged toward the iron steps going down, caught her heel and yanked it out. Parmenter was still looking at her sadly.

"It wasn't that I wanted to come," he said with his hands out, his bristly Adam's apple bobbing. "It was what I had to do, to come here to Chicago, to seek and find. You think it's so easy? I was in that place." He pointed to the door through which they had come and went on.

"I know what it is when a man can't fight off the animal that's in us all. The blood cleans the blood. I know who you are. It is for you I came."

Now he was pointing a bony finger at her, and the wind did an even wilder dance through his hair and screeched through the alley. Somewhere on the street beyond, in the still cold morning, a car squealed and skidded, and Parmenter paused for the crash that never came.

"For you I came," he repeated, taking a step toward her.

"Don't touch me," she said through clenched teeth. She pulled her purse back ready to hit him.

He reached out for her and she struck. The purse hit him in the face, and the loose strap broke. He staggered back, and for an instant she thought he would stagger over the railing and to the cement alley below. She backed down the steps, reeling in her purse, and watched him recover, his moist eyes moving to her. She imagined herself going over the railing.

Then she turned and ran down the fire escape.

"Stay away," she shouted, over her shoulder. There seemed to be no clink of shoe on metal behind her, but she didn't stop to look until she was on the ground and at the turn in the alley leading back to Clark Street.

He stood high above her, leaning over the edge of the fire escape, the wind blowing his flimsy jacket, lifting his hair. He looked as if he were in a pulpit delivering a sermon, for his mouth was moving and he was looking toward heaven. Then his eyes adjusted sharply, clicked and focused on her, and his mouth closed into something that might have been a sorry smile, and she ran.

◇ *ELEVEN* ◆

"Boy have I had a rough day," Angie said with exaggerated weariness as she climbed into the Aspen next to her mother.

Jean's laugh must have sounded a little hysterical because Angie took off her white woolen hat and gave her mother a quizzical look.

"What's so wild about me having a rough day?" Angie asked. "You feeling all right? You're not upset because of what I told you about Dad?"

Jean looked back at her daughter and leaned over to tuck a wild string of hair back behind the girl's ear. She had forgotten about Angie's announcement of Max's possible wedding plans. Well, she had forgotten about it consciously, but certainly it was there. It may even have been one of the factors that made her pursue Parmenter.

"Tell me about your rough day," she asked, and Angie told her.

There had been an argument with Elizabeth, but that seemed to be all right now. There was some question about transferring her credits for the year because she was moving in the middle of a semester, but that was probably going to be all right too. Someone had poured salt all over her sandwich at lunch as a joke, and at that point

143

she was fighting with Elizabeth so she had had to settle for her hard boiled egg, juice and an orange. There were more problems, but they were minor compared to these catastrophes.

When Angie slowed down her chatter, Jean asked her a question without looking at her.

"How'd you like to have a kind of moving vacation? We'd stay at the Holiday Inn, meals out, swimming in the pool, and I'd drive you to school the days you've got left. Let's see, three days. Tomorrow we'll go to your new school and take a look."

Angie was quiet for a second.

"Are you still worried about Klinger, what happened to Klinger I mean?"

"Nope," Jean said honestly, "just the whole idea of getting away from the neighborhood. I had a little run-in with Mrs. Park this morning too. What do you say?"

"It's going to cost a lot," practical Angie said.

"Your mom's going to be a star, remember? I don't think you'll believe it till you see me on television. Come to think of it, I won't believe it either till that happens."

"When?" asked Angie as they drove into the alley behind their apartment.

"Now," said Jean. "We go in there, pack the things we need in the suitcases and leave the boxes. I'll strip the beds and put the sheets and blankets in a carton and off we go. I'll come back with the movers on Monday."

Jean opened the garage door and pulled in. When she came to a stop in the darkened garage, she looked at Angie, and Angie looked back with a question. There was something Jean wasn't telling her, but this wasn't the time to ask for it. Angie could see all this in her eyes.

"This means I don't have to go with you to the station tonight," Angie said. "I can stay in the room and watch television. Do they have ON-TV or HBO?"

Jean got out of the car with Angie behind her.

"I don't know," she said.

"One more request," Angie said as they pushed through the back door and into the kitchen. "Can't I please do one minor little nasty thing to Martha?"

Jean was tempted, but she controlled herself and said no. The line between them and us has to be drawn some place, she thought. It took only forty minutes or so to pack the rest of their clothes, strip the beds, empty the refrigerator and take a last look. They had already packed the curtains, and the place looked particularly bright with the help of the sun, which had come out for a brief visit.

They stood at the door and Jean said, "Anything you want to say to the place before we go?"

"Not even good-bye," Angie said.

They checked into the Holiday Inn in downtown Evanston, which did have a movie channel. The evening movie was *Four Seasons*, which Angie had never seen, so that settled her evening. Dinner was a pair of Big Macs and a shake at McDonald's. Then Jean deposited Angie back at the room and said, "No walks, no wandering and no one in the room, not even room service, till I get back."

"I know the routine," Angie said. "See you later."

Parmenter had not followed her. She was sure of that. There would be no missing that old car. Besides, she couldn't keep a twenty-four-hour watch on her daughter. He'll be gone in a few days, she told herself, and headed for the station.

Roger was waiting for her with more news about Alexian and CBS. Everything looked fine. He hadn't talked to Alexian directly about Mel, but he had talked to Alexian's assistant, a woman named Mangione, who said she thought it was a possibility. Roger had already discussed it with Mel, which was evident as soon as she stepped into the studio, waved her fingers at the beclouded Ted Earl and got a cheerful "Hi" from Mel.

"I know there's no guarantee," Mel said in his deep voice, "but if it comes off, the best thing about it might be that CBS is a talk and news network. I'm getting to hate all-music."

Gary Burghoff, Jean thought, that's who played Radar. That's the actor Mel looked like.

"Favor," said Jean, sitting down and pulling her note cards. "If our friend Paul calls, don't put him through. You can signal me, but pass him by."

"Granted," Mel said, cocking his head and looking at the speaker in the corner. Ted had turned the volume down in the studio, but some of the sound always came through.

"I think it's Andy Williams," said Jean, glancing at her card. Her preparation was down to nothing. That promised writer would be a welcomed luxury.

"No," said Mel. "It's Jack Jones. And now that he's finished, thank you Jack, get on your mark 'cause here we go."

"Sigmund Freud once said that humor is the only decent reaction to the inevitable," she began after her introduction. "With the end of winter not all that far away, I thought we might brighten the long night with your favorite jokes, and we can try to do a little analysis of them and how the jokes and humor help us get through the day, week and our lives. Since we have to keep the jokes clean, take a minute before you call in, and I'll start out by telling a few of Freud's favorite jokes and what he thought of them, right after these messages."

Ted threw on a trio of taped commercials, and Mel said, "That's taking a chance. You're going to get Polish jokes, dumb jokes, Irish jokes, antifeminist jokes. You are a brave woman."

"The moon is full, and the werewolves are baying," she said. "I'm ready for them."

The show was rather disappointing. The worst was a man who kept laughing nervously while he told his joke and saying, "and now listen to this part." None of it was funny, and it turned out to be a near classic case of anal retention. She couldn't think of a decent way to tell him, and no alternate interpretation came to mind.

There was a Polish joke from a woman who said she knew lots of Poles and they didn't mind. After the joke the lights went wild on the phone with Poles and non-Poles who did mind.

It turned out to be the least humorous show she had ever done, and she made a mental note never to repeat the idea on CBS.

With a little less than five minutes to go, Mel took a call and looked over at her with a nod. It was him. Mel was about to cut the call off, but apparently the caller said something, and Mel reached for his pad and wrote it down before pushing the button for another caller, another complainer about Polish jokes.

When they signed off, Mel handed her the note he had written:

Wanted you to know I left another surprise for my old friend right where I put the other one. Birds of a feather

"No doubt about it," said Mel, getting ready to take a break for a taped show, "he's a bona fide ding-dong."

Jean read it again and then read it once more. It could mean a lot of things, but it probably meant only one. She ran for Roger's office, burst in ignoring him and called the Holiday Inn. Angie answered on the second ring to the room.

"Ange, are you all right?"

"Sure," Angie said. "Are you done?"

"I'm done," Jean said, looking at a surprised Roger, "but I've got to stop back at the apartment for something, and then I'll be there. How's the movie?"

"Terrific. Do you think Alan Alda wears a wig?"

"No," said Jean. "See you in a while."

She hung up and looked at Roger.

"I've got to check something back at the apartment," she said with a very dry throat. "Will you come with me?"

Roger stood up immediately and moved to her side.

"You look . . ." he began. "What are you checking for?"

"A present I don't want," she said and let him take her hand.

They drove in Roger's car, leaving Jean's parked in front of the station to be picked up later. It meant spending more time with Roger and possibly bringing him back to the hotel to pick up Angie and go out for ice cream or something. Roger's feelings for her were something she could lean on like a soft pillow and that, after what had been happening, was a nice thing to have.

There were no spaces on the street, at least not in the immediate neighborhood, so Jean suggested he pull into the garage. The Parks' red Ford was tucked in, making it tight for Roger, but he made it without a scratch and they got out.

"I don't think this is anything," she whispered. "If it's not, I'm going to be one very relieved woman."

"A little relief can go a long way," Roger said, taking her hand as they made their way in the dim light across the yard and up the back steps. She opened the back door, walked quickly to the wall and turned on the light, then looked as casually as she could into the darkness of the front rooms.

"This will take just a second or two. I'll check the boxes, see if I left any windows open and off we go," she said, looking over her glasses with a thin smile, a trick she had picked up when she was about fourteen. It probably didn't look coy and cute any more, and she had put it on her list of things to stop doing, but it had become defensive and habitual. Give the daddy figure a little-girl smart-sexy look and he'll melt, she thought, flipping on lights. Roger strolled behind her.

"Place really looks big with everything out of the rooms," he said as she stepped into her bedroom, reached over and hit the switch.

Roger was a few steps behind her in the dining room, adjusting a cardboard box on top of two others that looked as if it might fall.

She stepped out and looked at him, but his head was averted as he pushed the carton.

"Some of the smaller things . . ." he began.

"Roger," she said softly, maybe so softly that it didn't come out.

". . . we can just put in the trunk of your car," he went on, starting to turn to her and wiping a smudge from his palm, "and Jerry or I can—"

His face had turned to hers, and he stopped. She was leaning against the wall outside the bedroom, her glasses in her hand, her mouth open.

"Jean." He took the three steps across the room to her.

"Are you sick? What . . ."

"Roger," she repeated, and this time she could hear herself. "Call the police. See if you can get that Detective Lieberman. If not, get anyone and tell them to get here fast."

She slumped back and started to slide down the wall but he grabbed her arms. She thought, with surprise, that Roger was deceptively strong, which was just what she needed.

"Why," he asked. "What should I tell him?"

She tried to speak, but her voice wouldn't come, only the taste of bitterness, the bile that sometimes warns you that you are about to vomit. She turned her head toward the bedroom, her eyes still wide. Roger held her firmly with one hand and looked into the room. There was nothing left in there, just two beds and two mattresses. But on one of the walls was a massive inkblot of dark red, and on the bed below the blot lay a figure, a thin figure staring at him with wide, startled eyes. The red of blood curled in the figure's hair, and a dark trickle flowed down its nose across the right eye like a tear. From somewhere a draft raised a wild frill of the corpse's white hair and set it dancing like the down of a bird.

◇ *TWELVE* ◆

She sat in the kitchen at the table. She had unpacked the instant coffee and some pots and boiled water. Lieberman, who had just arrived at midnight, sat across from her, holding a hot cup in two hands. Behind them, around them, police were walking through the apartment, talking, taking pictures, pausing to ask questions. The most startling thing was that they acted as if nothing much had happened. They talked to each other, made jokes about mutual friends, talked about what they would do the next day, and went about their business.

She had talked to four or five policemen before Lieberman came. The first one there was Selig, the young uniformed cop she had met before. He had been surprisingly gentle and asked very few questions. Then others came. She couldn't remember them.

It had been Jean who had called the police. Roger had come out of the bedroom looking more shocked than she imagined herself to be. The sight of Roger had shaken her into action. She had taken his hand and led him into the kitchen.

"My God," had been his only comment as he looked up at Jean for an explanation she didn't have.

Before the police, she had called Max, then Lloyd. Fran answered and said Lloyd was out but expected back soon and what was wrong with Jean, her voice sounded so . . . Jean didn't want to explain, talk. It was like walking in cotton up to your waist or making your way through curtains that fell apart when you touched them.

"Fran, this is important," she had said, trying not to look back down the hall toward her bedroom. What if Parmenter were faking and rose, coming out of her room with that wild look, his face and hair covered with blood? "I know it's late, and I know it's far, but Lloyd has to go to the Holiday Inn in Evanston, Room three-oh-four, get Angie and bring her to your house. I'll call Angie and tell her. You have that?"

"Yes, but—" Fran began.

"Fran, please," and the plea worked.

"Okay, but I want you to call back and tell me what's happening."

When she hung up, Jean had called the Holiday Inn.

"Ange, listen. Things have changed. Uncle Lloyd is going to pick you up some time in the next hour or two and take you to his house."

"What?" Angie had said dreamily. She had obviously been asleep.

Jean repeated her message and Angie hazily asked, "What's wrong?"

"Roger's feeling a little sick," she said. "I might have to stay with him a while." Roger, in fact, had looked very sick. He had been staring down the hall toward her room.

"Okay," Angie said. If she were more awake, the questions, arguments would have come. Jean had hung up and looked at her trembling hands and then at Roger.

"Who . . ." Roger had begun. "My God, I've never seen anything like that."

"I have," she said, "but it's been a long time." And then the words to the song the Dark Man had evoked came back to her.

151

And then they had sat in the kitchen, saying very little, until the first policeman, Selig, came. And then things had moved quickly. No. Roger was sitting in the same chair, Lieberman next to him and Jean at the other end of the small table as the police whirled about.

I'm moving, she thought, who cares if they mess up the floor. The thought almost made her giggle with its absurdity, and she knew she was, once again, holding off hysteria.

Lieberman looked even older and more droopy-eyed than the last time she had seen him. His gray suit was rumpled, his white shirt wilted and his tie off. He sipped his coffee and looked from Jean to Roger.

"So you're all right?" he asked.

"Considering the circumstances," she said.

"I'm all right," Roger said, though no one had asked him. He seemed to be trying to reassure himself.

"I've got a suggestion," said Lieberman. "Mr. Nash, why don't you go home? We've already got your statement and we can send someone tomorrow to talk to you again. I'll come talk to you."

"But Jean . . ." he said, looking at her.

"She'll be fine. We'll take care of her," Lieberman said.

She reached over to Roger, brushed the hair away from her eyes and said, "I think that would be a good idea, Roger. We'll get together tomorrow."

"You sure?" he said, rising uncertainly.

"I'm sure," she said. She walked him to the back door, gave him a kiss on the cheek and pointed him toward the stairs. Over the railing and through the break in the walkway, she could see a few neighborhood people in a huddle, looking up curiously past the flashing squad car in the alley. She turned to Lieberman as she closed the door.

"Nice fella," said the detective.

"Yes," agreed Jean, going back to her seat.

"Not exactly the Rock of Gibraltar," added Lieberman. "No offense meant."

Jean lifted a hand to show she wasn't offended.

Lieberman drank some more coffee and made a face as if he had just downed a jigger of Scotch.

"I'm not usually on homicide," he explained. "You talked to Lieutenant Clavey, the one with the vest and mustache, remember?"

She nodded agreement though she wasn't sure.

"It's probably his case, but he agreed I should go ahead since I know the parties concerned."

"Meaning me and Parmenter," she said, trying to focus on the conversation and wondering when they were going to take Parmenter's corpse out. She half-watched down the hall, feeling that the breath she couldn't quite catch would, might come when his corpse was gone.

"The truth is no one likes to write reports," he said. "And this one is going to be long. You know why? Because we've got complications and suspects. Suicide is unlikely. Can I talk about it?"

"Talk about it," she said, lifting her eyes to his.

"To kill himself he would have had to stand on the bed and bash his head against the wall, the back of his head, hard."

"He was psychotic," Jean said. "Psychotics are capable of remarkable things, destructive things. Carl Jung had a case once in which a young woman spent most of her time trying to find a way she could shit on her own left heel."

"Her heel?" asked Lieberman, raising his droopy eyes and touching his mustache.

"Anal retention problem. Am I making sense? I'm almost hysterical." She got up and poured herself some more hot water for coffee.

"We'll see what the medical people say," said Lieberman, rubbing his lower back, "but it's murder."

"He called me," she said. "That's why I came here tonight. You can see I'm moving out. My daughter and I went to a motel, but he called the station and . . ." She reached in her purse, but the note wasn't there. She looked up hopelessly and Lieberman fished the note out of his own pocket.

"You gave it to Lieutenant Clavey," he explained. "Two things are possible. He called you and planned something else. Who knows what? I met the man, remember. I'd testify he was not in his right faculties, to put it delicately. So, he planned something after he called, came here and someone did this. We'll come back to that. The second possibility is that he didn't call you, someone else did, whoever did this. You didn't talk to him this time?"

"No, Mel, the announcer at the station, took the call and the message."

"A whispering man," said Lieberman. "That's no great problem. The problem is, who did that to him? I've got the beginning of a list of possibilities that could keep me busy a month."

"Suspects, but who?" Jean asked, trying to come back into focus. She had the vague memory of Roger giving her a pill to calm her down and that he had taken one too.

"How many fingers you got to count on," Lieberman sighed. "We can start with the boys across the street, our playmate Carl from down in the hall. He might have let it fester and decided in spite of the Mafia to come over here and teach you a lesson. Maybe he got high on something, and that gave him courage. Maybe he broke in here and found Parmenter and bashed him.

"Or," he went on, holding up two fingers, "Parmenter's sister might have followed him or come with him, tried to talk him out of whatever he was planning, got into a fight when they got here and instead of stopping him for a while, she stopped him for good. A big strong woman. I admit, not a good suspect. I've yet to meet her husband. I have no great hopes for him either, but you know in this business . . ."

He shrugged and went on, seemingly thinking of all this as he went along. Jean watched and listened with fascination.

"That brings us to three or maybe four," he said, holding up fingers and then wiggling them a little to show that counting was getting in the way. "In the category of those who might have played handball with Mr. Parmenter because he was bothering you. Your brother—"

"Lloyd?" she interrupted.

"Why not?" Lieberman's question came back in answer to hers. "Excuse the directness, but those were his parents too, remember, and his sister and his niece were being threatened."

"Lloyd wouldn't . . ."

154

"Lloyd wouldn't," Lieberman repeated, closing his eyes. "And Mr. Nash, Roger?"

"He couldn't have," she explained. "You saw him."

"One wouldn't, one couldn't" said Lieberman. "Your former husband? Max . . ."

"Allen," she supplied.

"I don't know what the state of his affection for you might be, but his daughter's involved."

"Max is a lawyer," she said incredulously.

"So lawyers never commit murder? I don't keep statistics, but as a profession I'll make you a bet they're right behind the doctors."

"I think if it was a matter of protecting Angie, Max might railroad someone like Parmenter, drown him in law suits, maybe even lie, you know, ends justify means, but he'd never . . ."

"From what I gather, everyone I've suggested is big enough and strong enough and might have a reason, but now we come to our A-number one suspect."

"You," said Jean, feeling the edge of her mouth threatening a tic.

"Me?" Lieberman's hooded eyes sprang open, his mouth dropped for an instant and then he smiled.

"You," she said. "You're not big but you're violent. I've seen you, and you know more about death than anyone you've named. You knew about the threats, met Parmenter and you like me. If I may be a bit shocking and bold though at the same time clinical, you have some kind of feeling for me, paternal, maybe vaguely incestuous. You could have followed Parmenter here or been here waiting to protect me, something."

Lieberman was smiling as he said, "Look at the brain on her. How can you not be Jewish? To tell you the truth, it's not bad, but that's not who I had in mind."

"Who," she said, "is left?"

"You," he said, still smiling.

It was Jean's turn to be surprised. She put down her cup before it dropped, but she spilled some coffee on the table and looked around for something to clean it with.

A tree-trunk of a man of about fifty or fifty-five with steely gray

155

short hair came in and told Lieberman that they were through with the body and it was going to be removed unless he wanted another look. He said no, and the man moved back toward Jean's bedroom.

"We were saying?" Lieberman began. He rubbed his closed red eyelids and then, as if suddenly remembering, said, "Oh yes, you are the best suspect on the list."

"Have you considered a career on the stage or in movies?" she asked nervously.

"Our temple was thinking of doing *Sleuth*," he said. "They wanted me but I couldn't remember all those lines. Nobody could, so we did *The Cat and the Canary* instead. I got killed early. You want to know why I think you're a good suspect?"

"After you," she said.

"You got a reason," he said, cocking his head. "You can't deny that. The man killed your parents, threatened you. Who better? It's your apartment. You've got a key. You actually went to see the man in his own house. You never did actually meet him, did you?"

Jean hesitated and then said, "No."

Lieberman picked it up, stopped talking and stared at her.

"You did talk to him? When and where?"

"I didn't," she said, letting her head fall to the table, onto her arms.

"Means, motive, and you're a strong girl—"

"Woman," Jean corrected.

"Again I forgot. Woman, you're a strong woman, not just physically but look at you, what you've been through. You're tired, sure, shaking, who wouldn't be, but at the same time there's a, what can I call it, look of relief."

"I am relieved," she said. "He's been haunting me since I was a child, and now he's gone, dead. A weight off my chest."

"There, you see, the perfect suspect."

Jean nodded her head and wished that the need to giggle would go away so she could think, defend herself from this little man with the penetrating, droopy eyes.

"And when did I do it?"

"That's a good question," he said. "With a helper, Nash maybe,

156

or someone to call at the station and pretend it was Parmenter, it's easy. On your own, though, I'd have to work on it."

"And you really think I did it?" She couldn't help pointing to herself and she felt stupid doing it.

"No," he said, standing. "I don't think you did it. I'm not sure you didn't do it, but I don't think you did. I've been wrong more times than we have suspects here, but I'd say you're clean as the window in I. Magnin's downtown. Remember I'm a cop. You look good on paper, but I'm not going to spend a lot of time trying to put Parmenter in your lap. Sorry, a poor figure of speech."

"Thanks," she said with some sarcasm.

"Tell me the truth," he said. "You feel a little better going through that little scene we just did? You know what I mean?"

She did feel better. He had pried her mind from its spongy morbidity into attention and action. She nodded her head in agreement.

"So now, you put on your coat, and I'll drive you to that motel and you get a good night's sleep."

She agreed dumbly and put on her coat. He was moving toward the front of the house. That way they'd have to pass the bedroom, might even run into the men removing the body. Lieberman stopped, understood, and turned to the back door.

"This will be on television and in the newspapers, won't it?" she said wearily, a bit ashamed that she was asking the question, a bit guilty that she wondered how it might affect her future, CBS.

He took her hand and led her outside.

"Delusions of grandeur," he said. "Isn't that what you people call it? In this neighborhood guys get murdered every few days. If they picked up on the events back in North Carolina, maybe it would be a story, maybe not. If you were a big star, which excuse me, you are not yet, it would be an item. At the moment, the record and report will show exactly what the department likes these things to show while we're investigating accidental death, possibly justifiable homicide during a robbery or home invasion. We don't like the news people bothering us either. Feel better?"

"Sorry I asked," she said as they moved toward the front of the building down the narrow walkway at the side, the cold wind pinching her face. When they got to the front, a group of neighborhood people were looking up at her window. Then they spotted her. Wayne and Martha were in the small gathering. Pal was looking frantically from face to face. Martha leaned over to an old black woman and said something, glancing in Jean's direction. The old black woman looked at Jean with curiosity.

Lieberman led her back to his car parked in the alley across the street. It was well after one in the morning. They said little more on the ride to the Holiday Inn and Lieberman, mercifully, didn't turn on the radio.

"We'll talk tomorrow," he said. "Try to sleep. I'm going home and do the same. They called me when I was thinking about going to bed, right after Carson."

"Sorry," she said.

"You'll be all right alone?" he asked.

"I'm okay," she said.

He nodded, gave her a twisted, tired grin and drove off. The lobby was deserted except for the man behind the desk who gave her a key.

In the room, she called Lloyd. He answered on the first ring and had obviously been sitting up waiting for her call.

"Lloyd," she said with a tired sigh.

"Jean, what is going on?"

She explained quickly. He was silent through it all.

"He can't really think you had anything to do with it," Lloyd said when she was done.

"No, I don't think so but Lloyd, I did follow Parmenter today, did meet him, just after you left. He was in front of the apartment. I caught up with him, talked to him. He had almost no contact with reality. He was pathetic and frightening. And now he's dead."

"You want me to come over there? Or I could bring you here?"

"No," she said. "I don't want any more talk. I'll just turn on the television for a while and then go to sleep. You could do me one favor, though. In case I do fall asleep, call my office in the morning and tell them I'm not feeling well. Nothing about the . . . about Parmenter. You know Harold? Call him or Ida Schwimmer."

158

He agreed and said, "Try to sleep, Jean. We'll get together to-morrow. And don't worry about Angie. She's in good hands."

When she hung up, she wanted to make another call, do some-thing, keep her mind busy with details, but there weren't any calls to make. It was too late and there was no reason to call Max. She turned on the television. On a late movie, Alan Hale clapped his hand against Humphrey Bogart's back and laughed. Jean turned it off and lay on the bed, closing her eyes. The lights were still on. She planned to get up in a few minutes, take a quick shower and maybe try to sleep.

When she opened her eyes, however, it was morning and the phone was ringing.

"Lieberman," came the detective's voice.

"Kaiser," she said, rubbing her eyes and searching for her glasses. She found them on the floor near the bed and put them on. She needed them to talk on the phone. Somehow her senses had to be connected for her to be at her best.

"Glad you haven't lost your sense of humor," he said. "How are you?"

"All right I think. Maybe a little hungry and my teeth feel like true grit. You called to find out how I was doing, and that's it?"

"No. Can you come down to the station this afternoon?"

"When?"

"How about one? Wait, it's a madhouse in there at one. You know the T and L Delicatessen on Devon?"

"Little place a few blocks east of Western?" she said, looking at herself in the mirror on the wall.

"That's the fella. I'll meet you there. One, right?"

She wanted to ask him if he knew any more, but it was clear that Lieberman had said what he wanted to say. Jean looked around the room, at the reproduction of a painting of some women in a market place, at the television set, at her suitcase in the corner. She decided to call Angie after she showered.

The shower felt good, hot and hard on her neck, back and be-tween her breasts. She made it hotter and the near pain kneaded her muscles. When she had brushed her teeth and hair and dressed in jeans and a floppy gray sweater, she felt better, but she knew she had

159

to work to keep away the memory of Parmenter curled like a bloody fetus, looking at her, a mandala of blood like an exploding sun on her wall.

She had calls to make, to keep her mind busy. The first was to Angie. It was after nine so there was no chance she would be waking anyone. Fran answered.

"Jean, honest to God I don't want to pry into your private life," she said, "but what is going on? Angie thinks you're in trouble or you ran away and married someone named Roger or, I don't know what. Do you want to tell her what happened?"

The words had come out in a rush, and clearly Fran had been working on them for the past hour or so.

"Is Lloyd home?" she said softly.

"I'll tell him to pick up the other line. He's in the off—"

"I'm already on," came Lloyd's voice. "I've been hoping you'd call. In five more minutes I was going to call you. What happened? What did the police say, do?"

"There's a policeman named Lieberman investigating. I'm going to talk to him this afternoon. He'll be calling you or one of the people working with him will."

"Me?"

"Lloyd?"

"You are still a suspect, remember you have a great motive for killing Parmenter," she said, finding her shoes and putting them on. "To protect me and get revenge on him. But take heart, I've got an even better motive. He had, I think, been threatening me, remember?"

"Well, it'll be a first," said Lloyd after a pause. "I've never been suspected of a crime before."

"Before you quote Blake to me," Jean said, "the woods are full of suspects. Roger, Max, Parmenter's sister. I think Fran will make the list and maybe half a dozen others. There's a beady-eyed clerk at the Hi Neighbor who gives me the eye when I go there. Maybe I can get him on the list."

"It's not funny, Jean," Fran said, her voice low.

"I know. It's just easier to protect myself this way, at least for a while. Give me time. I promise I'll fall apart."

No one said anything for a while. Then Lloyd's voice came in. "I think you've got to tell Angie."

Jean was about to ask Lloyd to do that, but she stopped herself. That was the very thing she had worked to overcome, dumping it on a man and standing back to play little girl.

"I'll come over in an hour," she said after a pause. "I've got to meet Lieberman at one on Devon. Come to think of it I've got to ask him if I'll be able to have the movers come on Monday."

"Jean," Lloyd said, and she knew what was coming next.

"Lloyd . . ."

"I think it's time you told her everything, not details, but everything. Yesterday, Mom and Dad. It doesn't have to be graphic, but she's going to find out. It might get in the newspapers or on television. She's strong and bright. She can deal with it."

Fran caught her breath, and a sound came out as if she were going to say something, but held herself back.

"Lucy and Dotty know, don't they?" Jean said.

"They know," Fran said. "Not about what you just told us but about . . . what happened in North Carolina."

"Tell Angie I'll see her later for some straight shooting," she said and bade them good-bye.

She made the rest of her calls as quickly and efficiently as the people on the other end would let her.

Harold said May Swerdlow, the center director, wanted to talk to her about how little time she was putting in on the job, but Harold had lied, suggesting hospital tests, secret diseases. He needed her support on this when May finally reached Jean. Jean thanked him, promised to be there the next morning and said she would say her tests indicated that she would be all right and could return to a full schedule of work. She also said that the police might be calling Harold. They probably wouldn't, but it was possible.

"Why would the police call me?"

"A man got murdered in my apartment last night when I wasn't there. They think I might have done it."

Harold laughed. Then the laughing stopped.

"It's not a joke?" he said.

161

"It's not a joke, but I'd rather you not tell anyone at the center about it, including Ida Schwimmer."

"Especially Ida Schwimmer," he corrected.

Roger was in his office, and not at home. She had to pick up her car right in front of the studio, but she didn't have time to hold his hand.

"How are you, Jean? Do you want me to come and get you, stay with you?" he said earnestly.

"No, Roger, I'm all right. Surprisingly, I even slept well."

"I didn't," he said. "I screwed up last night, didn't I?"

She knew what he meant, but she acted surprised.

"Screwed up?"

"You know what I mean," he said, his voice low. "I behaved like that stocky black guy in the Charlie Chan movies. My eyes popped open. I started gulping and I almost threw up. Shit."

"Mantan Moreland," she said.

"The dead guy was named Mantan Moreland?" he asked.

"No," she explained, smiling to herself. "The actor in the Charlie Chan movies. He played Birmingham Brown. Listen, I'm going to have to spend the day with Angie and see the police. Can we get together tomorrow, breakfast?"

"Sure," he said glumly. "I'll even try to look you in the eye."

"Roger, you may not understand what I'm going to tell you now, but if you had gone strong and had taken over last night, I'd probably be having second thoughts about you this morning. As it is, I really want to see you. And please look me in the eye. You have very nice brown eyes. One more thing, the police will probably be calling you."

"They already have," he said. "Someone's coming to the station this morning, but I really don't have anything more to say."

"You are a suspect, Roger," she said.

"Me?"

"Everybody says that. You are a suspect."

"I can't decide whether I'm scared and shocked or a little happy to have that much respect."

The next and most difficult call was to Max. She caught him at the office about to head for the Federal Building.

Max listened without emotion, seemed to be taking real or mental notes.

"And," she added when she had finished, "you are a suspect."

"Of course," he answered matter-of-factly. "You have nothing to worry about here. I don't think you should meet with that detective unless I'm with you, and I can't get away by one o'clock."

"Hold your chariot, Max," she said.

"I wasn't going back to our old games," he said patiently. "That was Max Allen, your attorney talking, not Max your ex-husband. That was the same legal advice I'd give any client."

"I'll consider it," she said.

"Do you want me to take Angie for a while?" he said. "Let's see. It's Thursday. I was going to pick her up Saturday morning. I could—"

"Max," she interrupted. "I'm going to tell her. The past, my parents, last night, everything."

"No," he said flatly. She knew that sound and put her free hand to her forehead. "We agreed that she was not to know till she was at least fifteen. She doesn't have to carry that."

Please no migraine, she told her head. Not today. Conversations like this with Max brought on migraines for her as did chocolate, failure to eat properly, smoke-filled rooms and a host of mysterious things.

"We can't protect her any more. You can't protect her. She will find out. Too many things are happening."

Max was silent, planning, considering.

"All right," he sighed. "I'll tell her Saturday."

"No," said Jean. "I'll tell her today. You can talk to her about it on Saturday."

"Jean," he said firmly. "I've got to get to court. You've had a tough night and you want to be at your best with her. Leave it to me to—"

"Max . . ."

She heard a massive sigh from him and then he said, "Shit. There's no saying the right thing with you, is there?"

"Max, I'm sorry," she said. "I'm not trying to change your personality. I gave up on that a long time ago. Let's just do it my way."

"I've got to get to court," he said. His Georgia accent had crept in during the conversation and was in full bloom now. The word "court" came out "caught." "And don't talk to that detective."

He hung up and so did she. He would surely never learn. He had said the one thing which would guarantee that she would keep her appointment with Lieberman.

The temperature was in the upper twenties or low thirties when she stepped out of the Holiday Inn. The sky wasn't completely clear, but it wasn't threatening either snow or rain so she decided to walk after stopping at the YMCA cafeteria on Grove for a coffee and do-nut. She didn't worry about whether the coffee was decaffeinated or not.

The coffee seemed to help her threatening headache, but to play it safe she took a Fiorinal from the small bottle in her purse and washed it down.

In the summer, the walk to the station to get her car would have taken no more than twenty minutes or so. With slick spots, uncleared walks and slushy streets, it took her over half an hour, during which she did a rather successful job of dealing with her guilt.

The guilt was simple. She definitely felt relieved. Parmenter's death, no matter who was responsible, removed a threat. She had been through it with Dr. Hirsch many times. There was no reason a ten-year-old girl should have felt guilty about doing nothing while her parents were murdered in the room across the hall. There was nothing she could have done except get herself killed too. There was no way for her to be sure they were being murdered. And even if she could have done something, it was a hell of a lot to ask a ten-year-old to be responsible for. The guilty person was not Jean Kaiser but Benjamin Parmenter, and he was now dead, and she really didn't care very much who had killed him or even why, though she wasn't too pleased about the murder taking place on her bed.

Even beyond that, something about it was wrong, but she wasn't sure what it was and attributed the feeling to a lingering wish to hold on to her guilt and fear.

She almost had it, the lingering thought, when she crossed Dodge Avenue behind a black car full of teenage boys. Traffic was light and the car stopped, probably heading to Evanston High School a few blocks further.

One of the boys, a blond with a chain of some kind around his neck, stuck his head out of the side window and shouted at her.

"Hey lady, you want a nice cozy ride?"

Someone in the car laughed, and the boy had a dumb smile on his face.

"Sonny," she said, looking him in the eye, "don't even bother to come back when you grow up. My minimum standards are a clean face and a normal IQ."

The dumb grin twitched, and he looked like a little boy who had been slapped. Someone in the car howled and said, "That's telling you, Tookey."

And the car took off. Jean finished crossing the street, but the thought she had been reaching for and almost touching was gone. The car was where she had left it. Roger wasn't looking out of one of the front windows of the studio, and no one came out as she turned the key and drove away. She rehearsed her speech to Angie all the way to Oak Park. It would be a lot for a twelve-year-old, but it would, nevertheless, be a story, not an experience as it had all been for Jean. She ran through the scene again, satisfied finally but knowing that it probably wouldn't work out that way. It never did.

Angie had been waiting in the living room, sitting on the sofa, her bare feet tucked under her, a yellow ribbon in her hair. She didn't smile when Jean came in and didn't come to her. She just sat there, rubbing her tongue over her braces.

Fran greeted Jean with a hug and moist eyes.

"You want some coffee?" she said. "Lloyd had to go to the church for a while. He'll be back later." Then she whispered, "I think he's meeting a policeman there. He thought it would be better, you know?"

Fran nodded toward Angie and made a discreet exit toward the kitchen.

"Hi," Jean said, taking her coat and boots off.

"Hi," said Angie sullenly.

"We've got to talk," Jean said, moving to the girl's side. Angie turned her head.

"I know," Angie said, her eyes full of tears.

"Who told you?" Jean said, wanting to comfort her daughter and herself but keeping her hands to her sides as she sat on the couch.

"No one had to tell me. I could figure it out. You and Roger got married last night."

Jean leaned back, shook her head, and stared at the ceiling for a few seconds. Then she said, "Good God, there are some weeks when nothing seems to go right. Angie, I did not marry Roger. I do not think I will ever seriously entertain the idea of marrying Roger. What I have to tell you is far more serious, and it's going to take you a big step from being a little girl toward being an adult. Maybe it's a little early, maybe not, but we've got no choice. I've got no choice."

The corner of Angie's mouth lifted, which, Jean noted, was exactly what Max's mouth did when he was puzzled. Angie turned to her, attentive and having no idea what to expect. Jean reached out and took her daughter's cold hand. Angie didn't pull back, and their hands stayed together throughout the entire tale. Angie listened without a word, without a question. Jean even told Angie about having followed Parmenter to the movie, everything but the descriptions of her parents and the dead Parmenter.

"That's it," said Jean, her eyes fixed on her daughter's face.

"Mom," she said, "he killed Klinger. Oh God, I'm sorry. I should have been thinking about grandma and grandpa. I'm awful."

Angie began to cry, her lower lip quivering. Jean reached over and pulled her close to her breast.

"Nope, you're not awful. You're human. You never met your grandparents. You loved Klinger. Nothing to feel bad about, so don't."

"I'm glad that man's dead," she said, her voice muffled against Jean's gray sweater. "Is that terrible? Will I go to hell? I mean for thinking that?"

"I'm feeling a little of that myself," Jean admitted. "We can't help feeling it."

They didn't say anything for a while, and Jean found herself rocking Angie gently. Fran put her head through the door, saw the scene, exchanged looks with Jean and withdrew again.

"Mom," Angie said after a while. "I couldn't be as brave as you. I just couldn't."

Jean's first reaction was surprise. She had never thought of herself as brave. She knew she had a certain feistiness, but she had always considered herself someone who had to fight weakness.

"Honey," she said, "I didn't do anything brave. You either face the demons in your head and your life, or they keep chasing you until they catch you. Brave isn't the word. I'm not sure what is, but if you want to go on thinking I'm brave, I'll just sit back and enjoy it."

Angie gave her a hug, and Jean kissed the girl's head.

A few minutes later, Angie dried her eyes and leaned against Jean as they walked into the kitchen, where they joined Fran, who pulled out some milk and Walter's cache of Oreo cookies with double cream.

"My braces," Angie said, taking a cookie and starting to put it back. "I'll look awful."

"We won't look at you," said Fran, grinning. "Gobble up half a dozen and run upstairs and brush your teeth."

"Walter will have a fit," Angie said with a small grin as she reached for a cookie and the glass of milk.

"Who cares?" Fran said. "I can handle Walter. Besides, I'm going to run out and get him a new package before he gets home. I can handle him, but you have to be crazy to want to."

Angie laughed and so did Jean. It wasn't much of a laugh, but it was real enough. Things weren't going too badly. It looked as if Max had been dead wrong about Angie's reaction, which was a comfort. Jean forced herself to drink her coffee slowly and listen to Fran, who filled in the silence with stories about Walter. When it looked as if they were finished, Jean said, "Can't wait for Lloyd any longer. I've got to meet a policeman. Angie, you want to come with me?"

"I'm okay," Angie grinned, her braces stained with cookie crumbs. She realized what she looked like and closed her mouth. "I'll stay here. You take care of things. Are you coming back here tonight?"

Jean looked at her carefully to determine what answer she wanted.

"We're planning a big Scrabble game after Walter goes to sleep," Fran answered.

"You are a disgustingly wholesome family," Jean said.

"That's only a false impression we show the outside world," Fran said, "because Lloyd is a minister. Someday I'll tell you what Lucy went through last year and pull some other skeletons out."

"Good," said Jean, "I will take malicious pleasure in knowing that even you guys have problems. Ange, I may decide to stay in Evanston tonight at the motel and get some work done, if it's all right with you. Tomorrow I'll come by in the afternoon when I'm done at work and pick you up, and we'll have dinner. You still want to spend the weekend with your father?"

"Yes, if you don't need me," Angie said, finishing her milk.

"I'll be okay," Jean said. "Got to go now, kiddo. I'll see you tomorrow."

Traffic on the way back to Chicago was reasonably light. Jean got to Devon about fifteen minutes early. Finding a parking space was another problem. She had to settle for one on Western and walked back the three blocks. The T and L Delicatessen was small and narrow, with booths on one side and a serving counter on the other. The smell of salami, pastrami and warmth engulfed Jean as she stepped through the door.

Lieberman was sitting in a booth about halfway back. He was reading the *Sun-Times* as she sat down. He had on a green corduroy sports jacket over a tieless white shirt and dark green sweater. His hair looked as if it could use a good combing, and his eyes seemed as heavy as ever.

"You follow basketball?" he said in greeting.

"A little," she said, sitting.

"What's the use kidding ourselves?" he said. "The Bulls have to get rid of Gilmore. He's good, who's saying he's not, but the only way they're going to win with what they've got is to start running, running, running. They can trade with a front-runner for a good, fast center while Gilmore is still worth something. You agree?"

Jean shrugged, and a voice behind the counter across from them, a raspy male voice with a slight European accent said, "You get rid of Gilmore and you can forget the whole *farchadat* team."

Jean turned to the voice and saw a lumpy, sad-looking beagle of a man with white hair.

"You know from basketball like I know from nuclear engineering," said Lieberman.

The heavy beagle man shrugged and shook his head at the policeman. A customer stepped up, and he turned his attention to him.

"What does he know?" said Lieberman. "You hungry?"

"I'm hungry," Jean admitted.

"Hey, Maish, when you're done with the customer, bring us two bowls of the kreplach and two corned beefs with chocolate phosphates. Okay by you?"

"Okay," said Jean.

And Maish shouted, "I got two hands, two feet and I got a customer ahead of you. Hold your horses."

"Business now, or do we keep this up for a while?" she said, looking at Lieberman, who gave a little smile, folded his paper, put his hands on the table and looked at her. She could see the holster under his jacket now.

"Business," he said. "First, you didn't tell me everything last night. You followed Parmenter yesterday to a crummy little tease show on Clark and the two of you got booted out. I'm surprised at you."

"I was . . . I was afraid you'd . . ." she began.

"And you were right," he said. "I did. Should I guess what went on?"

"I wanted to know what he wanted, told him to leave me alone, but he was so insane there was no point to it."

The beagle-faced man behind the counter shouted something at his customer, claiming the man had ordered a pound of tongue.

"All right," Lieberman said. "We're talking, asking, looking. From my experience we'll push this maybe a week or two. You'll get pushed, others will get pushed. If we don't turn up something promising, it'll fade away. It will stay open but it will fade away. Parmenter was not the kind of man who the police get stirred up about."

Two bowls of steaming soup and a plate of rolls were served by Maish, who, when he emerged from behind the counter, was wearing a red flannel shirt and an apron.

The soup was hot and good, and they stopped talking while they drank, and then ate their sandwiches. Lieberman winced when Jean put ketchup rather than mustard on the corned beef, but it didn't stop his steady munching.

When they were finished, Lieberman asked her if she wanted some coffee, and she said no.

"I gotta tell you this," he said finally. "I know you're relieved that Parmenter is out of your life, but I don't like that he was found on your bed like that. Someone trying to protect you doesn't leave things like that. I don't like that the killer left him there like you say the bird was left."

"Whoever did it was in a hurry, just left him there, a coincidence. No time to . . ."

Jean rattled on, and Lieberman just looked at her.

"You see what I mean?" he said when she ran out of steam.

She nodded. It was the point that had been nagging at her earlier. She didn't want to think about who had killed Parmenter. It was obviously a friend or protector, at least that was what she had wanted to think, but Lieberman's words suggested an altered picture.

"Listen," he said. "It could be lots of things. I'm just giving you a for instance. Remember I told you I made enough mistakes in my life? I want to be careful, sure. It's probably nothing."

"But it might be something," she said.

He pulled out a notebook and began to ask her questions, dozens of questions, her life story practically, and he took notes slowly, carefully nodding as she spoke. Thirty minutes later he closed the notebook and said, "Can I drop you somewhere?"

"I've got my car," she said. "Thanks."

They both got up and Jean said, "How much is my half of the bill?"

"Nothing," Lieberman said with a wink.

"I pay my own way," she said. "That's the way I want it."

"Here I don't pay," he said.

She pushed her glasses back and nodded knowingly. Free meals for cops who come in and sort of keep an extra eye on things. Lieberman had stopped to look into her eyes after he tucked his newspaper under his arm. He shook his head slowly.

"I see what you're thinking," he said. "You are a conclusion-jumper. That can get you into trouble, psychology or no psychology. Maish is my brother. What's the matter, you can't see a family resemblance?"

Now that he mentioned it, she could see it. The beagle-faced Maish had the same droopy, bored eyes as Lieberman.

170

"It was very good," said Jean.

"My pleasure," Maish said sadly. "How many pretty ladies you think I get in a day? I get grumpers and old cops is what I get."

Back on the street Lieberman looked both ways and into the sky as he pulled on his coat.

"You going to be at the Holiday Inn tonight?" he asked.

"I think so," she said.

"Right. If anything turns up, I'll be in touch. Take care of yourself and your daughter."

He hunched his shoulders against a shot of cold wind and went slowly down the street away from her. Jean found her car with a ticket on the windshield. She had forgotten to feed the meter. Ten bucks shot to hell, but that didn't worry her. For the first time since last night, she was actually and actively curious about who had killed Parmenter.

She called Dr. Hirsch from an outdoor phone booth, but he was busy with a patient so she left a message that she did plan to come for dinner on Sunday but there was a good chance Angie would be with her father. The answering machine said nothing, not even good-bye. Jean hung up.

The rest of the day was spent shopping for the new apartment, and picking up the key from Ann Kruth, who had a lease for her to sign and a hand ready to accept the first month's rent and the one-month security deposit. She took the keys and went to the new apartment but found that the painters were there, so she stayed only a short time, measuring windows and floors with the tape measure she had brought and marking down the numbers in her notebook. The painters, one black and one white, both about sixty, said nothing to her though they did return her hello and good-bye.

She had dinner with Roger, who spent the first twenty minutes in uncharacteristic near-silence, but soon warmed up when he was convinced that Jean was not hoarding some secret scorn over his behavior.

"I don't think I can figure you out," he admitted later when they went to the Holiday Inn. "I think that's one of the reasons I feel the way I do."

"There's an irony in this somewhere," she said. "One of the rea-

171

sons I like being with you is that I can figure you out."

They were in bed by eleven.

"In the Holiday Inn," she said, after they had made love. She let out a little laugh and looked over at him. He was close enough so she could make out his face and return a smile without her glasses. "It's like a soap opera. That may even be why I like it."

She gave him a quick kiss, got dressed and was asleep almost instantly. She had the vague feeling that Roger got up in the night and did something, took a bath or watched television. She wasn't sure what. In the moment that his movement brought her almost to waking she remembered that Lieberman had said Roger was a suspect. It was absurd, but someone had to be the killer. Her money was on the monsters from across the street, Carl and his brood. She tried to wake up but couldn't. Panic came and then she eased back into sleep and didn't wake till the next morning.

There had been nightmares, but she couldn't remember them. They weren't deep, and she was sure that if she paused in bed she would remember, and equally sure that it would be healthier to let them come, to take a look at them—but she didn't. Roger was dressed and sitting in the chair near the bed reading the *Sun-Times*.

"How long have you been up?" she said dazedly, reaching for her glasses.

"About an hour, had coffee but no breakfast. Nothing in the paper about it today or yesterday. I might have missed it, but if I did it was small," he said.

"You're worried about Alexian," she said, sitting up.

"A little," he admitted. "I don't want you to lose this chance."

She walked over and kissed him as he sat, and he beamed back at her.

"Don't invest too much in me, Roger. I'm not the Madonna of the Seven Moons and you look like a lovesick puppy."

Before he could answer she headed for the bathroom, closed the door and took a shower.

Breakfast went well, the day went well. She got to the center early, went to see May Swerdlow, told her a sad tale of illness, tests and recovery, lied beautifully and received sympathy. She was back at her desk waiting for her first client in plenty of time.

Harold had not been visited by the police, nor had he told anyone.

"The secret is ours," he said solemnly, holding his fingers to his lips and giving her a conspiratorial wink.

While she didn't exactly sail through the schedule, neither did she bog down and go blank. She managed to remain alert and attentive through tears, complaints, hostility, withdrawal and abuse. All in a normal day's work.

In the afternoon she went to the library for a while and did some preparation for her show. She and Roger had agreed that tonight would be her last show, that she would simply announce it, answer general calls and take a week off to prepare for CBS. She did make a few notes, though, just in case, and then when she returned to the motel called Angie, who seemed more concerned with Jean's emotions than with her own.

"You sure you're all right, Mom?" she said.

"Doing great. I went to the new apartment. They're washing it and doing some painting. I measured for curtains. The place is carpeted. Brown, dark and not too thick. You sure you don't want me to come there after the show?"

"Nope," said Angie. "Lucy, Dotty and I are going to a movie with Aunt Fran. Uncle Lloyd's got some work so he's staying with Walter. We're going to see *The Swamp Thing*."

"Sounds like fun," Jean said. "Say hello to everyone and I'll see you tomorrow. I love you."

"I love you too, Mom."

Jean rested in the room for a few hours before going out for a sandwich.

She got to the studio early and Mel was at the door waiting for her with a big grin on his young-old face.

"Who gave you a shot of what?" she said, returning his smile.

"Roger says Alexian gave the okay for me to move with you," he said. "He likes the way we work together and doesn't want to take a chance on breaking in someone new. I'll get a tryout on some off hours doing the news and maybe work into the slot in the evening."

"Stick with me," she said, heading for the lounge. "We're going places."

"See you in the studio," he said and hurried down the hall.

Maybe Mel did it, she said to herself, starting it as a joke and then rolling it around in her mind seriously. Maybe he's as strong under that baby face as his voice. Maybe, maybe I'm seeing killers behind every snow bank and potted palm.

It felt no different from the dozens of other shows. Ted Earl waved his dreamy wave. Mel did his usual introduction.

When she took over after the introduction she said, "Good news and bad news tonight. Bad news is that this is my last show on WSMK. I've enjoyed being here and owe a lot of the success of this show to my announcer and mediator Mel Trax, engineer Ted Earl, producer Roger Nash and to all of you. The good news is that I'll be on another station at the same time each Monday, Wednesday and Friday, in a somewhat different format with Mel across from me. We hope that you'll join us. So, for my last show on WSMK I though I'd simply leave it open. Questions, comments, problems. The time is yours."

Mel gave the number, and the lights on the board went on as usual.

The questions at first were about her, what was she going to do, why had she decided to change stations? Past callers called again to say good-bye and bring her up to date on their problems.

A few new callers came in with problems ranging from bed wetting—she advised professional help since the caller was almost thirty—to a husband who refused to have sex with his wife. The last one was a little tricky. Jean let the woman talk and then gave some sympathy and a few suggestions that probably wouldn't be much help.

"It's going fine," Mel said during the second break. "You know something? I think I can even face the Johnny Mathis album I have to play on the late show. Hell, I might even sing along."

They were back to the show and taking calls. A woman came on with a stern voice and said, "Jean, there are, I am sorry to say, times when one can simply not respond with humor to the adversity of life."

Jean was startled and tried to figure out where this challenge had come from.

"I'm sorry—" she began, and the woman explained.

"The other day you started the program saying that some doctor said you should laugh at your tragedies. I've been thinking about it since then and decided that it was not good advice."

"I wasn't giving advice," Jean said patiently. "I was paraphrasing Dr. Sigmund Freud and asking people what they thought. In fact, I'm rather inclined to agree with you."

"Then," said the woman, sounding very much like the stereotypical spinster schoolteacher in a scolding mood, "you should say so clearly."

"I think I just did. Thank you for your call."

She hung up and grinned at Mel, who put through the next caller.

"Jean."

The grin left her face. It was only one word, her name, but she was sure. It was him. He was dead, but it was him. It was the Dark Man.

"Yes," she said, looking at Mel and Ted who were still smiling.

"I'm sorry you're going to a new station," he whispered, "but I sent you a present the other day. Did you get it? I left it where you could find it easily."

"I got it," she said. Why were the two men in the room with her smiling like idiots? Didn't they recognize the voice?

"I know," he said dreamily. "I know."

"Paul," she began. This time when her eyes went around the small studio and into the engineer's booth, she saw a reaction in Mel. Ted sat smoking obliviously and grinning.

"No," the voice said, "not Paul. That isn't my real name. Call me John, John Fl—" he began and then changed his mind. "Just John from far away."

"What do you want, John?" she said.

"I really don't know," he said. "I thought I did, but I really don't. Isn't that strange? I just wanted you to know I was still here and to tell you that we would talk again and that I have another surprise for you. I'm sure you figured out that the friend I was talking about before was you."

"Yes," she said. "I figured it out, but why—"

"Good-bye for now," he whispered and hung up.

Mel took over on his microphone, said the show was over and that a new show would be announced for this time slot over the weekend. He nodded to Ted, and a commercial came on.

The green light went on in the studio, and Ted's raspy voice said, "Hey, you cut out four minutes early."

"Double up on commercials," Mel said, looking at Jean. Roger hurriedly crashed through the door into the studio.

"Jean, are you all right? I was listening and—"

"Definitely not," she said.

"It was just someone imitating him," Roger said, kneeling next to her. "A copycat. Anyone can whisper like that."

"No," said Mel. "It was him."

Roger looked at Jean and she nodded.

"It was him, Roger. It was him."

"Good-bye for now," the Dark Man's voice repeated, and Roger reached over to turn off the reel-to-reel tape recorder on his desk.

"You want to hear it again?" he said.

Jean was sure she didn't want to, but the question wasn't addressed to her. It was aimed at Lieberman and the man he had brought with him, the homicide detective named Clavey who was somewhere in his thirties, dark, mustached, well-built and, Jean decided, definitely not her type.

"That's enough," said Clavey in a voice that matched his appearance. "We'll take the tape with us. What do you think?"

The question was directed at Lieberman, who had been sitting back in one of the black leather chairs and looking at the machine. His lower lip was out.

"I think it's the same voice," he said. "We can run the whole thing through one of those voice machines I hear you have downtown, but it's the same."

Clavey nodded his agreement.

"We'll run them through."

Clavey looked at Roger, who was standing behind his desk.

Roger got the idea, removed the tape from the machine and put it into a box before handing it over.

"I'll get the others," he said. "Jean had Ted, that's our engineer, put them on a single tape."

He left the room nervously, and Clavey turned to Jean with a knowing smile.

"That was a good idea, Mrs. Kaiser. Any help we can get will be appreciated."

Was there a suggestion, the hint of trying to start something? Perhaps, Jean thought, but she didn't give a damn. She took off her glasses and looked at them to see if they were dirty. The intention was to show Detective Clavey that her glasses were more important at the moment than he was. She glanced up at his now blurred image, and he backed away, still smiling, as if he held a great secret.

"So," said Lieberman with a sigh to show that he had been thinking while they had been playing. "Whoever this is made the other calls, probably killed your little girl's bird, probably killed Parmenter, but what's all this 'long ago' business? Was he trying to suggest he was Parmenter?"

Clavey cleared his throat and said, "We can talk about it on the way back to town."

Lieberman looked up at him wearily.

"She's not stupid," he said. "If we can figure it out, she can figure it out. In fact, since she's the one in the middle, she could very well have better ideas than ours."

Clavey didn't like discussing this in front of Jean, but he didn't want a public argument with Lieberman. He folded his arms and shrugged. Roger returned with another tape and handed it to Clavey, who nodded without saying thanks.

"Well," said Lieberman, standing, "it's been a long hard day for all of us. Unless Detective Clavey has something more, I'm going home."

"Nothing at the moment," Clavey said, lifting his coat from the rack in the corner. "I don't think it's necessary to put a man on you. What do you think?"

The last question was directed at Lieberman.

"I think you'd find it difficult to justify," Lieberman said. "Besides I think Miss Kaiser is in good hands."

Roger was back standing behind his desk and smiled at what he took to be Lieberman's compliment. Lieberman leaned over to Jean and whispered, "I meant your own hands."

The two policemen started out the door, and Jean followed, calling back to Roger, "I'll walk them to the door. Be right back."

"We'll be in touch," Clavey said, looking at her. "If anything more happens, call right away."

With that Clavey pulled his coat tight, strode away and out the door.

Lieberman was shaking his head and looking after the departing detective.

"Look at him," he said, leaning toward Jean. "Who writes those lines for him? He's perfect. They should star him in a series like that guy in Philadelphia. What's his name on 'Trapper John,' the Harrison kid could play him? I don't know."

"Well," Jean said, "we eliminated some of your suspects. Mel, Ted and Roger."

Lieberman reached for the front door and shook his head no.

"But they—"

"You told me the announcer and the engineer were in the room with you when the call came, but Mr. Nash ran in after it was over. There's more than one telephone line in that room. There are four. He could have dialed one line from the other."

"I can't believe—" she began.

"Right," he said. "Don't believe. Just keep thinking. Now go back to your motel. I'd suggest you go alone and get some sleep, but it's up to you, you're a big . . . a big woman? That doesn't sound right. Sounds like an insult. Anyway, we'll talk tomorrow."

He walked slowly out the door, his shoulders leaning forward, and Jean turned back to Roger's office.

"He still thinks you're a suspect," she said, looking directly at him when she reentered the room.

"Good," he said glumly.

"I'm going to the motel and get some sleep," she said.

"You want me—" he began.

She broke in with, "Not tonight, Roger, thanks."

When she got to the motel, it was too late to call Angie at her brother's, and she really didn't feel like talking to anyone. She took a very hot bath, shampooed her hair, and did her exercises. She hadn't been getting enough exercise since all this started, and what she was doing now really wasn't enough but it would have to do. She didn't work up a sweat. That wasn't the point. She just wanted to feel a bit loose. Instead she felt tighter.

Jean had just turned the light out when the phone rang.

Lieberman with something new, she thought, or something's wrong with Angie, or Roger has to talk to me.

"Hello," she said.

"Good night," returned the voice of the Dark Man, and he hung up.

"You bastard," she hissed at the dead phone. She slammed it down and turned on the light to look at it with anger. She knew she should have been filled with terror, cowering under her blanket, calling Roger, but she also knew that was what the Dark Man wanted. He wanted to frighten her. That was at least part of his goal. He had not attacked her physically. You rotten son of a bitch, she thought, putting her glasses on. She also told herself to calm down and think it through, figure out what the problems might be of a man who gained satisfaction by terrorizing a woman. What would Hirsch say? Hell, what would Freud say?

Freud would say sex, that's what Freud would say. She sat looking at the phone, forcing her mind to move slowly, rationally.

He remains hidden and he attacks me, she thought. He leaves bodies on my bed. Sacrifices? Offerings? He wants me submissive, frightened because he is afraid to make himself known. He is afraid and he gets a sick satisfaction, maybe even orgasm from these threats. Then something chilled her like an ice cube against her temples. He's calling more often. He's coming closer. He had not attacked her physically, but maybe he was trying to build himself up to it.

Some of the fear was back, but most of the anger remained and with it something else. He had been pursuing her, watching her. Now she would put her abilities to work, try to analyze the Dark Man's calls, his behavior. Now she wished she had kept the tapes or made another copy. Maybe she could get them back or volunteer to help. She was a professional.

"You may be after me," she said to the telephone, "but you're looking in the wrong place because I'm going to be right behind you."

She took off her glasses and reached over to turn off the lights, but hesitated. She withdrew her hand and put her head on the pillow, knowing that the only chance she had for sleep was if the lights stayed on.

◇ *THIRTEEN* ◆

Saturday morning. Her eyes opened to light. The light of the sun through the windows whose drapes she had forgotten to close, the nearby table lamp she had left on in case she woke in terror, the light inside her head from the ache of pain, the shooting light and the pulsing pain. Only once before in her life had she awakened with a migraine, but she couldn't remember when that had been. It was one of the tricks of the headaches that they acted like a drug, making her forget when they came and went. She only knew that they had been there like a small, sharp-clawed demon perching inside her skull, his head in his hands, a contented grin on his bearded face.

She groped for her purse, found her pills and put one into her mouth before reaching for her glasses. Then she remembered that she would need water. She staggered to the bathroom, unwrapped a glass and washed the tablet down.

There was a knock at the door. The pain stopped her from answering, but the doorknob turned. She considered a blind rush at it to keep it closed, to lock him out. This isn't fair, she thought. At night, in the dark, that's when you're supposed to come. She had taken no more than three steps when the door pushed wide open.

"I'm sorry," said the maid. "I didn't know you was here."

She was a thin black woman with her gray hair tied back tightly.

"You all right?" she added, looking at Jean.

"Just a bad headache," she said. "Forget cleaning the room today. I'll just rest."

"Sure I can't get you something?" the woman asked with what sounded like real concern.

Jean tried a smile but felt every tiny muscle tighten.

"No thanks. A few hours rest. I have some medicine."

The woman departed, and Jean moved over to the window to close the drapes, to cut back the painful light. As she did she saw a few bundled people on the sidewalk below, heavily dressed, lumbering, their breath clouding in front of them. She went back to the bed.

Things to do, she said or thought, she wasn't sure which. You want this headache. The pain, the blotting-out pain. You want it because it locks out the world, the Dark Man. The thought of him brought a new kick inside her skull, and she lay back, groaning. It was one of the things she had worked through with Dr. Hirsch. There always did seem to be something that she wanted blocked out when the migraines came. Often it was a decision to make, a triumph she felt she didn't deserve. It made sense, but the knowledge didn't stop the headaches from coming.

It was too painful to let her head touch the pillow so she sat up again with a groan. The phone. She had to make the calls. Before she reached for it she tried the self-hypnosis technique. It seemed to help, but the pain didn't go away completely, and the angry demon fought it mightily. Then she tried deep breathing, which she knew would help a bit, but which couldn't be continued for very long.

She decided to call Angie.

"You've got one of your headaches," Angie said after the first greeting. "I can tell. You sound like one of those fake fortune tellers on TV mysteries. Did you take your pills?"

"I took them," Jean managed to say. "Ange, call your dad. See if he can pick you up in Oak Park. Tell him I'll come for you tomorrow night around eight, okay?"

"Okay. Mom, Uncle Lloyd said he wanted to talk to you."

"Can't handle it, baby," Jean said. "Tell him I'll call him back

182

later. Have a good time and say hi to your father for me. Tell him not to call."

"I could come there and take care of you," Angie said.

"Nothing to do for it, Ange. I'd just make you be quiet, and you'd have to listen to me groan for a few hours. I'll be all right by this afternoon. Have a good time."

She wanted to hang the phone up but Angie hesitated, something hanging.

"Maybe Roger could come over and help you," she said sincerely.

"If I wanted help from anyone, it would be you. I'll call you later at Dad's and let you know I'm all right, but don't hang around waiting for my call. I'll be fine. Always am. Bye now and thanks for the offer."

They hung up and she groped her way almost blindly back to the bathroom, each painful step pulsing blood to nourish the demon. Without turning on the light she ran a hot bath, dropped her clothes on the floor and climbed in. She sat forward, still wearing her glasses, and allowed herself the luxury of a series of groans. Then she went through the self-hypnosis, meditation and deep breathing again. In a few minutes the pain eased, but she didn't think it was over. It came in cycles. It was fooling her.

The phone rang. Angie? Lieberman? The Dark Man? Roger? Max? Lloyd? The Nielsen Survey? It didn't matter. There was no way she could get out of the tub and make it. All she wanted was for it to stop ringing. Eventually it did.

She let her hand drift in the water and watched the ends of her hair dangle and float on the surface. She imagined herself standing a few feet away watching, seeing a painting. What? Woman in the bath? The murder of Marat?

She let out some hot water and ran some nearly boiling water in. A pain peak came and went and then another, and she found it most tolerable to simply give in to it, not deal with it, moan, let it attack, have its way and its say, and depart.

The phone rang two or three more times at intervals that could have been anything from ten minutes to an hour. At one point she managed to doze in the tub but her head lolled back and hit her with pain.

Then came the first sensation of cessation, the feeling that the lull might last or that when the pain came back it wouldn't be so bad. It wasn't. The demon was leaving his perch, though he wasn't quite ready to take wing. He'd reach back to scratch with sharp claws and teeth as he fluttered around outside her head, but he would go.

When it did go, gradually so that she couldn't quite pinpoint when she knew it was gone, she felt that familiar languid sense of relief, the weakness and joy. She let the water out and listened to it drain and gurgle away before she got carefully out of the tub, marveling at her withered fingertips. It wasn't a trick. The headache was gone. She pulled a towel around herself, tucking it in over her breasts, and made a tentative step out of the bathroom.

The phone started to ring again. This time she went to the bed, sat down and picked it up.

"Yes," she said.

"Miss Kaiser?" came the voice of a young man.

"Yes," she repeated carefully, looking for her watch. It was after noon.

"This is Jerry Cannon at WSMK. We met once. The Christmas party."

Now she remembered him. He was a tall, gangly kid with a birthmark on his cheek. He had just joined the station, right out of the University of Illinois, or was it Missouri.

"I remember, Jerry. How did you find me. What—"

"Mr. Nash gave me your number," he said. "I'm doing the morning show at the station, got about forty minutes to go. I've been trying to reach you for hours."

"I had a headache," she said. "Why were you trying to reach me?"

"Some crazy woman has been calling here all morning. Maybe fifteen times. I keep telling her you're not here and I'll get a message to you, but she keeps calling. I didn't want to give her your number there. Mr. Nash agreed."

He obviously wanted reassurance that he had done the proper thing.

"Thanks, Jerry," she said, feeling very, very hungry and knowing she had nothing in the room but a small piece of chocolate bar in her purse. Or had she eaten that? "Who was the woman? What did she want?"

"Mrs. Bratcovick," he sighed. "I don't think I'll ever forget the name. She made me write the message. 'Come right away. I know who did it.' She hasn't called back for about half an hour so maybe she gave up. Miss Kaiser? Are you there?"

"I'm here," she said. "I'll take care of it. Thanks, Jerry."

She hung up and looked for the phone book. The after-headache weakness was there and would be for an hour or so. It would help if she could get something to eat. She found the Bratcovick number, dialed nine to get an outside line, and dialed the number. It rang two, three, ten times. She hung up and redialed. Maybe she had dialed incorrectly. But the result was the same.

I'm not going to see that woman alone, she thought, remembering the menace the last time they had come together. This might be some trick to get Jean in hand and punish her for Parmenter's death. Or maybe she did know something, or maybe she was as mad as her brother, driven over the edge by his death.

She called Lieberman's number at the police station. He wasn't there, but the raspy-voiced detective asked if he could help. She thought of asking for Detective Clavey, but she didn't like him, didn't want the tension of dealing with him. She insisted that she had to reach Lieberman and the detective said wearily that he would find him and have him call her back.

"It's urgent," she said, wanting to say "life-or-death," but she couldn't bring herself to use the cliché, though it might very well be apt.

"Stay by your phone," he said and hung up.

She found the small square of chocolate and washed it down with cold water. Her legs were still wobbly, but her head was without pain though unusually light. She turned on the television set and watched part of a basketball game. The announcers were excited. The fans were excited. The score kept flashing on the screen, but she couldn't quite grasp it.

The phone rang. It had, according to her watch, been about ten minutes since she called the station.

"Miss Kaiser?"

"Don't you think you can call me Jean?" she said.

"All right, Jean," Lieberman said, "providing you don't call me Arthur. Or Lieberman. Detective Lieberman sets just the right tone. What's up?"

"First, he called last night, here at the motel. He knows I'm here."

"What did he want?"

"To say good night. To frighten me."

"And you didn't call me last night or this morning?" he asked.

"I was more angry than frightened. But that's not the urgent business. Mrs. Bratcovick called the radio station, left a message for me. She says she knows who did it. I assume she means who killed her brother. I'm not sure I believe her. She wants me to get over to her apartment fast."

"Progress," Lieberman said drolly. "You called me instead of running over there."

"Detective Lieberman, I just finished having a doozy of a migraine. I could do nicely without the sarcasm. What do you want to do?"

"Can you drive? You all right for that?"

"Yes."

"Good. Come over to the station. It's on the way. I'll be waiting in front. We'll take my car."

"I'll be there in about half an hour. I've got to dress and grab a quick sandwich somewhere."

She hung up and decided what to wear, not really caring. Jeans, blue blouse and blue sweater and out she went. On the way she stopped at Burger King for a Whopper with cheese, fries and a Coke. It tasted great. She gulped it down, feeling some strength returning, anxious to hear what, if anything, Ellen Bratcovick had to say. It was cold enough that Lieberman, standing in front of the station looking for her, wore his knit cap pulled down over his ears, his mustache stiff and gray.

"Just leave it there, in that space," he called. "And come on." She paused to drop two dimes in the meter by the space and dashed after him. He had jumped into his car and started the engine.

They said nothing on the way. There was nothing to say. The

186

traffic was light, and they were on the street in front of the Bratcovick apartment in about ten minutes. He found a space and got out with a little grunt. She followed him.

When they got to the door, he pushed the bell, and Jean heard it ring deep inside the apartment, as she had heard it the other time she had been there. There was something old-fashioned about it. Not a chime, but a simple bell, metal flapping against metal. No answer. Jean looked at the detective, who rubbed his cold hands together and looked at her. He moved to the porch window and tried to look in.

"Too dark," he said.

"Maybe she changed her mind or went out shopping or saw you with me through the window," Jean suggested.

Lieberman shrugged and tried the door. It opened. Standing in the small hallway, Jean looked down at the cracked white tiles under their feet while Lieberman pounded on the door and said, "Mrs. Bratcovick. It's Jean Kaiser and Detective Lieberman."

He tried the apartment door and it, too, was open. He closed it and said, "You open it and invite me in."

She looked at him, puzzled.

"There are things police can do that ordinary citizens cannot do, and then again, there are things ordinary citizens can do that police can't. A friend called you, left the door open, you went in and brought a friend who happened to be a policeman."

They stepped in. Lieberman closed the door behind them.

"Mrs. Bratcovick," Jean called.

They made their way from the dark, old-fashioned living room into the even darker dining room. The tiny grotesque statues made by Parmenter looked like chilled marionettes ready to spring into lifelike action.

Lieberman nudged her and Jean called again.

"Mrs. Bratcovick?"

The furnace below them hummed into a cycle, and Jean thought she could feel the floor vibrating softly.

Both she and Lieberman had been here before and knew how to get to the kitchen. On the way they looked into the Bratcovick's bedroom, but no one was there.

"I'll take a look in his room," Lieberman said, nodding toward

Parmenter's room off the kitchen. "Then we'd better wait in the car."

Jean nodded in agreement and waited while Lieberman moved forward, opened Parmenter's door and stepped in. She expected him right back out, but he didn't come. A minute, maybe two passed.

"Detective Lieberman?" she called, and took a step toward the door. He came out almost immediately, closing the door behind him.

"We better go in the car before she walks in and finds us," Jean said.

Lieberman looked around for something in the room.

"She won't come in and find us," he said. "Sit down."

She started to ask a question, but he motioned with his hand, saw what he was looking for and moved to the wall behind her. She sat down. He picked up the phone and dialed a number.

"Vinnie? Art Lieberman. Find Clavey. Tell him we've got a homicide at 1544 Lorien. First floor. I'll be here. He'll know."

He hung up the phone and turned to Jean who was looking at him with her eyes wide.

"Mrs. Bratcovick," he said.

Jean slumped and he put a hand on her shoulder.

"You all right?" he said.

"Definitely not," she whispered. "What . . ."

"Beaten. A real mess. Bloody mess. I've seen, I don't know how many hundreds. You go through phases. First you're indifferent, a little smug, maybe proud that you can take it. Then it starts working at you and you get a little scared. Then, much later, after many more, you look at them as if there's an answer to the whole thing, the mystery of life and death and they've got that answer, but they're not telling you. They've had to pay so much they're not going to give the secret away."

"You're talking to keep me from falling apart," she said.

"Partly," he agreed. "It's also true."

"I'm not going to fall apart," she said. "Tell me."

"You been in there?"

She nodded yes. He removed his knit hat and rubbed his gray head.

"Well," he said. "Parmenter had a heavy iron cross on a table. Looks like someone used it to beat her to death."

All Jean could say was, "Oh."

Lieberman looked at her from under his droopy eyelids.

"I might as well get to work," he said. "Don't follow me into that room and don't answer the phone if it rings. You need anything, feel uneasy or something, give me a call."

"When is it going to end?" she said.

He was almost at Parmenter's door, and she had thought the question was a whisper only for herself. But Lieberman answered. "It doesn't end," he sighed. "You just come to times when you can rest for a while."

◇ *FOURTEEN* ◆

"All right," said Clavey, one hand on his hip, the other holding a finger up as he paced around the room in his three-piece suit. All he needed was a gold watch chain and a jury. "You made those calls to the radio station, pretended you were Ellen Bratcovick. You went to her house, beat the shit out of her with that crucifix, went back to your hotel and called Lieberman. That's how you did it."

"And the calls to my show?" Jean asked reasonably, glancing over his shoulder toward the back of the Bratcovick apartment, where two policemen had just led a squat man with a red face and bushy mustache. They had almost been holding him up, which led Jean to the conclusion that it was Mr. Bratcovick, the bartender. A deep, loud "No" screamed from the back of the apartment seconds later, confirmed or helped to confirm his identity. They hadn't brought him back out yet.

"You've got an accomplice," Clavey said, leaning toward her.

Jean looked over at Lieberman, who sat or rather sank into a dark old chair and watched Clavey pace without moving his head. Only the brown eyes under the droopy lids moved. He looked amused. A

190

Parmenter statue was perched on the mantelpiece of the walled-up fireplace behind Lieberman's head.

The plaster statue, about two feet high, was of a man desperately trying to pull his hand from a cross on which he was nailed. The other hand was free, and the man's head was tilted back with his mouth open, a silent scream to the cracked white ceiling. It looked like a self-portrait.

"Miss Kaiser," Clavey said, dripping with sarcasm. "Are you paying attention to what I'm saying here? It is rather important."

"I'm sorry, Lieutenant," she said, adjusting her glasses and looking at him. "And this accomplice of mine helped me kill Parmenter? Why would I go through all this rigamarole? Phone calls, fake phone calls. Wouldn't it be easier to just go out and kill Parmenter, away from my apartment? And why would I want to kill Mrs. Bratcovick?"

That was the moment Bratcovick the bartender came back into view through the dark shadows of the dining room, kicking, possibly by accident, one of the plaster statues on the floor. Jean wondered how much of the conversation he had heard. When she saw his face she knew he had heard none of it, probably would absorb very little of what went on in the world for a while. He was, she could see as he stepped into the living room with the two cops behind him, older than she had thought, perhaps close to seventy. He had the scarlet-faced look of the tavern owner who at least two or three times a day had to accept a drink from a happy or sad customer. He looked as if he could use some of his own wares now.

"I warned her," he said, interrupting Jean. Warned who, me? Jean thought because the man was looking directly at her. Then he went on. "I warned her not to take him in our house." He had a slight accent. "He brought this on my house. What can I do? I'm not young."

Jean got up and stepped toward him. He had been addressing her, she realized, not because he knew her but because she was the only woman in the room and he had just lost his woman. It didn't matter what she said, just so she gave him something. She took his limp, rough hand and held it.

"We're so sorry," she said sincerely, and it was sincere. She had not liked Ellen Bratcovick, but she had recognized her despair, her fear, and now she was sorry for this little man.

"You knew my Ellen, you were her friend?" Bratcovick asked, staring at Jean, who looked like no friend he imagined his wife having.

"We met," Jean said, looking at Clavey, who had leaned back against the mantelpiece, his hands folded, patiently waiting for the scene to end so he could get back to work. Apparently, he had not thought of Bratcovick as a possible suspect. She looked down at Lieberman, whose eyes were almost closed. Certainly he wasn't asleep?

"You met?" Bratcovick answered dumbly, looking at the carpet. "How can I sleep here tonight?"

"Don't you have any other relatives? Brothers, sisters? Anything?" she said softly. One of the two cops who had led Bratcovick in nodded his head no.

"A friend, partner," she tried.

"Shweivka, the baker, across the street from my place. He lives down the street, but he's not home. He's working. What day is this? Saturday?" He considered Saturday, still looking at the rug. "Maybe he's home."

Clavey pushed away from the mantelpiece and said, "Bill, see if this Shweivka's home and take Mr. Bratcovick over there. See if they'll keep him for a few days. When he's up to it, get a statement. Anybody door-to-door?"

"Miller," said Lieberman from his chair. "I'll give him a hand."

Bratcovick looked over at Lieberman, who got up, gave the bartender's arm a squeeze, and walked past and out.

"He's a policeman?" Bratcovick asked.

They led Bratcovick out in a daze from which he might never recover, and Clavey went back to work.

"Remember where we were?" he asked with a weary smile.

"You were going to tell me why I wanted to kill Mrs. Bratcovick."

Jean went back to her chair, folded her hands in her lap and looked up at him, waiting.

"This isn't funny, Mrs. Kaiser," he said.

"I was trying irony and sarcasm," she said, "and doing a lousy job at it. Lieutenant, I didn't kill anyone, and I really don't think you think I did. Sure, you can come up with some idea of why I'd kill her. Maybe I was afraid that she knew I killed him and that she would seek revenge."

"Don't stop," he said, a smile curling the corner of his mouth. "You're doing fine."

"Can I go now? You've asked me questions. I've given you answers. I had a bad migraine this morning, and I'm having a hell of a time trying not to imagine what Mrs. Bratcovick looks like back there."

Clavey's hands came up in a what's-the-use gesture.

"Go back to your motel. We'll call you there if we need you," he said, turning toward the back of the apartment. "If you go anywhere else, let them know at the desk so we can find you."

"Thanks," she said.

He gave no answer other than to disappear into the darkness. Jean took one last quick look at the statue of the man with one hand fixed on the cross, and then she went out.

She had no car, since Lieberman had driven her. So, she could either wait for him or get back on her own. The day was clear, and the air was cold but not painful. It was probably good for her head. She walked the five blocks to the Logan Square rapid transit station, paid her fare and got on a waiting train, which pulled out right away. Thirty minutes and two transfers later, she was at Davis Street in Evanston and heading for her motel, the motel where the Dark Man knew she was staying. When she stepped into the lobby, she looked around. There were two clerks behind the desk, a woman with a small boy who was holding back tears, and a large, heavy man sitting in a chair reading a newspaper. He looked over the paper when she glanced at him. His eyes caught hers, and his eyes were very cold indeed, she thought.

She moved to the desk past the crying child whose mother was saying, "You've already got one. You don't need two."

The heavy man with the cold eyes walked up behind her as she asked for her key and any messages. There was a message, to call someone named Susan Templer, and a number.

She almost collided with the big man when she turned. He

grabbed her arm to keep her from falling.

"I'm here," he whispered.

She started to sag, wondering how mad he could be to attack her in the afternoon in a motel lobby. She was about to throw her knee into his groin when he said quickly, "Lieberman said I should let you know I'd be watching."

"You're a policeman?" she asked.

"Do I look like an English professor to you?" he said.

She considered asking him up to her room, but she couldn't have this cop part of her life even if he was going to guard her.

"Thanks," she said softly. "I'm going up to my room to make a few calls and get some rest."

"I'll be down here if you need me," he said. "Fronti will take over at nine. He's a wiry guy with glasses. He'll introduce himself if you come down."

"Thanks," she said, giving him a smile with lots of teeth. He nodded, apparently unmoved, and headed back to his newspaper while she stepped into the elevator.

The next question was, who is Susan Templer? Someone had to have given her this number, said she was at the Holiday Inn. The center? No, they were closed. Cops, radio station? Hell, she thought, and dialed the number, and a man's voice, with a hubbub of voices and machines behind him, said, "City."

"Susan Templer please." A policewoman?

"Templer," came a high, young voice.

"This is Jean Kaiser. I'm returning your call."

"Oh, Miss Kaiser," she said. "Police business."

"I've already talked to Lieutenant Clavey and Detective Lieberman." She kicked off her shoes and sank into the blue armchair, placing the phone on her lap.

"I talked to Clavey," Susan Templer said. "I still have some questions."

"Okay. Go ahead."

Susan Templer was thorough, Jean had to give her that. The call lasted about fifteen minutes, during which time they went over just about everything, including the deaths of her parents in Carrboro, Parmenter's harassment, and the meeting with and death of Ellen

Bratcovick. When she was done, Susan Templer said, "That's great. You've been a big help. With a little luck I can still catch the first edition for tomorrow."

"First ed—" Jean began. She sat up and put the phone on the table. "I thought you said you were a policewoman."

"I never said or implied that, Miss Kaiser," Susan Templer jumped in politely and firmly.

City, Jean remembered. City desk.

"How did you know I was staying here?"

"Easy—I talked to a cop I know who was working on the preliminary report, found out you worked for WSMK, called there, told them I knew you and they gave me the Holiday Inn."

"Susan," Jean said evenly. "This will probably get me no place, but I'm going to make one try. If you put all that together and print it, my peace of mind, my future, my daughter's well-being and who knows what else will be up for grabs."

"And it's my job and future if I don't go with this story and my boss finds out I've got it—and he will find out."

"In a day, two days, no more than a week, you'll forget this story and go on to something else, but I'll have to live my life with it and you know what my life has been. Hell, I just gave it all to you. Don't you feel something?"

Susan Templer paused for less than the flutter of an eyelid.

"I'm sorry. It's a good story. If I listened to your argument, I might as well quit the business. Try and see it from my end of the phone."

"Good-bye, Miss Templer. Enjoy your byline." She hung up before the reporter could get in the last word.

She called Max on the chance that Angie would be in.

"Can I talk to Angie?" she asked immediately.

"You told Angie everything," he said. There was something in his voice that Jean recognized from their years together, a hesitation, something withheld.

"And a good thing too," Jean said. "I'm afraid it's going to be all over everyone's breakfast table in the morning. It shouldn't make Sunday brunch particularly palatable, especially if they have photographs."

"Oh crap," Max hissed.

"I'll live with it and so will Angie, Max. Now let me talk to her."

"Jean, all this confession may be good for the soul, but it doesn't do the body a hell of a lot of good. Since we're on it, there is something I'm going to have to talk to you about."

"A confession," Jean said, now pacing the floor near the bed.

"Yes," he said, but before he could go any further Angie was on the phone.

"Hi Mom, how's it going? We're going to that indoor miniature golf place tonight."

"Sounds like fun, kiddo. Shoot a few birdies for me."

"Those things move mighty fast," she said in a fake bass, imitating Bubba Smith in the Lite Beer commercial. Then she laughed.

"It's going to be in the newspapers tomorrow morning, baby," she said. "Everything I told you about and a little more. You want me to be there with you? I think your dad may try to keep you from seeing it, but I want you to know."

"I'll be all right," she said. "You just get some rest or go out with Roger, but be sure to come get me tomorrow night." Then in a whisper: "Dad's feeling down about something. All nervous. Not like him at all. I want to try to cheer him up, you know?"

"Let me talk to him," Jean said.

She heard Angie's voice, slightly away from the phone, asking her father to get back on. He said something and Angie's voice was on again.

"He says he'll tell you some other time. It can keep. So long."

She hung up. Jean considered calling again and pushing Max— this was no time for enigmas beyond the enigmas she already had to deal with. But she knew Max. If he didn't want to talk, he'd go all macho man and might never tell her. She would have to wait, and there were other things to think about.

She turned on the television set, but Saturday afternoon on television proved to be a bust. Her choice was between a tape of a college rowing meet, a round-table discussion with three Chicago Latino leaders about cuts in federal job assistance, and a German western dubbed into English.

Around six, she decided to change clothes and go out for something to eat. She was about to call Roger to see if he wanted to keep her company, when the phone rang. Her hand was almost on it, and she pulled back as if shocked before picking it up.

"Hello," she said.

There was no answer on the other end, but the line wasn't dead.

"Hello," she repeated. Still no response, but perhaps, yes, breathing. "It's you. I'll grant you one thing, you've got me frightened. But let me give one back. I want you caught now. Paul or John Fl—or whatever your real name is. You can breathe into phones and play games as much as you want, but they're going to catch you, and I'm going to help them. Shove that where it will do the most good, you . . . creep."

The phone went dead.

That's telling him, she thought. You were about as articulate as the cop downstairs. The call did have one distinct result. She decided not to spend the night in the room alone. She wanted to be with her family.

She packed her things, checked out of the hotel, paid her bill, and informed the cop that, since she was going to go stay at her brother's house in Oak Park, he would no longer be needed.

"Can you hang on," the cop said, folding his newspaper, "while I call in and check. Only take a minute."

She agreed, and he went to a lobby phone to call. It did take about a minute.

"I'll help you get that stuff to your car," he said. "Lieberman says if that's the way you want it, okay. He doesn't want us over in Oak Park anyway. He says he'll give you a call."

The cop carried her suitcase and Angie's to the car, plunked them into the trunk when she opened it, and waited in the underground parking garage. He was doing his job to the end. She thanked him and waved. He neither waved back nor smiled. In the rearview mirror she did see him throw his newspaper into a garbage can and yawn as she pulled away.

She got to her brother's at dinner time, was greeted warmly and sat down to eat; dinner was a dark stew which was one of Fran's specialties. She was a good cook. Jean threw a look to Lloyd, who took off his glasses and nodded, knowing that she had something to tell him privately and not right now.

Walter ate quickly and left most of what he had been given. Before anyone else was even deeply into the stew, Walter was pushing for dessert, which Fran—unwisely, she admitted—had told him was strawberry ice cream.

Lloyd told the boy firmly to stop asking or he would get none. So Walter stopped asking, but he squirmed magnificently and pouted professionally.

Lucille and Dorothy talked about Lucille's new boyfriend, and Jean simply ate and let the family soak into her, comforting, boring and warm.

After dinner she caught Lloyd for a moment and told him first about Mrs. Bratcovick and second about the newspaper reporter. Lloyd took off his glasses, rubbed the bridge of his nose, put his glasses back on and touched the top of her head the way he had done when she was a little girl.

"Jesus wept," he said. "We'll just have to make do. I'll tell everyone about it later."

Later Dorothy and Lucille went next door to the Wentroff's house to feed the cat. The Wentroffs were in Florida because Mike Wentroff's mother was sick again. Walter went to bed early with a slight stomachache from too much ice cream, and the three adults talked, deciding how to break the news to the girls.

When the girls came back, they said the Wentroff's cat was getting testy and lonely and hissing at them. Lloyd told them to take a seat, and proceeded to tell them everything, quickly and efficiently.

Lucille moved to Jean's side and gave her a hug.

"We're going to be famous," Dotty said.

"I hope not," said Jean, hugging Lucille. "They may not even mention you. Depends on how they decide to play it."

The rest of the evening went quietly, with everyone staying away from the subject. For a while Lloyd went into the rec-room office to finish up his sermon, which he thought might need some altering after the morning papers came out. He'd know after talking to a few early arrivers and judging for himself.

At nine, Lucille got an idea, excused herself, and dashed off after her mother told her to be right back. She was back ten minutes later with the early editions of both the *Sun-Times* and the *Tribune*. Any hope Jean had of being quietly tucked away inside was dashed. She was page three of the *Sun-Times*, page two of the *Tribune*, and her name was right in the dead middle of it along with a photograph of her at least five years old that came from God knows where.

The phone was ringing downstairs, behind her closed door and deep inside the house. It was Sunday morning, and the phone wouldn't stop ringing. Jean put her second pillow, the one she usually hugged, over her head. She had no idea what time it was and didn't care. They had talked till almost two, at first trying to ignore the newspaper stories and later facing them. When she had finally gone to bed she had been convinced that things weren't so bad. Lloyd was particularly good at making one's troubles seem slight in relation to the enormity of history and the world's problems. The trouble was that Lloyd's wisdom was rather like a half-dozen chocolate chip cookies: fine when you were eating them, but only a sweet memory in the morning when you had to face a day without them.

The damn phone kept ringing. They were probably all in church. Then it stopped, and Jean buried her face in the second pillow, ignoring the sunlight through the closed curtains.

"Aunt Jean," came Dotty's voice after a gentle knock at the door. "Are you awake?"

"Do I have to answer?" she said.

"The phone's for you," Dotty said.

"The phone has never been for me," Jean replied, sitting up and finding her glasses. "It's a tool of the twentieth century I could do without. It's a demanding son of a bitch, interrupting conversations, sleep, work, ordering you to fill space and time with sound. You know the word 'phony' comes from the word 'telephone.'"

She had found her robe and was putting it on. Dotty was in the room, leaning against the wall.

"I didn't know," said Dotty, interested.

"Man or woman?" Jean asked, taking a deep breath, removing her glasses and cleaning them on her pajamas.

"On the phone? A woman," said Dotty.

"Hell," Jean sighed. "You know there was a mass murderer a few years back. Shot about thirteen people, then barricaded himself in the house with a bunch of hostages, raving that he was going to kill them.

199

A reporter found the phone number of the house and called him. The killer paused in his firing at the cops to answer, and was very polite, telling the reporter that he was very sorry but he was too busy to talk right then. I think that's a reporter on the phone."

"Should I tell her you don't want to talk?" Dotty said, opening the door.

"No, I'll talk to her. I'm a creature of the twentieth century. I can't resist the Bell system."

Dotty led the way to Lloyd's study, where the nearest phone was. Jean knew the room reasonably well. It was small and dark even with one window beaming in a track of light. And it was cluttered with books, notes, papers. The phone rested precariously on a tottering pile of three or four books.

"Good luck," said Dotty, disappearing.

Jean nodded and picked up the phone.

"Yes," she said.

"Miss Kaiser?" It wasn't the reporter, at least not the same reporter.

"Yes," she replied, glancing at an open book on Lloyd's desk.

"Hold on please, Mr. Alexian is calling."

There was a click of some kind, a pause and the hoarse whisper of Alexian.

"Jean," he said.

"It's Sunday morning," Jean answered.

"The television stations, radio stations and the newspapers don't stop on Sunday morning," he said. "Let's talk. This won't take long."

Jean assumed she was about to be fired before the job began. Thinking quickly, she hoped to at least have the last remark in the conversation, something pithy, perhaps a quote that would haunt Alexian. One of Lloyd's Blake collections was on the desk, but there'd be no time to find the right comment that would devastate Alexian, who was probably stroking his beard and eating an early-morning egg salad sandwich with little crumbs entwined in the gray strands of his hair.

"You want me to come down to the office?" she said.

"I'm back in New York," he said.

"You mean this was big enough to make *The New York Times?*"

"Hardly," he said. "I got a call from the Chicago office last night."

"And I'm fired," she said.

"You may be a fine-looking woman and a clever psychologist, but you've got very little business sense. You give up too easily. What you should have said was, 'So,' or 'Do you think the publicity will help in promotion?' or something like that. Damn it. You, believe it or not, are not the only problem I've got. We live in an insane world, which ultimately is good for both your business and mine. I want to know how this has affected you, how you're feeling. Not false sentiment. I'm concerned with my investment in you."

"I'll survive," she said.

"Right," he said, taking a bite out of something. "I thought I could see that in you. Now I'll give it to you straight. I don't know what this is going to do to your image. It might make it impossible for you to do the show at WBBM or it may make you a celebrity."

"And all the ghouls will tune in, right?"

"You seem to have a harsher attitude toward human curiosity and guilt than even I do. I thought you were the shrink."

"I've had a hard day's night," she said, pushing Lloyd's book aside and losing his place. The pages flipped and opened on a well-worn page. Hell, Lloyd knew it well enough to find his page.

"So where are we?" he said. "I'll tell you. We see how this all carries in Chicago for the next few days, how it gets resolved. The papers aren't going to let this story drag on for more than three or four days. I know something about news. If there aren't any developments soon, you'll be forgotten, but when you go on the radio, some reporter will make the connection. It's an easy one. Our problem will then be whether we get accused of exploiting your name, of using you because of all this. No one's going to believe us when we say we had this in the works before some lunatic began bludgeoning people all over town. Richard Nixon made disbelievers of us all."

"You're a philosopher," she said, sitting in Lloyd's wooden swivel chair and leaning back.

"And you're being a sarcastic—"

"Bitch," she finished. "I'm sorry. You're being very reasonable."

"All right," he said. "We'll try to work something out. You are a good property. How would you feel about moving to another city if it came down to that or dropping you? This story won't mean anything in New York or Philadelphia."

"I . . . I don't know. I'll have to think about it."

"Think about it," he said. "One last thing. Roger's doing a fine job as your manager."

"I'm glad," she said, watching the dust dance in the sunbeam through the window.

"Don't be," he went on, biting whatever he was eating again. "He's doing a great job for me, not for you. I'm suggesting you get yourself another manager. I'll even give you some names."

"Why do you want to suggest that if Roger's doing what you want?"

Alexian chuckled slightly and put his hand over the mouthpiece to say something to someone, probably the woman who had placed the call.

"I've had a lot of experience," he finally said. "If we work together, a time will come when you figure out that Roger has screwed you up. Then you'll get your teeth sharpened for me, and somewhere down the line we'll have bad blood and a hell of a fight. I'd rather get it all taken care of now. You're not that expensive a package either way. However, I have people over me who don't see it that way and would have me under the ax if I offered you more than you and your manager asked for."

"Thanks," Jean said.

"Good business," he replied. "And to think I started out as a reporter for the *Champaign-Urbana News Gazette*. The Chicago office will keep me informed. If you want to reach me, they'll know where I am. Stay alive."

He hung up, and Jean let out a puff of air. That had turned out better than she had feared. She would have to call Roger, tell him about the conversation, minus the suggestion to dump him. Roger would be hurt that Alexian had talked directly to her and not gone through him, and Jean had no energy to nurse Roger's ego.

Pick a page at random, an omen, a sign, the way people, her father, used to ask God to guide his hand through the Bible to the right passage or line, the way Dr. Hirsch had suggested she flip through the collected works of Freud for inspiration. Only her father

202

had not been making a joke. She reached for Lloyd's book, flipped and read:

My mother groand! my father wept.
Into the dangerous world I leapt:
Helpless, naked, piping loud;
Like a fiend hid in a cloud.

Struggling in my father's hands:
Striving against my swaddling bands:
Bound and weary I thought best
To sulk upon my mothers breast.

No inspiration there. She flipped a few more pages, where something caught her eye, but she had had enough of poetry for one morning and a voice was calling her, Dotty's, asking if she wanted some breakfast.

Dotty was the only one home. The others were at church. It had been decided that Dotty would stay with Jean, keep her company, and run interference if she needed it.

"Besides," Dotty explained, "he's doing 'With every bounteous deed there is a price to pay,' which I've heard variations on since I was seven. Furthermore Dad's head has not been in his sermons recently. He's started talking again about teaching poetry somewhere."

Jean sipped some coffee after dipping a toasted English muffin into it and commented, "Maybe all of us should pack up and look for new pastures."

"Maybe," agreed Dotty, who was playing with the gooey remnants of an omelet.

Fortified with caffeine and a fifty-fifty chance of not losing the CBS deal, Jean combed her hair, brushed her teeth, dressed and faced the telephone.

She prepared herself for Max's onslaught of advice, warning and admonition. But he didn't answer the phone; Angie did.

"Did you see the papers, kiddo?" Jean asked.

"Yeah, ecch," said Angie. "Are you all right? Dad is bananas but pretending it's not important. He's a good actor, but not as good as

203

you are when you're trying to hide something from me. He was on the phone this morning with Phyllis."

"Let's please forget about Phyllis for a while, Ange."

"Are we still moving tomorrow?" Angie asked. Death and transfiguration were not as important as tomorrow, which was fine with Jean.

"I don't know," Jean said. "We might be making a longer move in a while."

"Longer?"

"Another city, but not until this is all cleared up."

"I don't think Dad will like that," Angie whispered.

That was what Jean was afraid of. Max knew the law, and he had the right to have Angie on weekends.

"Let me talk to him," Jean said. "We may stay at Uncle Lloyd's tonight, or you may have to stay with your father. I'm sorry."

"I think I'd rather be with you," Angie whispered. "Dad's a little weird today."

Jean was about to question her when Max's voice came on with a bit of its confidence eroded and his down-home accent strong.

"Jean, do you need anything, any help?"

"No," she said firmly.

"I . . . we've got to talk," he said. "There's something we've got to work out."

"Okay, let's work it out," she said.

"Not now," Max half-whispered.

"Because Angie can hear you?"

"That's right," he said.

"All right. I've got to talk to you about some things too, but they can wait a day or two. Can you keep Angie tonight?"

Max said he could, and Jean promised to call later that evening to check and report. When they hung up Jean was more than uneasy. It wasn't the Max she had known. There had actually been a sense of need, God help him, maybe even a hint of weakness in his voice. The conversation had been brief, but Jean had sensed it.

It struck her as painfully ironic that someone who disliked the impersonality and mechanism of the telephone should be so tied to it personally and professionally—as she was.

She called Dr. Hirsch with the idea of canceling dinner that night, but he had read the newspapers and urged her to come without Angie. She finally agreed, knowing that she wanted to agree when the call began but feeling she had to put up strong token resistance. She immediately told Hirsch what she had done. It was the curse of patient and analyst; the truth had to be told.

"So, you're coming," he said. "Let's forget about analyzing it. There's a basketball game on, Celtics and Lakers. We'll talk tonight. My wife wants to know if you like veal."

"Veal is fine," she said.

They hung up.

She didn't call Roger. There was no need. He would be calling her as soon as he felt it safe to assume she would be up.

His call came when Lloyd, Fran, Walter and Lucille returned slightly after noon. Walter was announcing over and over again that he would not go somewhere and Fran was responding patiently that he would.

Roger's voice dripped with sympathy and he asked if Jean wanted to spend the day away from the city, away from telephones. It was tempting, but it meant mothering Roger, which she didn't feel up to. Alexian's suggestion that she get rid of Roger as her manager stabbed through the conversation though she tried to put it away, determined that she would keep Roger no matter what. But deep down something was saying that she knew Roger would have to go, had known it before Alexian had suggested it, not because of the money and the deal, but because Roger never really represented anything permanent. She needed him now and felt guilty that she was using him for her emotional and, damn it, physical needs, but he would survive. She didn't mention Alexian's call, promised to get in touch the next day, claimed she needed a day to relax and finally got off the phone.

"That looked painful," said Lloyd, his eyes hidden behind the glasses catching the sun. He gave her a supportive smile.

"Could have been worse," she said. "How was the sermon?"

"Christians won again," he said. "They always do when I tell the story. How are you this morning?"

Jean told them about her call from Alexian and her decision to have dinner with the Hirsches. Fran suggested that she stay away from the phones, maybe go out for the day. She considered it and agreed, promising to return after dinner.

It was at this point that Walter decided Jean should take him to the Brookfield Zoo. The boy was oblivious to the cold. He reasoned that the animals were there winter and summer and winter was a good time. Lucille told him that it was almost zero outside, or hadn't he noticed? Walter had not noticed.

After lunch Lieberman called.

"I think," he said, "it would be a good idea if you tell me where you're going to be all day. Sort of stay in touch. I'll give you my home number. And to make me feel better, how about letting us send somebody around to keep you company. I know a nice detective with no brains and nothing to do. He's sitting at the station now reading the funnies."

Jean refused, promising to get back to him and assuring him that she would be with people all day and night.

It was cold, and she had trouble starting the Aspen, but it finally agreed, jerked a few times, stopped at the corner, started again with some urging and skidded sideways, stopping inches from a parked van. When she straightened out slowly, she checked the rear view mirror and spotted the dark car behind her. After three right turns, she was sure the dark car with a man driving was following her. She could see his face clearly when she stopped at the light at Austin Boulevard and recognized him as one of the policemen who had been at the Bratcovick apartment the night before. So, either Lieberman was taking no chances, or Clavey was keeping an eye on her—suspect or potential victim, it made no difference.

She and the cop saw an afternoon movie, *Victor/Victoria*. She had planned to see *You Ought To Be in Pictures*, but decided that it was unlikely fare for a cop who looked like this cop. He sat three rows behind her, his arms folded, looking like a compact refrigerator. She considered talking to him after the show, but she didn't know the protocol for the situation and didn't want to embarrass him, though he looked as if he were beyond embarrassment.

Later in the afternoon she headed for the Hirsch house in Wilmette and got there just before five.

Mrs. Hirsch, whom she had met a few times before, was a buxom, well-groomed woman with short, straight white hair. She nodded frequently while people talked as if she were listening carefully and finding everything quite reasonable.

"We've got one of those video game things," Hirsch said, leading Jean into a den. "My grandson comes over and plays it with me. I thought your Angie might enjoy it if she came."

"If she knew about it I wouldn't have been able to keep her away," Jean said.

"You want to try a game of Space Demons?" he said with a slight smile.

Jean declined.

"Computers, video games, video recorders," he said. "The bionic age is upon us. It's time for someone to write a seminal psychoanalytical text on the effect of all this on the psyche. It's a revolution."

"Started with the telephone," Jean observed.

"Probably," he agreed, offering her a soft, worn chair.

The room was large, rust and white.

"Okay," he said. "Busman's holiday. We talk. No charge. The difference is that here you get a hell of a lot of my opinion."

They talked—or mainly, Jean talked—about the murders, Alexian, Roger, Max and Angie, and even Lloyd and his family. At one point Myra Hirsch stuck her head in, saw they were talking, and left after depositing a bowl of hot pizza rolls.

"They'll kill me," Hirsch explained, popping one into his mouth, "but I'm hooked."

They washed the rolls down with ginger ale, and Jean leaned back in the comfortable chair. She had been talking nonstop.

"Like having a good bowel movement," Hirsch said, crunching a pizza roll in his mouth. "Feels good to let it all out."

"Feels good," she said. "So, you have some advice?"

"Yes," he said, searching the bowl for a few crumbs and sighing when he found none. "Your unconscious is already working on the answers. It will present an answer at the conscious level and convince you that whatever decisions you make are arrived at rationally. But they are not. They are totally intuitive and arrived at in such a complex way that you would never know how they came about without a review of the history of the universe. I could make you think I'm a genius-genius by taking a good guess at what your unconscious will tell you to do and then suggesting that you do it. After all, I've had a good deal of time to play games with that mind of yours, but I don't want to play the magician. I'm still hungry and you, if you will recall, always wind up resenting the advice."

The three of them ate dinner—tender slices of veal, salad and green beans with a little wine—and talked about Hirsch's family and the new book he was working on. Myra Hirsch let him clear the dishes while she showed Jean some of her drawings and art work. Jean knew that Myra was an artist and had done book jackets, but she had never seen her work and was fascinated by it. Hirsch joined them in her studio at the back of the large house.

"I'm not allowed to analyze them," he said, pursing his lips and looking at the dozens of paintings on shelves and walls. "Maybe she'll let you if you're interested."

Jean was fascinated by the wall-to-wall color. The room was like a greenhouse of paint, and the paintings were amazingly varied. One large painting was of a man's callused hand holding a delicate flower. Jean recognized it as the cover of a novel whose title she couldn't recall.

Another smaller painting was of a broken doll, its head split, and wearing a grotesque grin. Jean didn't recognize that one but guessed it was for one of a string of grizzly popular novels about malevolent children.

"It's too much for me," Jean said. "I'm overwhelmed."

The response seemed to please Myra.

"My wife has the ability to let her spirits talk to her, take over. As Hillman says, we are mainly the creatures of our creation, fragmented and held together by social pressure. Schizophrenia is usually cited as a mental disorder, but in fact, the ability to experience multiple personalities is but an acknowledgment of the truth. It is society which forces us to present a oneness. One god. One personality. One boss."

"And one lecture per night," Myra Hirsch added, touching his arm.

"It's fascinating," Jean said and meant it.

"It is better to let the demons out than let them gnaw away at you from within," Hirsch added.

"Hey," his wife said, poking his arm. "Your lecture is over. Let's have some coffee."

"Cake too, cake too," he said, leading the way.

The evening ended comfortably. Jean felt much better and remembered only at the last minute as she approached the door that the policeman might still be outside waiting for her. She told the Hirsches, and Mrs. Hirsch wrapped up a piece of cake and filled an old thermos with hot coffee.

They said good night to Jean at the door and she promised to see Hirsch in the next week; then she noticed the car across the street. It was no problem to spot it. The street was residential, and since each house had a driveway there were no cars on the street except the one. Hers was in the Hirsch driveway. She walked in the light of the street lamps, shivering against the blast of cold from the lake wind, and stopped in front of the car. The policeman had left his motor on and the car was probably eating gasoline. She tapped at the window and he lowered it. She almost dropped the cake and coffee. It wasn't the same man who had followed her.

"I . . ." she said stepping back.

His face was broad and dark.

"Are you a policeman?" she whispered.

He gave her a bored nod of agreement.

"I took over about an hour ago," he said.

She handed him the cake and thermos and he took them with a "Thanks."

"I'm going back to my brother's house in Oak Park," she said. "You really don't have to stay there all night."

"Don't plan to," he said, screwing off the top of the thermos and taking a drink. "I'm supposed to see that you're tucked in with a locked door for the night. Clavey's orders."

He said he knew the way, but he had to follow her. She told him she would wait in her car till he finished the coffee and cake, and his jaw twitched slightly, which may have been the suggestion of a smile.

She was back in Oak Park by eleven. She parked in front of her brother's house, got out, locked the car and went to the porch, where

209

she waved to the policeman who had parked behind her. She couldn't see if he waved back. She had been given a key so she went in quietly.

Fran and the girls were watching a movie on television, and they urged her to join them. Lloyd, she learned from Dotty, was at Oak Park Hospital visiting a sick parishioner. Jean tried the show for a few moments, but she couldn't keep her mind on Goldie Hawn. Something was picking at her mind, hinting, teasing. Some answer was trapped, looking for a way through to understanding and words.

She was sitting in the kitchen about ten minutes later when the phone rang.

"Who can that be at this hour?" Fran asked from the other room.

Jean put down the cup of warmed-over coffee and picked up the phone.

"Hello," she said.

"Hello, Jean," the Dark Man answered. "I've got your little girl."

◇ *FIFTEEN* ◆

She was still holding the phone in her hand when it rang again. Lost in what she had just heard, the idea that the phone could be ringing pushed through, an insistent puzzle. She realized that it was the second line and turned the button.

"Hello," came Lloyd's voice.

"Lloyd," she said, her voice soft, almost erased, but he didn't seem to notice.

"Jean, I've spent one devil of a half-hour. There is a limit to the consolation you can give to a woman who is having minor surgery for gallstones."

Jean tried to focus on something in the room, anything, the coffee cup, the magnetized can opener on the refrigerator, the frost on the panes of the back door. She wanted to speak, to stop her brother's patter, to tell him, but she was frozen and her hand had a white-knuckle grip on the telephone receiver as if she were under some posthypnotic spell that would not let her loose without the proper command.

She imagined Lloyd wiping his hair back as he went on.

"I think the Lord set himself a goal, like Jerry Lewis, a thousand operations a year."

"He has Angie," Jean whispered.

"Jean, what's . . . ?"

"He has Angie," she repeated, her voice cracking. "Are you deaf or something? You go on about gallstones and that madman has my daughter."

"Tell me," he said, his voice changing, growing suddenly serene and professional, probably the same sympathetic tone he used with the woman in the hospital, Jean thought and then realized that she was being unfair.

She let the feeling of near anger pass. It had always been a trait of hers, but one she knew was shared by most people. If you can't reach the object of your anger, use the person closest by to take it out on.

"There's nothing to tell," she said. "That crazy bastard has Angie. He just called. He's going . . ."

"But Angie's with Max," Lloyd said.

She noticed a small crumb on the white formica table and picked it up.

"Maybe he was just trying to frighten you," Lloyd went on quietly. She tossed the crumb in the general direction of the sink.

She had called Max as soon as the Dark Man had hung up, but she had been sure that the voice had not lied.

"How's Angie?" she had asked when Max picked up the phone.

"How's . . . she's with you, isn't she? Roger called about an hour ago and said you wanted Angie downstairs quickly because you had last-minute packing to do."

"Are you sure it was Roger?" she had asked.

"Sure it was . . . No, I don't know your boyfriend's voice for Chrissake. What's this all about?"

"Nothing," she said. "Angie's all right. I was just a little upset that you let her go without checking."

"I'm sorry, Jean," he had said with more petulance than regret, "but I told you I've got a lot on my mind. You sure Angie's all right? Can I talk to her?"

"She's taking a bubble bath. I've got to go. I'll talk to you tomorrow."

She had depressed the button to cut him off and then let it go to listen to the dial tone. That was when Lloyd had called.

"I've talked to Max," she told her brother. "Angie's not with him."

"I'm calling the police," Lloyd said firmly.

"No," Jean hissed, trying to keep hysteria away.

"Jean," Lloyd pleaded.

"He said he'd kill her if I called the police."

"How can he know if you call the police?" Lloyd said softly.

"I don't know, but I can't take a chance. Lloyd, he's crazy. He wants me to come to him now, tonight."

"All the more reason to call the police, that Lieberman."

"He told me what I had to do to keep him from killing Angie, and I'm going to do it."

"But Jean," Lloyd tried.

"I'd rather think it through here, Lloyd," she said, "but I'll hang up and go right out the door if you don't stop trying to humor me. He told me where to go and said I could bring one person with me, one unarmed person. If more come near, he'll kill her. If he thinks we're armed, he'll kill her. I've just gone through the list. Roger isn't home. Max would call the police. Dr. Hirsch is too old, and Lieberman is a cop. I couldn't trust him, besides there's no time. . . . Lloyd, will you meet me there?"

"Yes, sure," he said, "but for God's sake, let me call the police or you call them."

Jean's head gave a firm negative shake before she said, "No."

"All right. Wait for me. I can be home in ten or fifteen minutes," he said.

"That might be ten or fifteen minutes too long for Angie. Meet me there."

"Where?" he asked softly, resigned.

"The apartment on Seeley. That's where he has her, if she's still alive."

◇ *SIXTEEN* ◆

Jean made an excuse to Fran and the girls, mumbled something about a fight with Max, and dashed out before the questions in their eyes could be turned into words. She forced herself to drive reasonably, not slowly but reasonably. Her mind kept thrusting pictures of Angie in front of her: Angie in her red and yellow Chapel Hill T-shirt with the 44 on the front, her smile tentative to hide the braces. If Angie were dead, Jean would always remember her with braces.

No. She fended the image away and tried to concentrate. Why did he want Jean to come to him? Why the apartment? Why allow her to bring someone?

The windows began to defrost by the time she hit the Eisenhower Expressway. Traffic was thin, but slick icy spots kept it moving slowly. Jean knew that the same idea as before was teasing at her consciousness, hinting at an answer if she could hold back her panic long enough to let it out. Or maybe it was a trick of the mind. Maybe there was no answer, just the hope of one.

She tried to keep calm, to listen to her breathing as her eyes looked to the right into the black infinity where Lake Michigan should be.

Slow motion up Sheridan Road, past Loyola University. Six minutes later she made another left on Seeley past the Hi-Neighbor. A gust of wind spun an old drunk comically and Jean prayed that he wouldn't fall and crack his skull, forcing her to stop. The drunk went up on one foot and slid on his behind into the front door of a dry cleaning store.

Jean gunned down the narrow street, ignoring the intersections. There was no light on in the front of the apartment. Martha and Wayne's light was on, but the rest of the building was dark.

The dashboard digital clock said 11:45 when she skidded into the alley and bounced gently off a telephone pole. She didn't bother to check the garage. Instead she parked in front of it, far enough over to let anything but a truck pass.

She opened the door and stepped out. The silence was sliced by the wind and a faraway backfire or crash.

She closed the door as quietly as she could and crossed to the concrete sidewalk alongside the garage. There was often an obstacle course of dog shit, but Jean ignored it, her coat open as she hurried and almost slipped.

No lights in the back. Eyes? A face in the window? She couldn't tell. She went up the stairs trying to be quiet though there was no point in being quiet. If he were there, he would see and hear her.

She reached for the doorknob and told herself, "Be careful. For Angie. Be careful."

She turned the knob. The door was open, and she stepped in. Jean could hear the beating of her heart. It was clear, very loud, insistent.

Jean had seen Parmenter's body and that of the bird. She knew the strength of the Dark Man, his fury. Her heart was, she was sure, beating visibly against her chest as she reached for the light switch with some deep fear that a hand would reach out and grab her wrist or come through the floor.

The light came on with a ping. The room was empty except for the kitchen table. The cupboards were open, empty. The light cut only a foot or two into the darkness of the hallway to her right and the dining room in front of her.

"Angie," she said, almost crying at the weakness in her voice.

215

She wanted to shout but her voice could only father the wish for a shout. "Angie."

Then the anger and fear broke through.

"Angie. Where are you? And you, you bastard, step out where I can see you. No more hiding on the other end of a telephone wire."

There was no answer, no sound. She thought of a weapon, but the knives were packed in the dining room. A car passed by on Seeley, sending a dance of shadows into the living room.

She moved to the sink where a bottle stood that Jean and Angie had used to store used Brillo pads. She had forgotten to throw it away or pack it. She dumped the Brillo pads in the sink and held the bottle. An eerie silhouette popped up against the muted light as another car passed outside.

"Let's go," Jean told herself and stepped toward the rear bedroom, Angie's bedroom. With the bottle in her right hand, Jean reached in and flicked on the light. The bed was still there, and the dresser. The walls had been stripped of her posters, and her things had been packed. Jean could feel her glasses slipping. She reached up quickly to push them back and stepped over to the closed closet. She opened it, bottle held high, catching her breath. Something was . . . no, nothing leaped out. The closet was dark. There was no crumpled form on the floor, no dark figure.

"Where are you?" Jean said aloud, moving quickly back into the little alcove near the bedroom, looking into the small rear bathroom and stepping out.

She went through the kitchen and paused at the entrance to the dining room. Someone could easily be behind the wall to the right or left. She leaped forward, turning quickly and swinging out with the bottle.

"Hahh," Jean heard herself, not trying to keep it back, but there was nothing there.

Her back against the wall, Jean slid along and found the light switch. The single light bulb behind the frosted ceiling fixture came on. Jean's eyes turned to the pile of cartons but they revealed nothing. The next stop was her bedroom, the room where Parmenter's body had been found, where Klinger's body had lain. She had known from the start that it was the most likely place to find Angie if he had killed

216

her, but she moved quickly to the door and spun into the room just as the lights went out.

"No," she moaned softly, backing into the wall. Her head thumped where she knew a photograph of herself and Angie had hung days before. If it had still been there, the back of her head would now be filled with shards of glass.

Caution was gone. She was losing the battle to hold back the hysteria. Had Martha and Wayne heard her and gone back to their old tricks? Had the Dark Man done it? Was he now on his way up the stairs?

"Angie," she said, trying to see the bed. Some light came through the window from the apartment across the way. Jean pleaded with her eyes to adjust quickly.

There was nothing on the bed. Her feet clattered hollowly on the now bare wooden floor and Pal began to bark furiously as she moved to the closet.

Wayne's voice was distant but carried through the floor.

"Who the hell can be up there?" he said. "I'm going to call the damned police."

The heat was off in the apartment but Jean knew that her face was covered with perspiration. She jerked open the closet door and stood back. No one leaped out.

He's playing a goddamn game with me, she told herself, clenching her fist. She moved into the dining room and then, by the street light outside, took the final few steps into the last room, the living room, where she stood just inside the door. Pal barked furiously as her shoes clapped against the bare floor. The room was large and empty.

"Probably that Jew bitch getting some things," came Martha's voice. "Shut up and go to sleep. And you shut up too." The latter apparently said to Pal, who did not shut up.

The room was still, the light of the nearby street lamp illuminated the center of the room through the six uncovered windows.

"He's not here," she heard herself saying with a sob. "Not here." She pounded her fist helplessly against the wall. Pal went mad and Martha shouted, "Shut up, up there. If you're burglars, we called the police."

No time to cry, Jean told herself. Not now. She stood catching her breath and the noise in the apartment below stopped. But there was another sound now and she willed herself to stop hyperventilating so she could make it out. It was a creaking, a familiar . . . Someone was coming up the stairs, the front stairs, coming up quietly, slowly from below.

She turned to face the door a few feet away. Was it locked? Had he been here earlier? Left it open? Should she try to move those few feet, throw the chain? Would it keep him out?

She pressed back against the wall holding the bottle in two hands, knowing her knuckles were going white and might crush the glass. She thought of crying out for help to Wayne and Martha, but knew they wouldn't come, wouldn't listen.

Then the footsteps stopped and she knew he was just beyond the door, as she had known he was a lifetime ago when she was a girl and her parents . . . The doorknob turned. A pebbly thrust of light from outside ran down the door and she could see the knob turn and turn and turn and turn. And then the door began to open and she wanted to see and didn't want to see and she saw him standing there as the door swung open.

Jean let one hand fall from the bottle and a sob of relief came to her throat.

"Lloyd," she whimpered, and took the three or four steps to him. "He's not here. Angie's not here. I think we'll have to call the police, Lieberman."

Lloyd pushed the door closed behind him and said nothing.

"The phone's been disconnected," she went on. "We'll have to go to the Seven-Eleven."

In the gray half-light Lloyd looked almost amused. Jean repeated to make it clear. "He's not here."

"He's here," said Lloyd. It was not her brother's voice, but that deep voice that carried with it the suggestion of a distant echo, a dark cave.

◇ *SEVENTEEN* ◆

"No," she said, leaning against the wall.

"Yes," he whispered. "Oh, yes."

"Where is Angie? Lloyd, what did you do with Angie?"

"She's sitting in the lobby of the Holiday Inn in Evanston," he whispered. "I called Max and said I was Roger. When she came down I just picked her up, took her to the motel and told her to wait in the lobby, all night if necessary."

"Stop whispering," she said. "Stop that voice."

"I can't," he said. "It's an old, old voice. Older than my other one, perhaps older than time."

"Why? Lloyd, why?"

Instead of an answer he reached out, tore the bottle from her hand, and brought the edge down against the wall. Shards of glass flew, and below them Wayne's voice sighed, "Oh, Jesus Christ. I'm calling the police."

In the light from the window Jean could see half of her brother's body and face. The other half was in darkness, and from the darkness into the light his hand reached out, clutching the end of the bottle. Blood, black, snaked down his sleeve from his cut hand. The ends of the bottle, two slivers of glass, caught the light, and she looked at his face.

"How?"

She could speak in nothing but single words. He looked like something, someone from the past but she didn't know . . . Her father. He looked like her father now in the near light.

"Oh Lloyd, there's . . . Don't you see there's something wrong? Why are you doing this? Why have you been doing this to me? I can understand your killing Parmenter after what he had done to Mom and Dad. Even his sister, but what are you doing to me? Why?"

He laughed. It was a low, whispered laugh and Jean realized that it wasn't Lloyd she was dealing with, but at the same time it *was* Lloyd.

"You still don't understand, do you?" he said.

"Understand?"

"Parmenter didn't kill our mother and father. I did." He took another step forward, and she moved to the far wall as he stepped into the full low light of the street. It was soft and luminous.

"No," she said. "You need help, Lloyd. You didn't kill them."

"But, dear sister, I did. I most certainly did, so long ago and far away." He looked at her face, and she could see herself in the windows of his glasses, a distorted, pale woman's face. Two of them against a white wall.

"I'll tell you about it," he said. "I've wanted to tell you for a long time. Maybe that's why I called you that time. I only remember calling you that one time, you see. You sounded so sure of yourself on the radio. You went through your life with psychiatrists, learned how to deal with it, turned the horror into a career. I had the horror in myself too. I learned to control it. So simple and no one thought for a moment, not for a moment. You were out with your friends tubing on the river. I flew in from Chicago, drove to the house in the afternoon. I told them about the girl, about Evelyn. I killed Evelyn. I really killed her. And now my hand is bleeding."

"You killed someone named Evelyn?" she asked. Maybe Wayne would call the police and they'd burst in if she could keep him talking, but she also wanted the answers. Inside this man whom she had known as her brother were answers to the terror of her life.

"I met her when I was in Divinity School here at the University of Chicago," he said. "I never wanted to be a minister. It was his doing. I was too weak to fight him. You know what he was like. You were just a little girl, but you know."

"I know," she agreed, moving toward the window, considering a leap through glass, a one-floor drop. It probably wouldn't kill her.

"Evelyn wanted to marry me. She was older than I was. She had a child, a little boy. And she was Jewish. What more could have been wrong?"

He laughed, a sobbing laugh.

"Your arm is bleeding," she said, "let me—"

"It doesn't matter. I've got to finish telling it now. Don't you see that?"

"Tell it, then. Take your time."

"About Evelyn there's not much more to tell. I killed her. One night we got into a fight, and she started to push me, force me to face Father. She didn't know what he was like. I couldn't face it, or her. Maybe she slapped me. It was a long time ago. It should be clear but it keeps changing when I see it, imagine it. I hit her, beat her while the little boy was sleeping in the other room of the apartment. I remember the address clearly. You want to hear it?"

"If you want to tell me," she said.

"It's not important," he said. "Not to you. The next morning I called Father and Mother, told them I had to come home and see them. They said you'd be out for the day. I came right to the house from the Raleigh airport. Did I say that?"

He was inches from her now.

"I don't think so," she said softly.

"Do you know what he said when I told him? Come on, guess what he said, our father, when I told him about Evelyn."

"I don't know," said Jean.

There were no sounds now from below, and she had heard no voice making a phone call.

"He said I should turn myself in, tell the police what I had done. I told him about Evelyn. Blake described her.

"A Woman Scaly and a Man all Hairy
Is such a Match as he who dares
Will find the Womans Scales scrape off the
    Man's Hairs.

"You see what I mean? Can you imagine what the police would have done to me? And our mother. All sympathy in her eyes but no argument with him. I knew her power. His was nothing compared to hers. Her eyes moist and her mouth still. They said I had to turn myself in by the next morning or he would turn me in. He had no choice, he said. God gave him no choice. What the hell did he know of God? I wanted to kill them. 'Sooner murder the infant in its cradle than nurse unacted desires.' The cowardly critics say Blake meant that metaphorically. He didn't. It was literal. There is no good and evil. What we call evil is creation. We suppress it. Without creation and destruction there is nothing. Can you begin to see that?"

"I understand it, but—"

"I found Parmenter that night in Chapel Hill," Lloyd said, looking toward the window as if seeing the events again. "He was wandering, a drunk. I led him to the woods beyond our house, gave him a bottle and sat him down. Then I got the ax out of the shed and came into the house. I thought you slept through it, but you didn't. I drove back to the airport, went back to Chicago and called in the morning. I was calling when you walked into the room and discovered them. I was calling to establish where I was."

"Oh, Lloyd, and you've lived with this," she said, starting to put out a hand to him. He backed away.

"It would have destroyed me if there were such things as good and evil," he said. "Their lives meant so little. They are neither in heaven nor hell, reincarnated nor at peace in nothingness. They don't suffer. The living suffer. You suffered. I had it all controlled until he got out, until Parmenter came to Chicago looking for me. It was me he was looking for, not you. It was me he was following, not you. He remembered my face, but they told him it was father he remembered. He began to put it together. Then he came for me. I think in some mad way of his he was even trying to protect you from me. And so I called you at the station, got you to start thinking it was you he was after. And you believed it, you went after him."

"And," she said. "You killed him. And his sister?"

"It's not clear. Oh, Christ, I'm bleeding a lot. What did you say? His sister? I don't remember his sister. Not well. I went to search his room. She was there. I don't remember what I did."

"And tonight?" she picked up as his voice trailed off. "If I had suggested that I bring someone else here besides you?"

"I didn't think you would," he said. "I was right there. I'm your brother. But if you had, I'd have found a way. Suggest something."

"Lloyd, what are we doing here now? You've told me. Why don't we sit down somewhere light and talk some more?"

"Maybe I'm mad, but I'm not a fool. You'd simply go sit with me over a cup of coffee at the Copper Coin after bandaging my hand and we'd talk about my murders calmly. Would we share a cheesecake? No, no, no, you'll turn me in. Or you'll do what they did. You'll tell me to turn myself in."

"Lloyd, what choice do you have?"

"It's so simple," he said. "I kill you. Then you're not here to haunt me, to remind me of long ago and far away. You're not here with your Roger and who knows how many others reminding me of the lust I killed with Evelyn. When you were a child, it was all right. I protected you. When you were a mother and a wife it was all right, but you became that voice, that professional knowing voice and then Parmenter came from the past."

His hand, the right one without the broken bottle, came up swiftly and pointed to the wall near her head. He began pounding the beat as he recited in a sing-song whisper:

"Prisons are built with stones of clay. Brothels with bricks of Religion.

> "The pride of the peacock is the glory of God.
> The lust of the goat is the bounty of God.
> The wrath of the lion is the wisdom of God.
> The nakedness of woman is the work of God.
> Excess of sorrow laughs. Excess of joy weeps.
> The roaring of lions, the howling of wolves, the raging of
>   the stormye sea, and the destructive sword are
>   portions of eternity too great for the eye of man.
> The fox condemns the trap, not himself."

Jean reached up and touched his pounding hand. Below, Pal was at it again, and Wayne and Martha were arguing, but she couldn't make out the words, wasn't listening to them.

"I knew it was you," Jean said gently.

Lloyd's glazed eyes looked down at her, and his pounding fist stopped.

"No." he said.

"Yes," she said, still holding his hand. "When you called the station and said your name was John Fl—When I was in your study this morning I flipped through one of your Blake books. There were poems dedicated to John Flexman. He was Blake's best friend. I knew, but I didn't let it come to me. I didn't want it to. But I knew."

She touched his other hand, the one holding the bottle, and her fingers felt blood.

"Lloyd, let it be over. Put the bottle down. Rest, please."

His head was shaking, and his eyes had turned from her, though he didn't pull his hands away.

"My family. Jean, I've been a good father, a good husband, a good minister. I have." Now his eyes turned to her, and his voice was almost his own. The whisper was fading, there was a plea buried deep.

"I know."

"They'll suffer," he said, and the sob was clearly there in the shadowy face he turned away. "I have to."

She let go of the wrists and touched his face. It was wet with tears and the bristles of his unshaven cheeks pricked her hand.

"No more," she said, forcing his face toward hers. His eyes were bewildered and she knew this was the moment, the moment that determined if she would live or die, the moment he would crumple or else plunge the broken glass into her face or stomach. She tensed and felt the stiffness in him flow downward. He was starting to slip toward the floor, but she held his face firmly, urging him to stand.

"Lloyd, you brought me here to help you," she whispered. "You wanted my help. I'm giving it. I want to give it."

"Damn you," he hissed, his eyes wide. "You don't understand. You mock me by playing a whore's Christ. I don't want your forgiveness. Forgiveness is the horrible burden of the forgiven. If I accept you now, all that I've done is without meaning. Don't you understand that I must be cleansed in blood? You are the reminder of the mocking worm that won't stay buried, that burrows up through my bed at night and takes small bites. You are the past that has to die before I can be whole. I should have known that when you were a child. You know what I want from you? Hate. Hate me."

She couldn't tell if his final words were a command or a question.

"I don't hate you, Lloyd."

"Then damn you," he sobbed, his right arm rising slowly, the jagged bottle catching a twinkle of light from outside. Two black lines of blood streamed through the hairs of his arm and Jean watched the rivers join at his elbow as the arm stretched upward.

Jean kept her hand from going up to hold off the slash.

"I don't hate you," she repeated, looking into his eyes. His hair had fallen forward and he looked like an angry child.

"Hate me," he screamed, hand high, threatening.

She shook her head no and forced herself to keep her eyes on his.

"Hate me," he pleaded.

Something crackled on the floor behind Lloyd near the dining room, broken glass. Lloyd's head spun around to face the sound and darkness. A short figure stepped out into the dim light carrying something in one hand. The something was a gun and the figure was Lieberman.

"Reverend," Lieberman said gently, "you've got yourself a bad cut there. Why don't you just step back, put down the bottle and let us give you a hand."

Lloyd's head shook and the Dark Man's voice spoke: "It's almost finished. If I stop now, it will always be there, the last word of the sermon never written. The prayer without 'amen.'"

"Reverend," Lieberman repeated wearily, "there's no place to go with this."

Lloyd turned back to Jean. She didn't look at the bloody right hand holding the thick sliver of glass.

"You understand," Lloyd said softly so that only she could hear.

And she waited for the slash of glass against her neck, the bullet's

225

scream that would kill her brother, the whimper that would be no end or beginning. Below her the dog barked madly over Martha's shouting voice. She wondered what Lloyd's family would think, how Angie would feel.

Then Lloyd made his decision and flung the bottle toward Lieberman's shadow.

"Reverend, don't," Lieberman shouted as the bottle shattered behind him. Lloyd's hand touched Jean as he turned, took three long steps and hurled himself against the center window. Instead of flying out, his stomach hit the wooden cross frame while his head crashed through the upper pane.

"For Chrissake," screamed Martha hysterically from below. Lloyd staggered back into the room, his face lost in blood as a rush of frigid air from the broken window slapped Jean's face.

Her brother's face was a moist dark mask of bewilderment.

"Lloyd," she said, urging him to something she couldn't put into words but which he seemed to understand as Lieberman pushed past her and moved toward him. Lloyd ducked and plunged head first through the lower window pane. A single sliver of glass swung madly in the wind, catching the light of the street lamp outside. Jean could clearly see a drop of blood dangling on the glass just before the sliver let go and followed Lloyd through the window.

Gun in hand, Lieberman leaned out the window, carefully avoiding the jagged shards. Jean moved forward and looked down at the body of her brother. Lloyd lay in the dark, dirty snow. A bone from deep within him had erupted through his shoulder and pointed like a guiding finger at the corpse's open eyes, asking Jean a final dark question that had no answer and would last forever.

She heard a door open below, sensed the dog running out and hovering over the body, was aware of some movement at her side. She could smell the Fourth of July of long ago, the burnt smell of the firecrackers in front of the town hall in Carrboro. It was the only answer that came to her.

"Are you all right?" she heard Lieberman ask. "The officer watching you called in when you came here and your ex-husband called and said your daughter—"

She turned her head from the face of her brother and looked at the policeman who had stopped speaking in midsentence.

"Hey, are you all right?" he said, gently reaching out to touch her shoulder.

The cold air tightened her cheeks and she said, "I'll survive."

◇ *EIGHTEEN* ◆

Fran had been stronger than Jean had anticipated. It was almost as if the revelation were not a surprise but a weight she had waited all her life to bear. After the tears and first shock passed, Fran heaved a sigh and found real or imagined strength. She didn't know what Fran told Walter and the girls beyond what they must surely have read in the newspapers or seen on television. She did know that the link that held her to her brother's family was gone, that she had to back away from them, maybe forever.

"We had an idea it might be your brother," Lieberman told her over coffee at his brother Maish's restaurant two weeks after the funeral. "Parmenter's room, the fact that he was hanging around there, some of the things he said. But nothing was sure."

"His life was a hell, must have been a hell," she said.

"It wasn't all that great for Parmenter and his sister," Lieberman said, sipping his coffee and looking at her with half-closed eyes. "Not to mention your parents."

She looked up at him sharply.

"Look," he said. "He was your brother. Feel about him the way

228

you want, the way you have to. I'd feel the same way about the *zhlub* behind the counter. He's my brother, so maybe I'd feel that way. I'm a cop. I didn't become a cop for fun. It stopped being fun the second day. I think there's good and bad. You do bad, you pay. You do good, you deserve a reward though you don't often get it."

"You wouldn't like William Blake," she said.

"Never met the fella," Lieberman replied, reaching for the remnants of a cheese danish.

"He was . . ." she began, and Lieberman's eyes widened with anticipation, and she knew he was putting her on.

"And what do you believe?" he said, motioning to his brother for two more coffees.

"I don't know," she said honestly.

"And you're a psychologist," he said as his brother approached and put down two fresh coffees. "And a pretty good one from what I saw the other night."

"Enough already," Lieberman's brother said with a wheeze. "An old fart like you keeps bringing this good-looking young woman in here, my customers are going to start talking. Take her to one of those fancy places you take all the other women."

He turned away, and Lieberman feigned a sad-hound-dog face.

And that had been the last time she had seen him. She had anticipated the biggest trouble with Max. She had talked to Alexian, and the two of them had decided that she would move to New York City and launch the show from there. That would take care of Roger, who had no plans for giving up the radio station. Mel could, if he wanted to, come with her, and she was sure he would.

The problem was Max, for Max was a lawyer and a good one. Max was also a father and a good one: he had custody of Angie on weekends and he knew his rights. Their meetings since Lloyd's death had been awkward, as if both had had something to say and neither knew where to begin.

One afternoon Jean determined to bring it up, but Max beat her to it.

"You know I've been wanting to talk to you about something, Jean, and it might as well be now. I know you've got a lot to deal with, but I can't hold this any longer. I don't think Angie should stay with me on weekends for a while. Someone is moving in with me," he explained, looking away.

"I understand, Max," she said. "I really do. I've been thinking of moving to New York. I have an offer there from CBS. Angie and I could—"

"Just for a while," Max said, clearly relieved. "When you think she can take it, understand."

"Of course," Jean said. "We'll keep in touch. Meanwhile, I'd like you to put off having your friend move in while I resettle in New York, find an apartment. I'd like you to keep Angie for a week or so. She'll miss a little school, but she's a bright kid."

"Of course," Max said enthusiastically. "And I'll take care of your lease in the Evanston place. No problem there."

Angie was excited about moving to New York. She didn't talk much about her uncle and what had happened. She didn't know about the night in the apartment. She didn't really know about Lloyd's killing of her grandparents. Lieberman had kept that much from the news people. She'd have to be told some time maybe, but not now. The tale to Angie was that her uncle had lost control and killed Parmenter, who had been harassing her mother. There would be plenty of time for the rest when she got older.

That left only Roger to take care of, and he proved to be the most difficult of them all. The most awkward moment was *not* that last night in bed in his apartment. She had seen it as a farewell, a moment, not unpleasant—far from it—before she took off for New York. The catch was that he asked her to marry him.

"You knew I'd ask you," he said, rolling over in the bed on one elbow.

She touched his cheek in much the same way she had touched Lloyd's and said, "Not now Roger. Maybe I love you, but not now. I have to get away from here. New York is perfect. We'll stay in touch and maybe down the line . . ."

He nodded, touching her bare shoulder. Without her glasses she could barely make out his face, but she knew that defeated look even in the blur before her.

Two weeks later, Max and Angie drove Jean to Union Station.

Max had made a vain attempt to get her to fly, but had given up more easily than he usually did.

"Nobody rides Amtrak," he said.

"Next time I see you, kiddo, you'll be free of the braces," Jean said to her daughter. "I hope I recognize you."

"I'll be so changed in two weeks that I'll walk right by you in Grand Central Station and you'll think you just saw Brooke Shields," Angie said, hugging her mother.

"We're going to be fine," Jean said, touching her daughter's cheek.

"We're going to be fine," Angie repeated. "And the first thing we do when I get there?"

"New York School for the Performing Arts," she remembered. "I'll pull strings and get us a tour."

"'Fame,'" Angie explained to her father.

"I know," said Max.

The train ride was quiet, uneventful. She had one of those small sleeper compartments, claustrophobic for some, but she had always liked small rooms and felt uncomfortable in large ones. She read David Shobin's *The Unborn* and a biography of Agatha Christie.

It was morning when she arrived in New York and caught a cab. The cab driver had a name that could have been Arabian or Indian, and he seemed to be confused as he drove through the late winter rain, but he found the right address on East Seventy-seventh Street and dropped her off.

She paid him and gave him a generous tip compliments of CBS, took her two small cases, and went into the building, greeting a woman stepping out with an umbrella as if they were old friends.

Jean took the elevator up to the fifth floor, anxious to get in and get the feel of a new home. Someone at CBS had found it for her. She had taken it sight unseen with the understanding that if she didn't like it and could find something else, they would get her out of the lease. They warned her, however, that places like this were hard to find in Manhattan even for the astronomical rent she would be paying.

She found the door at the end of the hall, a clean, white-walled corridor with dark tile floors, and put her bags down to open the door with the key they had mailed to her. The phone was ringing inside, and she hurried, making a mistake, turning the key the wrong way. She fumbled for almost a minute, but the phone kept going. Finally she got it, pushed the bags inside, shut the door behind her and looked around for the phone.

"Coming as soon as I can find you," she said.

The room off the hallway was the living room. It was large, modern and bright, and her furniture had been arranged in it in a reasonable, if incomplete, way. The rug was even on the floor, and on top of it were her boxes, the same ones that had been piled in the old apartment when she last saw them. She knew that there were two bedrooms beyond, and a dining room that could serve as an office, but the phone was hidden and still ringing.

"Okay," she said. "Where the hell are you hiding?"

She followed the sound to the corner and found a cord and then began to follow the cord through a door into an even brighter corner room with two large picture windows. Perched on top of her old desk was the telephone.

She picked it up in the middle of a ring and said brightly, "Hello."

"Hello," came the man's whisper on the other end. "Welcome to New York."

"No," Jean gasped.

"No?" returned the voice of Alexian. "You've been in town an hour and you're already disillusioned?"

Jean looked out of her window into the rain and a smile touched her lips as she said, "Sorry, for a moment I thought you were some-one else."

LITTLE FALLS PUBLIC LIBRARY

706 East Main Street
Little Falls, New York 13365

(315) 823-1542

MEMBER

MID-YORK LIBRARY SYSTEM
Utica. N.Y. 13502